Praise for *The Voices of Heaven*

"... A complex, uniquely Korean love story that shouldn't be missed."

–Kirkus Reviews

"This book is perfect for book clubs, which will find its emotionally wrenching story the opening to spirited discussion."

–Shirley Christian, Pulitzer Prize–winning Journalist and Author

"[An] illuminating power that is very rare."

–David H. Lynn, Editor, *The Kenyon Review*

"Maija Rhee Devine's narrative style is spellbinding as she captures the rules and mores of an ancient (and more contemporary) culture both in its injustices and its tenderness. Her use of language brings to life the very smell of the food she describes and invites the reader into a deep understanding of the spiritual rituals, as such rituals accompany both the ordinary and the extraordinary events of the novel. Readers will come to care about what happens to these characters as the plot unfolds, but they will also notice the sheer poetry of Rhee Devine's descriptions."

–AAUW, Kansas City, MO,
36th Thorpe Menn Literary Excellence Award Committee

"In the midst of the gritty realism of the Korean War, Maija Devine has created a dreamlike . . . gripping read and the most imaginative vision of the Korean world I have read."

–Crosby Kemper III, Executive Director,
The Kansas City Public Library, Kansas City, MO

"Maija Devine's *The Voices of Heaven* is not just a great read; it's also a riveting portrayal of a culture and a time that we would do well to understand better."

–Mark R. DePue, Director of Oral History,
Abraham Lincoln Presidential Library, Springfield, IL

"Maija Devine [is] both hilarious and thoughtful, as is the book. Details, color and smells arise, as does love when you least expect it."

–Delta Willis, Author & Conservationist

"It is fascinating from beginning to end. So much cultural information. The rotation of the different narrative voices was astutely handled."

–Wanita Zumbrunnen, Poet and Adjunct Professor,
Lindenwood University, St. Charles, MO

The Voices of Heaven

1-22-2020

For Bruce (부르스
in Korean),

May the spirit of our GP workshop
bring us lots of good results!

THE VOICES OF HEAVEN

Maija/이매자

An Award-Winning Autobiographical Novel By

MAIJA RHEE DEVINE

The Voices of Heaven

Published in the United States of America by Seoul Selection USA, Inc.
4199 Campus Dr., Suite 550
Irvine, CA 92612, USA
Tel: 949-509-6584
Fax: 949-509-6599
E-mail: publisher@seoulselection.com
Website: www.seoulselection.com

ISBN: 978-1-62412-003-9
Library of Congress Control Number: 2013939057

Printed in the Republic of Korea

In memory of my loving parents,
who adopted me and gave me life

Contents

PART I

BEFORE THE WAR

The Voices of Heaven

The day before the wedding, Seoul, June 1949

Soo-yang

"Stifle your laughs," Mrs. Chong told her daughter, Soo-yang.

Laugh? Why would she laugh? Tomorrow, she'd slip into bed with another woman's husband, his wife lying in a room three feet away behind thin, rice-paper doors. That's how her life as a mistress was to begin. So, what happy tune would she be wriggling her shoulders to, giggling like an idiot who couldn't tell red beans from black beans?

"Never show your teeth," Mrs. Chong said. "Breathe quietly, and keep your eyes turned down to your toes." Her mother was shampooing her hair in reed-scented rainwater in their yard in preparation for her arrival at his house. It was an important occasion, even if it could hardly be called a wedding.

Tomorrow night, as Gui-yong would loosen the tie of her bedtime blouse, she'd remember neighbors' gab about him and his wife, the mandarin duck sweethearts, just like in the fairytales. What misfortune to squeeze between the two, still love-struck with each other even after fifteen years of marriage!

"Such love, as sweet as the sounds of harp strings," her mother had said, "could work for you, too. Harp-string love for one woman could sing the same tune for another. A man who glues himself to one woman like sticky rice will do it again. It's a good sign."

A good sign? What kind of a spineless man glued himself to two women? Soo-yang, Weeping Willow, wanted him to have some balls. *Oh, my.* She blushed. If he had them, he wouldn't tear his affection away from his wife so easily. Still, she'd rather yield herself to a loving man than to one as cold as a lizard.

Her mother had washed her hair the same way for her wedding eight years earlier. Soo-yang clenched her teeth to keep the memory of being jilted by her groom out of her head. Bent over the basin, her hair shielding her from mother's eyes, she let tears drop and blend into the water.

"Your new life will try to break you because *this* time, you'll be the second woman with his wife living right there with you." Her mother's serene voice annoyed her. How could she keep calm on a day like this? At twenty-five, Soo-yang should be a married woman with one son running around in trousers with a poop hole, one in a piggyback blanket on her back, and another in her belly. Instead, on her wedding night . . . A sob hiccupped out of her. To cover it up, she whipped at the water.

"Even if you get the luck of having a gold-filled pumpkin drop on you," her mother said, "and you bear sons as sturdy and cute as toads, you'll have heartbreaks. Your name will never go on your husband's record, not as his wife nor as the mother of your children. You mustn't gnash your teeth when their names appear next to his and his wife's. You know why? Because you'll have more urgent matters to attend to. You'll teach your children to call his wife 'Big Mommy.' You'll teach them to think of her, not you, as the tongue in their mouths that they have only one of and can't do without. When they grow older, you'll teach them how to bear the shame of having been born to you. I know you know all this like you know the palms of your hands, because this is the rule of our land. But let me tell you again: don't pamper yourself with tears. If you do, even worse heartaches will come, one after another like beads on a necklace."

Her mother blew her nose. "I shouldn't have to repeat," she continued, her voice flat, "'Obey your mother-in-law and your husband to death.' You must please their every whim, and their stomachs and spleens, too, because this is the rule of our land. But, I must repeat, remember to obey his wife. Even if her words to you come across as coarse as mugwort cake, you must take them as though they were as sweet as peeled plum. If you treat her as you would a Buddhist nun, she'll treat you like one, too. But if you hurt her feelings, you know what they say about women's grudges: They can make even a June day freeze over. Never look her in the eye, be sure to hand her things with both hands, and eat in the kitchen by yourself. If you were to eat with them, you'd look brazen. Remember, they know what happened to your last marriage, and they're taking you in out of kindness. But none of these things matter. The one Buddha-true thing that matters is you don't have a guarantee you'll bear them a son. Do you? So, what if you don't bear a son? You know as well as any three-foot-tall child knows you'll be sent back to us. And what if you bear only girls? Will they keep you and give you more chances to bear a boy? House God have mercy. And even worse, what if you produce no child at all? The only way they may still keep you is if you serve them as though you were a slave who's loyal to them until death. I know you know all this, as this is the rule of our land."

Yes, they were generous to take her, a reject. She was like spoiled meat spat out, even if the wedding had never been consummated. The groom had been seventeen, too immature to not be scared off on their wedding night by a gouged-out dip in her thigh. Who could've foreseen a scar from a fall and a botched treatment would cause her groom to never enter her room again? Yes, she must pour her guts into serving her in-laws and Gui-yong's wife.

Mrs. Chong ruffled Soo-yang's hair with a white towel that had been set on the hearth ledge to warm. Her parents had a son, as valuable as a gold nugget, but she was their precious jade.

"Remember." Mrs. Chong kept on. "Once you set your foot in his house, your body and ghost become his. While you breathe the air and even after you stop breathing, you die as *his* ghost. We took you back from your groom once before because you were just a child, your umbilical cord practically still attached." Her mother handed her the yellow blouse with a maroon collar.

"You feel ashamed of being the second woman? Angry at your fate? Just say to yourself, 'I'm already like a steamed pig. Boiling water can no longer burn me.' Because that's truc. You became a boiled pig, and I did, too, that day your groom cast you out."

Mi-na

"You're going to be one happy girl, aren't you? Little Mommy's coming. She'll give you a baby brother to play with in no time!"

Grandma's fake teeth were as brown as her fingernails, and her lips moved sideways because of the pipe in her mouth. Grandma smoked before the magpies sang in the morning, after her meals, before going to bed, and while she sat in the outhouse.

Hearing about the baby boy made Mi-na's belly button feel mushy, like when she dropped down on a big swing. At least Grandma smiled instead of complaining about what Mi-na had forgotten to do, like empty her ashtray. Once Grandma began talking about the woman who was coming, she stopped yelling at her.

Thinking of having to share Daddy with a boy baby made her feel like she had a bean sprout caught in her throat. What if Daddy stopped giving her horse rides on his back?

The clinking sound of Mommy's dishes drifted in from the kitchen. The sesame seed oil smell made the flies make a propeller noise as they flew between the kitchen and the bean sauce jar stand. Her kindergarten wasn't fun today. Nothing new. Just drawing the first five letters of the alphabet over and over. They sang the "Mountain Rabbit" song twice, hopping and flapping their cupped hands.

"When is the woman coming?"

"Mi-na! You mean Little Mommy, don't you? Say, it, Mi-na: 'Little Mommy.'"

"Why should I call her that? She's not my Mommy." Beginning tomorrow, grown-ups would call her Mommy the "Big House Person."

Mi-na lifted her belly off the wood floor of the sitting room, where she drew a toad on a piece of paper.

"Little girl, she'll give you a brother, and the mommy of your brother will be your mommy, too."

She hated Grandma. She hated anyone who sprayed spittle, going on and on about boy babies. *Gochu, gochu, gochu*! Stupid wee-wees. She'd seen one of those peppers on Auntie Jin-i's baby. It looked like a worm that had grown too fat. *Eeek!* She hated anything that moved without legs. That's why spiders and centipedes didn't send her screaming, but worms did.

She especially hated Mrs. Bang across the street. Every time she saw her, Mrs. Bang clicked her tongue and said, "You should've been a boy." Lately, Mrs. Bang had been saying, "If you were a boy, Little Mommy wouldn't be coming." But what could she have done to have been born a boy? Could she go back into Mommy's tummy and come back out a boy? She'd asked Mommy about that. She said it wasn't Mi-na's fault. But Mrs. Bang thought it was. She hated her, and she hated Grandma.

She loved Grandma's stories, though. At night, she told them until Mi-na fell asleep. Her favorite was about Simcheong, who saved her blind father. The Heungbu and Nolbu story, about a poor brother who gets beaten by his rich brother but becomes richer than the rich brother, was good, too.

"I'm going out to play five-pebble game, Grandma." At the stone step, she slid on her rubber shoes.

"Stop! Before you go, say 'Little Mommy.'"

Mommy stuck her head out the kitchen and said, "Listen to your Grandma."

All right, she'd do it for Mommy. "Little . . . Little . . ." She skipped out without finishing. It was too hard. The minute she opened the gate, she ran smack into the tummy of Mommy's best friend in the neighborhood, Gae-sun—Mrs. Lee, or Auntie to her.

"Sorry, Auntie. Looking for Mommy?"

"Workers are digging a bomb shelter for us . . . Maybe your Mommy wants them to do one for her, too."

"Yes, she will!" Grown-ups had been talking about Commies a lot. She even had a nightmare one day, and Grandma had shaken her to wake her up. Mi-na came back into the house with Mrs. Lee to hear about the bomb hole. Anything would be funner than being told about her missing penis.

Mommy came out of the kitchen.

"Mommy, can we have a hideout hole dug out, too?"

"The workers are doing our house . . . and they can do yours, too . . . but you've got enough going on around here . . ."

"I'll talk to my son," Grandma said from the room she was fixing for Daddy and the woman who was coming. "But I doubt we can do anything for a while. Pray for us, Mrs. Lee. Hope those rotten sons of bitches up North don't start a war before we get a grandson born to us."

So that was the end of the bomb hole talk. Mi-na followed Mrs. Lee out.

Eum-chun

"Welcome to my husband's bed." Eum-chun practiced the words she must say to the woman coming tomorrow. "Bear him a son," she added.

She darted out the kitchen and, holding onto the cement rim of the sink in the yard, heaved. A thread of spittle ran down to the drain. She kneaded her chest. Charcoal—burning, burning, burning. That's how it felt there.

If the rumors came true, North Korean Communists could make a pile of dry leaves out of the South with machine guns and tanks any day. Seoul would turn into waterfalls of blood. And what was she doing? Dillydallying over having to share her man—as if not having borne him a son wasn't her fault.

Dull peach colored the dawn sky like persimmon juice spreading through gauze. The curved edges of the gray tiles on her roof gripped the back ends of the others, making neat rows moist with dew. Without a son, a family would be like a roof with missing tiles.

Fifteen years ago, when she saw her husband for the first time on their wedding night, oh, how effortlessly she fell for him. During the day, her eyes had been glued shut with honey to keep her from drawing bad luck by peeking at Gui-yong. A warmth that develops slowly between a man and a woman during the first years of marriage would have been good enough for any newlyweds, but instead, she flung her heart open the moment she saw him.

Below his bushy hair and brows, she caught his eyes. They glinted with a look of having seen her before, but he couldn't have. His eyes were small—how she favored large ones!—but there flashed humor. His upper lip curved slightly, revealing something he was holding back from her, teasing her. She giggled. Sweetness welled.

She stepped into the kitchen and dropped another dried whiting fish into the water for the wedding soup she'd make tomorrow. The two fish she let soak earlier had softened. At the poke of her chopstick, their sides flaked away, but the eyes remained whole and stared.

Dumb fish. "Don't fall apart like them," she said to herself. "What right do you have to behave so childishly?" Having had one miscarriage and no son, she had left gaping holes in the roof of their house large enough for hail to pelt through. Without a boy to shoulder her husband's family line, how could they survive in this life, and the next? When they grew old, who'd bring them steaming rice on a cherry wood tray? When they fell ill and the money dried up, who'd keep them from begging on the streets? After their death, who'd help them to enjoy eternal life by offering ancestral rites three times a year? Daughters were as good as wet straw shoes. Once married, they became outsiders.

The least she could do to redeem herself was to hold a wedding party nobody would deem shabby, like a model wife. Not to do so would be like lying on her back and spitting into the sky. The spit would spray onto her parents' faces, too. Gods knew she'd never want that.

The sweet life she had with Gui-yong settled into her bones. It was all she had to hold her up. One might say fifteen years of marriage was a long time—considering it only took ten years for mountains to change their shapes. But her life with Gui-yong seemed as short as a summer nap.

She stirred the rice in the pot to keep it from sticking before her mother-in-law and daughter got up to eat. Ah,

Mi-na. Mi-na, her daughter, her treasure, as precious as a jade leaf, her child who fell from heaven. One dawn five years after her miscarriage, someone laid the infant girl at her doorstep. Now that Gui-yong would take another woman, Mi-na would become the only one belonging wholly to her. More importantly, she would grow and prove that a daughter could become as good as a son. Would that be possible? Could she become a woman judge? A member of the National Assembly? Could she show the mothers bragging about their sons that one dazzling daughter could become ten times better than a son? A daughter could never serve as the celebrant of ancestral rites, but with a good education, why couldn't she outshine boys? It was a wild hope, but many fortune-tellers had predicted Mi-na would do just that. She planned to live for that day of salvation. That would only be possible if Mi-na didn't find out about the adoption. If a child learned her own flesh and blood had given her away, how would she grow normally and excel? No, she must never, never know.

She shoved a piece of pine kindling into the fire and ran a wet dish rag over the pot lid. The black metal sang a soft *ssssss*.

Before Eum-chun quit elementary school, back when the Japanese made Koreans speak only Japanese, her third-grade teacher had asked, "Anyone know what glue Chinese and Koreans used to hold bricks together to build their fortresses? After thousands of years, they stand strong."

"Cement," a boy answered.

"Mud mixed with straw and rocks," said another.

"No. It was the glue made from sticky rice," Mrs. Jin said. "Nothing can pull two things apart when they're glued together with that. You can read it on a plaque at the Nanjing City Wall."

The children giggled, but Eum-chun believed her; the teacher's name meant truth. Now, she prayed her and Gui-yong's love for each other would remain indestructible like the fortress walls glued with sticky rice, even after the new woman began living with Gui-yong.

Tomorrow, every dish must look cheery, full of hope for the sons his second woman must bear.

May North Koreans kill us all today, she wished. Then she would not have to face tomorrow.

May your Aunt Hong's gods strike you dead for your self-pitying, her good-wife voice said.

She sat on her straw seat on the dirt floor and stared into the fire.

Kim Koo, who thousands thought was a Red, was defeated in the vice presidential election. His opponents said he ought to be hung upside down and bludgeoned to death like a dog on the hottest summer day for advocating cooperation with Kim Il-sung. But thousands backed him, and one of the fifty parties formed in the National Assembly was actually a Communist one. So her wish, as shameful as it was, could come true, and that would give her what she longed for—no tomorrow.

The dawn light brightened and added a shine to one side of the pot.

In their darkened bedroom, Eum-chun ran her fingers across Gui-yong's lips. At the dip below his nose, his day-old stubble felt like salt sprinkled on dried seaweed. When she stroked his lips the other way, he grabbed her hand and pushed it down his chest, and down, down, down. Would his new woman do the same with his lips? The image of his hand moving hers down bear-pawed through Eum-chun's mind.

She jumped up and grabbed a fish out of the soaking pan on the ledge, slapped it into her grain masher, and turned the handle.

I'll grind it up. Throw it down the outhouse hole. She felt like screaming, *Lock me up and starve me to death. I want to die.*

A passing mangy dog will laugh at you, a voice inside her said. *Thousands of other women faced a day like yours before for at least the last six hundred years. Some did it like a queen, some like a dried-up tree, some like a bitch-rat. How will you do it?*

She slid the fish back into the water.

Gui-yong

Something was wrong with his balls. Sooner or later, everyone's six organs or other vital parts were bound to wear out. In his case, his balls did. Why else, then, would Gui-yong's private parts turn to acorn jello when he pictured himself bedding down with Soo-yang tomorrow? Shouldn't his body be trying to bust out of his trousers like when he'd first seen Eum-chun before their wedding? By all accounts, his lovemaking with her should've lost steam by now, but he still lusted after her. Luck and love seemed to work that way; they favored some men over others. The unlucky, like Noodle Leg at the office, grumbled about the "wife smell," which he said drove him to other pussies. Gui-yong had his share of chances to fool around with other women. If it hadn't been for what he had with his wife, he would have, too.

He parked his truck by the Quonset hut of the City Hall Transportation Division. He'd get a short route today. He wanted to get home for dinner with his wife one last time without the new woman.

Fifteen years ago, to get a glimpse of Eum-chun before their wedding, he had pried her address from the matchmaker and prowled her neighborhood. Why? Not seeing their brides' faces until their wedding day didn't drive other men crazy. A week before the wedding—on the third day of the third lunar month, when swallows returned from the south—he finally saw her. Behind the bush clover fence of her home, she was taking clothes off the line.

Swallows went *kkkaaawww kkkaaawww.* He saw the side of her face, her lavender blouse and black skirt, and her braided hair tied in a purple ribbon. Her height, taller than most girls, surprised him. When she came close to the fence, he saw her round face. How disappointing! The ends of her eyebrows arched downward, too, another letdown. Why then did his heart do flip-flops?

Before he could see more of her, she walked away. That night, when he tried to remember more details of her, his heart did the dance of a drunken pig. It was as if his mind had seen more than his eyes had. The groove under her nose ran unusually deep, causing her lips to look pouty—he loved that. Her small nose set off her large eyes, but their tail ends tapered off. "Flowing eyes. Tears flow into them," his mother had said. He now knew what she had meant. But his and Eum-chun's horoscope fit that the fortune-tellers had predicted was good enough for his mother to ignore the tears. His sign was a dragon, hers a snake. Ordinarily, that wouldn't strike a good match, but her February birthday made her a sleeping snake, improving the pairing. His mother then bragged that those eyes were also called the "phoenix eyes," known to usher in wealth.

Her breasts? The cursed skirt band that pressed them had made it impossible to guess their size. But his body had felt them and swelled. Tomorrow, he'd touch Soo-yang's. His wife, who was on the high-strung side, would lie in the next room alone. *May her nerves not give out.*

He took a deep breath and stepped into the dispatcher's office.

"You lucky, large-testicled boar!" Noodle Leg shouted at Gui-yong for all to hear. The women blushed. "But me? I get a bloody nose even when I fall flat on my back."

Gui-yong looked up from the dispatcher's counter.

"Taking tomorrow off and want a quick route today, too?" The dispatcher frowned.

"What's he got, boss?" Noodle Leg butted in. "Switch his with mine. I'll do the long haul. Tomorrow's his 'noodle day,' boss. He's marrying again."

The dispatcher scribbled on his pad and grunted. "Namwon, then. Office things, paper, ink, and pads. Auto parts to army posts. No lumber. Coal on the way back."

"Thanks, boss," Gui-yong said. Namwon? What a fluke to head there today. Even children knew about the Joseon Dynasty love story that happened in Namwon between Chunhyang, the daughter of a *gisaeng* entertainer and Lee Mong-ryong, the son of a noble family. Realizing their love was impossible in the world they lived in, they shed enough tears to create the Yocheon River. It ended with them living happily ever after, though. The writer must have drunk himself dumb. In real life, there was no way that affair could have had a happy ending. Naturally, the Chunhyang story was his wife's favorite. Would he and Eum-chun be able to keep what they had even after Soo-yang joined them? He didn't know how. What if the women didn't get along? Whose side must he take if they didn't?

Noodle Leg wheeled his glance, made sure their division chief, Soo-yang's father, was not in earshot, and grabbed Gui-yong's shoulder.

"Up to handling two women tomorrow, pal? Need some help?"

Phone Pole whisked by and slapped Gui-yong's coveralled back. "I'll pitch in, too, buddy."

Behind their desks, the women giggled. Miss Chin's cheeks turned pink. She was only fifteen, worked days, and went to school at night.

Gui-yong faked a smile. *Let'm have fun.* The sick yellow-sky feeling in his gut was his business, not theirs. If anyone got wind of *that*, he'd call him a Noodle Penis. Noodle Leg and Phone Pole had wives and sons, but they womanized. They'd like to set up rooms for their favorite pinkies but couldn't afford to. Besides, having borne sons, their wives might gouge out the pinkies' eyes. So whenever they could scrimp on rice money and toss it to the women, they saw them on the side. Gui-yong had met Noodle Leg's most recent pinkie at her rice wine joint. Soon after that, his wife stomped into the stall and tore hair off the woman's head. Noodle Leg had chuckled and said, "If a man doesn't fool around, what kind of a man is that?"

Gui-yong picked up boxes and walked out to the Quonset. The breakfast of bean sprout soup Eum-chun had spiced with red pepper flakes, just the way he loved it, lapped in his stomach. He belched.

"Hey. I'll give you a hand." Noodle Leg clopped behind him. Polio, Gui-yong had heard. Noodle Leg rolled his mud-colored shirtsleeves. "Save some energy for tomorrow, for your bedtime feasting."

"I'll take one of your long runs sometime."

"You'd better." He limped over the step.

How could he just swagger into Soo-yang's room and sleep with her as though it were as simple as gobbling peeled pine nuts? The sun threw barf color around the dome of City Hall.

Noodle Leg plopped a box next to the five Gui-yong stacked on the truck bed and slapped his back. "Take it easy. Don't squander energy!"

They finished loading fourteen crates of stuff for desk wimps. Gui-yong would drop off the red-lined notepads, carbon paper, and inked stamp pads at the village and city offices. Batteries, spark plugs, cranks, and spare tires went to the Jeolla-do military posts.

"Don't run into any Communist guerrillas, pal. They're crawling in the mountains down there." Noodle Leg pounded on Gui-yong's back.

Gui-yong took the steering wheel. As he backed up, he saw in the rearview mirror Noodle Leg flicking his fist with the thumb thrust between the index and middle fingers, the "good fuck" sign.

Mi-na

When Mi-na skipped out the gate to find someone to play the five-pebble game with, she found Sun-ja, Mrs. Bang's daughter, across the street, tossing bean bags in her courtyard. She liked playing with Kwang-ho better, a third-grade boy, because when Sun-ja lost, she sometimes turned nasty. But she didn't see Kwang-ho anywhere. The girls played the game outside Sun-ja's gate. They squatted under a wisteria tree right in the middle of its shadow, large as a straw mat. When Sun-ja lost three rounds in a row, she jumbled the pebbles, as Mi-na thought she might, jumped up, and kicked at the dirt. Dust flew into Mi-na's face, and she stood up, brushing it away. Sun-ja had done this before. But today she did something new. She screamed out a word that Mi-na didn't know at first.

"Changeling! Changeling!" Sun-ja slapped her palms together right before Mi-na's nose and loosened dust toward her eyes.

"Stop it!" Mi-na said, crying. "I'll tell my Mommy!"

"You gonna tell? Garbage! Go ahead, Garbage Girl. You don't even know who your real mommy is!" She stuck her tongue at her. "She threw you away! Na, na, na."

Mi-na flew into her house.

Mommy was spicing spinach salad, and Grandma was grating carrots. Mi-na fell into Mommy's arms.

"What happened!" Grandma and Mommy shouted at once.

Mi-na couldn't speak for a long minute from her crying, which didn't want to stop. Finally, she took a breath and blurted, "Changeling, Mommy! She called me a changeling. And Garbage Girl, too. Go spank Sun-ja, Mommy. She lies, Mommy. Right, Grandma?"

Grandma turned around so fast she whisked like wind that slammed the gate. She left words flying behind her. "I'll smash the girl's mouth."

A big cloud of a sigh puffed out of Mommy. She pulled her in tightly. In fact, so tightly Mi-na coughed.

"Not so hard, Mommy. I can't breathe! Snot's going into my mouth! Wipe my nose, Mommy."

"Sun-ja's a funny one, isn't she?" Mommy said, laughing a little and drying Mi-na's nose with a handkerchief she pulled out of her sleeve.

"Mommy! How can you laugh? She called me garbage!"

"Because Sun-ja's lie is as red as a monkey's butt!"

At that, Mi-na's nose wriggled a little.

"Look at your forehead sticking out. Isn't it Daddy's? Look at your hands. Aren't they boney like mine?" She spread her hand out before Mi-na's eyes. Look at your full lips. Aren't they like Grandma's? Sun-ja made herself as silly as a mouse with its tail caught in a trap."

Mommy had a way of making stinky things look not half bad. Now, if she could also stop the Little Mommy person from coming, Mi-na wouldn't mind being a girl so much.

Eum-chun

The gate creaked open. Eum-chun's neighbor Gae-sun poked her head into the kitchen.

"You all right?" Gae-sun asked, handing her a bowl of spring water mixed with honey. "Drink this. You need it . . . today." In her other hand squawked a hen, its legs bound in red ribbon and its eyes startled to pink.

"I know you won't be having a wedding ceremony, but a hen will bring good luck."

"Sweet of you," Eum-chun said, taking the bowl. Gae-sun

took the hen to the storage shed and set it there.

The mother of five sons and three daughters, Gae-sun was a woman of Eum-chun's dream. Not a womanizing wolf, her husband was a perfect man, too, even if he was a half span shorter than her and potbellied.

"Drink it. I'm not leaving . . . until you do . . . I can't have you collapse on us." Gae-sun's eyes kept closing mid-sentence, her narcolepsy more prominent to Eum-chun than ever. "Not today. Not tomorrow . . . Not ever." She ran her palm across Eum-chun's shoulders.

Her throat swelled, making the drinking hard, but she downed the nourishing liquid. When not closed, her friend's eyes sent waves of calm.

"Eum-chun, the Voice of Heaven," Gae-sun said, "Blessings will be bubbling out of your name . . . and Heaven wants you . . . to be strong." She squeezed Eum-chun's hand. How ironic her name should be so grand. Her father, a drunkard all his life, had once let it slip he got the name from a fellow drunk and a quack fortune-teller. Since then, Eum-chun swung between loving and hating her name. *I must make it good*, she thought sometimes. Today, a pepper-hot hate reared up. *Why didn't that Heaven bless me with a son, if it had to create the rule requiring a son?*

Eum-chun slumped onto the hearth ledge. As if she needed to be beaten down even more, last night's dream churned in her head.

"I think something happened to my sister," Eum-chun said.

"Did you get word about Jin-i's baby? This early?"

"No, but in my dream, I saw a mountain spirit. I was happy to see him. He came to comfort me, to give me strength, I thought. But when he smiled, his mouth was a black hole. Not one tooth remained. I think what we've all feared happened. Jin-i's lover took their baby away. Gave him to his wife to raise."

Gae-sun joined Eum-chun on the ledge and wrapped her arm around her.

"Seongju House God, have mercy . . . as if we need that trouble, too . . . Listen. Think only of yourself . . . and only of Mi-na." The words staggered out, held back by her friend's narcolepsy. "You've got to be strong for her, if not for yourself . . . Without you, she'll go . . . where no one can save her . . . with no flesh and blood of her own to save her . . . Let's just get through . . . tomorrow and . . . worry about Jin-i later. Alright?"

Gae-sun was right. After she left, Eum-chun wiped the top of the portable meal table and set it on the ledge. She felt it in her gut—Kim had used Jin-i only as a seed bearer and had now discarded her. But as Gae-sun said, she must think of Mi-na before anyone else. If anything happened to herself, who'd guard Mi-na like a tigress from finding out her own flesh and blood had given her away? No, no, no. From the "no, no, no" flared sparks of energy. This was no time to mope. If Mi-na learned of the secret, instead of becoming a lawyer, she would throw herself over the Han River. Then, what would the Voice of Heaven live for? No, no, no. After making it through tomorrow, she'd try to help her sister—to get back her infant son. But before that, she must prepare for the wedding party. She grabbed her bags and headed to the market.

Gui-yong had left extra early in his government truck. She longed to make him proud of her famous cooking skills again. She planned to make the wedding dish bright, with egg fried and sliced into gold threads, green onion strips, and rings of red pepper. Each bowl must look like a bride's tiara of ruby, amber, and jade beads. The guests would cheer, "A hundred years of happiness!"

After her trip to the market and a breakfast, she and her mother-in-law would finish laying new floor paper in the room where Gui-yong would honeymoon.

Honeymoon? Of course. May gods bless him and his new woman, Eum-chun practiced her prayer, *with a night as sweet as persimmon.*

Soo-yang

After the shampoo, back in her own room, Soo-yang took time tying the red silk bow of her blouse. Her mother's words had been uttered before, but today they rattled in her head like peach pits in a dry gourd. Still, she saw a flicker of hope—as small as a piece of earwax, but it was there. Because she'd be yoked to a man, her ninety-one-year-old ill grandmother would be able to close her eyes properly and die. She could fly to the Heaven in the West.

Dozens of daughters and granddaughters in folktales walked on frozen ground to buy dried centipede and toad vials to cure their ill elders. They cut their wrists and drained blood into the throats of their dying family members to save them. Considering that, what she'd agreed to do didn't amount to much. She swallowed her fears and pride and gave in to her parents' wishes for her to join Gui-yong's family. Straightening her shoulders, she sent a wish across the Han River to her grandmother. *Go. Fly to the Heaven in the West. Peacefully, like a crane.*

Another shred of hope came from what she had seen in Gui-yong the few times her father had brought him home after work. While arranging spicy squid strips on the portable table and pouring wine for them, she had taken sideways glances at him. He frowned after a sip of the wine as if it was sour, but he pumped food into his mouth like an A-frame-lugging porter. He was tall. His eyebrows were thick but stopped without warning, which made her cover her laugh with her hand. His wide forehead, though it narrowed at the temples, signaled he was a man with a big heart and of wit.

But once her parents' talk of offering her to him began, the humor left his eyes. But, over time, a corner of his heart might warm toward her. She'd try to be happy even if such a thawing happened only once in a blue moon. Would his wife begrudge her that?

She laid an iron the size of a spoon over the fire in a portable stove. After a bit, she took the iron, spit onto her finger, and touched the iron with it. The spittle gave a small hiss. She pressed the iron across the new willow-green blouse and skirt she'd wear to her new home. "A *cheop*," a mistress, people would call her. It would sound like the *plop* of cow dung hitting the ground. "A *sosil*," also a mistress, others would call her. It's an older, softer word that was as tear-streaked as the stories of Joseon Dynasty concubines trampled by their in-laws, their hearts broken over their sons who were treated as inferiors to those born to first wives. "A *si-at*," a seed bearer. It would make her a she-pig—which she was. Must she accept this fate as the law of the land? Should she fight it? Could she? No, then what? Jump into a well? Imagine the shame that would land on her parents and all their ancestors! She could shave her head and become a Buddhist nun. She admired nuns. But did she have the nerve to leave her family forever? Besides, she didn't think she could pray for more than half an hour a day. That would fall ruefully short. She also liked to eat beef, pork, and chicken at least once in a while. As for having a man—even if she shared one with another woman—maybe that was better than having none? So, she was back to square one. Accept the law of the land. What else could she do? She must live through her fate just as cows munched their way toward their end.

As she ran the iron down the full length of her skirt, her wrists weakened. Could she give Gui-yong even a pale imitation of the sweet love life he had with his wife? If she gave birth to only girls, would Gui-yong keep her at least long enough to name the girls "Ggeut-ja" or "Mal-ja," the Final Girl, and wait to see if the name would kick a boy baby into existence? How badly would Gui-yong's wife hate her? Some first wives beat second wives or used words viciously enough to break bones.

When the iron passed over the spot where her tear fell, it let out a soft *pssss.*

Eum-chun

Eum-chun walked out to the courtyard and looked up. The eaves of her roof cut the June sky into a rectangle. She tucked cloth bags under her arm and hurried out the gate. Her lips felt dry. A dozen blocks lay before her on a downslope. She could smell the market, and the taste of pickled octopus sprang to her tongue. Her mouth watered. If she could have some of that, her legs might feel steady, not hollow like bamboo. She imagined all that she could do with such steadfast legs besides just preparing a wedding feast. She could run to her parents. She could open a roadside stand or a rice wine joint. But did she have the money for it even if she dared? Would her parents approve? No. Besides, how would she pay back the shame she'd already piled on them by not bearing a son?

The prayers she'd recited all these months and a mouthful of octopus might keep her belly from folding over. If lips could wear out with prayer, she'd have no lips left.

At the end of the block, she walked past Mrs. Choi's house. She stared at the closed gate and wished she could see her neighbor's Buddha-like face.

"Not even fit for pigs!" Mrs. Choi had said about fermented octopus. As much as she admired Mrs. Choi, she was wrong about that delicacy. About everything else, she was as wise as a hundred-year-old tortoise. How else could she have personally picked a woman to become her own husband's live-in mistress while shedding tears as if the spiciest mustard had burned her throat?

The sons and daughters Mrs. Choi produced with her husband and the sons his mistress bore him lived together—without any squawking from anyone, as Mrs. Choi's hands smoothed every wrinkle.

Asked how she could do that, especially when she had borne her husband healthy sons, Mrs. Choi said, "Why let him waste money on loose women out to suck every penny from him?" How wise. But for Eum-chun, finding a second wife for Gui-yong was as difficult as trying to bite her own elbow. She should have spread the word long ago that they were searching for a woman with baby making hips. If she could see Mrs. Choi's face, she might know she could brave through tomorrow, too. If there was no way to skip over this thousand-foot fall, she might as well fall gracefully.

Eum-chun swallowed the water in her mouth. She'd not be greedy; she'd settle for two bites of fermented octopus. Buddha would understand.

In front of Seongdong-gu District Office, a dozen men stood before the newspaper bulletin board. What was making the news today? Not another Communist guerilla attack from Mt. Jirisan! Under their system, if fathers didn't see eye to eye with their sons on Communist goals, they'd send their sons to be tortured. And the sons would do the same to their fathers. Even dogs struck with rabies wouldn't do that. If Communists were that rotten, how could leaders like Kim Koo, the fierce Independence fighter against Japanese rule, Pak Hon-yong, and Yuh Woon-hyung support the Reds, as people accused them of doing? The guerrilla-infested Jirisan Mountain area was where Gui-yong had driven to this morning. She shivered like a sick dog.

When Gui-yong's Uncle Park visited them a month ago, he and several men gathered at Mr. Lee's house. At midnight, Uncle Park held up a mirror at a certain angle against the moon. A circular object appeared in the mirror, its upper part red and the lower blue. Slowly, the red grew legs, pushed into the blue. Soon, red took over. Silence fell. Crickets went wild with their cries.

"War's coming," Uncle Park whispered. "Communists will win."

House God, she prayed. *Please bring my husband home safely, even if he'll enter his newlyweds' room tomorrow.*

He'd close the rice paper door behind his back, the light would go out, and he'd take the new woman into his arms. What would she do then? Howl like a wolf torn by wild dogs? Sink to her knees, as though hit by a Commie bomb? Jealousy, the sewage tank of emotions barred from women for a thousand years, would swallow her up. Buddha forbid. Confucius forbid.

Past the stationery store, the shouts of the sellers rushed at her. She skirted around the tent stalls and apple crates set on the ground. Eggs peeked from the openings in the woven straw nests.

"Auntie, eggs! My hens laid'em an hour ago!" the woman with a baby sleeping in her piggyback blanket called out. "I'll give you an extra egg, Auntie."

"I'll get'em later," Eum-chun said, clutching her bags and passing her.

Shoppers elbowed her. She smelled raw meat, dried squid, and smelt. Chickens thrashed in wooden crates, their pupils dilated with fear. Steam billowed up from the cow blood soup. A man sliced beef and pork and chopped the bones.

"Intestines! Best for soup!" he yelled out while sloshing ropes of cow guts in water. His chopping board, dipped in the center from years of use, held a spoonful of blood.

An old saying gripped her: "You don't get pickled octopus at every market," meaning, you can't get lucky every time. She didn't dare wish for luck every time. Just this once. If luck could help her keep Gui-yong's love for a few more years and prevent her from becoming as unwelcome to him as a bowl of cold rice, she'd give up eating octopus.

She tripped over a seller's mat and tipped a tub, spilling spinach patties.

"Damn you! You blind, woman?" the woman shouted. Eum-chun reloaded the vegetables and bowed her apology.

As she tightened her skirt higher so as not to trip again, she bit down on her lip. It felt as though she cut her lip open. Labor pain might hurt like that, although she'd never know. The taste of blood in her mouth shot determination through her head.

No more whimpering! Do you hear me, Eum-chun? Come, you dog-shit fate. Even if a thief twists off a cock's neck tonight, dawn will break, and tomorrow will pounce upon me. Then I'll show you grace. Grace!

Gui-yong

Gui-yong barreled past Seoul Station and saw men and women, fresh from the countryside and waiting for Seoul folks to hire them. Since Liberation Day in 1945, Koreans who'd fought in the Japanese army in China, the Philippines, and Vietnam had swarmed back by the trainload. Students and workers who'd gone to Japan were returning, too. Some had also moved down from North Korea. Noodle Leg said 100,000 people had poured into Seoul in 1948 alone. Even with the Red bastards shooting at everything that moved along the closed border, folks starving from the taxes and forced labor the Russians and Kim Il-sung slapped on them kept milling down. He didn't understand what drove Communists, but he heard names like Marx and Stalin ping-pong around whenever men in the office got heated over politics, which was all the time.

"You lucky dog," Big Nose, one of the new drivers, said to him. "You don't have relatives stranded up North." Big Nose had fled from the North just before the Communists sealed the border. He left behind his wife, a son, parents, and grandparents. They were probably shot dead between their eyes for Big Nose's disappearance.

What luck that he had a government job, too. Good thing he learned to read and write after he was married. His wife taught him. Started during their honeymoon year. Without that, he'd be driving a taxi for a stingy owner for half his pay.

Just before turning in with Soo-yang, he'd have to look at his wife one last time. Or should he keep his eyes away, walk into the new room, and take Soo-yang's clothes off like he was doing nothing out of the ordinary? Despite his lofty name, Treasured Dragon, he was an idiot, worrying sick about what a grown man shouldn't. If he stopped men and women passing by City Hall and asked if he, Gui-yong, was right-minded to be worried about living with two wives, they'd yell, "Half ball!"

But other men must know life with two women wasn't easy. That's why they said tigers wouldn't eat the guts of a man who'd lived with more than one wife at the same time.

There was nothing better to clear his head than driving. What should he get for her in Namwon that would make her feel less like a shattered water dipper? If he said, "My love for you will not change," would she believe him?

An American army jeep flashed past. The driver's face was as white as rice flour.

"Did you know white men live with only one wife at a time and are happy even if they only have daughters?" Noodle Leg had asked one day while they stood beside their trucks.

How could that be!

"Some Christian thing. Westerners are Christians." Noodle Leg should know. He had education, up to junior high.

"You know what that means, don't you? Foreigners sticking with one wife at a time?" Noodle Leg spat into the dirt. "A penis gone like a pepper after frost. Ha, ha."

If he lived in the West, his life with only Eum-chun and Mi-na would've left nothing lacking. Not because living that way was moral, as Noodle Leg said Christians believed. If his mother or Eum-chun's shaman aunt heard him thinking this way, they would think he had sided with Christians and would dump a basket of red dirt on him, shouting, "Which five-clawed devil ghost possessed you?"

At the eastern crossing over the Han River, Gui-yong cut south onto the highway. Pear trees screened the view of the river, making the water flash by like chunks of sky. Pears were Eum-chun's favorite. If it were September, he'd buy her some.

Eum-chun

"Fermented shrimp!" the seafood woman shouted.

So what if her husband's new woman was ten years younger than her? Prettier? Oval-faced, too, the shape of a beauty? Eum-chun was pumpkin-faced, like her father, and not beautiful like her sister Jin-i.

But didn't Eum-chun have a nicely rounded nose and a city woman's mouth that was not as coarsely big as a peasant's? Her lips just right, not too thick or too thin? The new woman did have an advantage over her. She was wide-hipped, which Eum-chun's mother-in-law loved. "A body like that can push out a son as easily as a piece of oiled rice cake," she predicted.

Her beautiful sister had delivered her lover's son as easily as that. *Seongju House God, is my sister all right? Is her baby with her?* Her dreams had told of things to come, but this time she hoped it was a dream as silly as a dog's.

As much as she loved Jin-i, she could never understand how her sister got herself into such a trouble. How did their mother's daily lessons get lost on Jin-i? "Never let any boy or man touch any of these twenty-nine buttons on your dungarees," their mother had said. Jin-i had another child, a girl, whose father was a married man out having flings with wine house women. If the child had been a boy, he would've given him to his wife. Aunt Hong named the child Li-ho, Tiger by a Plum Tree, meant as a message: Go girl, bite your share out of life. If Eum-chun treated Gui-yong's new woman with kindness, would that good karma make Jin-i's lover not rob her of their baby?

"Ah, Auntie." The fermented fish woman greeted her while running a rag over the bellies of her five shiny red earthenware jars. "What do you need today, Auntie?"

Eum-chun sniffed each of the open jars.

"No pickled octopus today?"

"Ha! It's sold out. How about clams? They're extra gamy today!"

Eum-chun ran her free hand over the goosebumpy jar.

"I'll take some oysters."

Gui-yong would love them, the manly lover's food. Mrs. Choi said pork was. That's why she didn't serve it to her husband any more.

"Even without pork, he already got me into enough trouble to last me a lifetime," she said. But according to neighborhood gossip, he ate it behind her back at every meal, including breakfast. Mrs. Choi never served him chicken wings either.

"He chased after women's skirts and stirred up enough wind all by himself," she said. "God knows he doesn't need any help from pigs or chickens."

Eum-chun bought oysters and turned away.

"If you come back, the day after tomorrow," the woman offered, "I'll save some octopus. Just for you, Auntie."

That would be after Gui-yong spent his first night with his second wife. Would she feel enough like herself to walk to the market then? She'd better. She'd show the world what she was made of—guts, grace, blindness—and follow what Heaven laid out for her life, son or no son.

Back at the top of the incline, she passed Mrs. Choi's house. The gate was cracked open. Mrs. Choi must be up, smelling the steam from boiling rice. The urge to dash into her kitchen and see her face pounded Eum-chun. If she could see that face, she'd lay new flooring paper in her husband's honeymoon room, confident she'd find a hole to fly through even if the sky collapsed. But she had no time to stop now. Mi-na would be late to her kindergarten.

When she returned after walking Mi-na to school, she set vegetables apart from the eggs and meat.

"Back already?" her mother-in-law asked from the wood-floored sitting room open to the yard. Mrs. Rhee was smoking her long bamboo pipe.

Mrs. Rhee's usual scowl created two wavy lines on her

forehead. Had she been a man, she and her son would've looked like twins, except her son didn't frown. He was too busy teasing Eum-chun to do that. He joked about how the belt she tied on when doing chores made her behind look more to his liking. He teased her about Peach, too, who ran a rice wine joint on his southern route.

"Had to fight off Peach," he said, "and five other women to get home to you, *yeobo*, sweetheart. You should've seen the flirty eye smiles Peach threw at me."

He teased Mi-na about her forehead sticking out like his and his mother's.

"How're you going to catch a husband with a forehead like yours?" he asked, making Mi-na pout until he tickled her sides.

She passed Mrs. Rhee, who had finished smoking and was now gathering scissors, flooring paper, and bean oil. Eum-chun went into her room to fix her hair because the bun pinched at one spot.

"Let's get the floor done before Mi-na comes back." Mrs. Rhee's voice came.

"Yes, Mother."

After fixing her hair, she went back out into the sitting room and passed the apple crate-sized radio on the shelf. How happy those days had been when Eum-chun and her mother-in-law listened to their favorite *pansori* musicals together. Before the plan to bring the new woman firmed, they sat around and ate rice cake like mother and daughter, tight as the two halves of a walnut.

Mrs. Rhee went into the new room and put down the paper, brush, and rag. In the small garden spot beyond the faucet, Eum-chun's red-for-a-hundred-days flowers, zinnias, held up their bright faces. One hundred—a perfect number for flowers and a sweet number of years for marriage. At their wedding, his mother had thrown walnuts into the red skirt Eum-chun held out. She caught five—that meant they'd have five children. She and Gui-yong had hoped at least three would be sons.

Magpies swooped down to the eaves and broke into a jabber. *Tsssack, tsssack, tsssack.* "That means good news is coming tomorrow," Mrs. Rhee always said. Today, she didn't. She was being considerate of Eum-chun's feelings.

"Mother, I'll be right there."

She picked up a dry rag from the ledge and rice glue from the stove and went toward the honeymoon room, which had been used by guests in the past. Would the sounds Gui-yong and his woman make carry into her room? She remembered hearing his uncle from Suwon snoring when he stayed there.

With the wedding noodles she'd cook, she must wish Gui-yong and his woman well. *May your marriage bed be as satisfying as the noodles.*

Gui-yong

After three hours of pushing hard, he felt like stopping and peeing behind a tree, but he decided to keep going until he reached his regular stop, Peach's wine joint. Her regulars said her neck wore out from stretching like a heron's, waiting for him. Each time he ate there, after piling extra food on his plate, she didn't take his money. While she busied herself with cooking, he slid payment under a china bowl on her counter. If he looked at her closely enough, small pock marks showed around her lower chin, nothing a good-looking woman should feel shabby about. She was a typical southerner who sweetened the tail end of her words with *yooo*. Her hips nicely wide and her boobs pushing out even with her skirt band bound around them, she was the sturdy type.

"There's a woman," his mother would've cried, "who can push out boy babies as easily as peeled plums."

A year ago, when his mother slapped on her headache band and quit eating for three days in a row, he could no longer put off getting a second wife. He first thought of Peach. She'd have made the best seed bearer for him. He'd have let her stay where she lived and paid her living expenses. If she'd have given him a son, he would've taken him to Eum-chun where he belonged. After a while, he would've stopped seeing Peach. She'd have understood. Most seed bearers blamed their fate, not men.

Doing that to her, though, didn't feel right. Not because he was an especially moral man but because of how he felt about the trouble Jin-i was in. She might lose her newborn to her lover's wife.

So after stewing over Peach, he dropped the seed bearer idea. Now, whether he'd chosen her or someone else, he wished he'd have set her up anywhere but under his own roof.

He swung around a bend, passing rice paddies to the left and farmhouses to the right.

He parked the truck by a totem pole next to Peach's. Its eyes bulged as if it were seeing something too awful to see. He walked past several boys kicking a coin wrapped and tasseled in cloth. If he had a brother with a few sons, he could adopt a nephew. And of course no one outside the family would give up their sons for adoption. If he'd chosen Peach, he might already have a son. Soon he'd show him how to play the coin-kick game those boys were playing.

"You must've gotten an early start," Peach said, her eyes smiling, and wiped her hands on her apron. Two of her regulars playing chess, Ham, the dog butcher, and Min, the blacksmith, nodded at him. Peach brought two steaming mung bean pancakes, intestine stew, and radish kimchi, which he downed in a hurry. He stood up. The chess players were too busy to embarrass Peach by ribbing her about wasting her time on Gui-yong.

"You ate too fast! You'll get a sour stomach." Peach shot him a scolding look and held out barley tea. Gui-yong gulped and slipped money under her china bowl.

"How about a jug of your homemade rice wine? To take with me?"

"Good luck tomorrow, and have many sons," she said.

"Who told you?"

She twisted her apron. "One of your City Hall men came by yesterday."

He couldn't bring himself to say, "Thanks for your good wishes." He merely tipped his head, tucked the wine under his arm, and shuffled off. Before he got into his seat, he craned his neck. She stood by the door, her hands behind her apron like a nun's.

He passed the oak trees. Eum-chun would like the wine. He checked the back mirror; Peach was still there watching him. Only after he turned onto the highway did she turn back.

The first month after he told his mother and Eum-chun about Soo-yang, Eum-chun made his life as unbearable as sitting in a Buddhist hell. She poured tears onto his chest every night. But she'd handled tight spots before. One miscarriage. The adoption of Mi-na. His mother had banged her pipe on her brass ashtray and yelled, "You can adopt a child *after* I'm dead and dirt has filled my eyes." But they got Mi-na, and she brought so much laughter into the house that even his mother's heart melted. Eum-chun and his mother were tight as ever. Eum-chun would brave through tomorrow. He hoped he would.

He eased back into his seat and turned on the radio. Maybe he'd hear "Taepyeongga," the Peace Song. He liked the cheerful belting of its refrains. They weren't words, just sounds a happy person would make.

Nilliriya, nilliriya, ninanooooo!

His shoulders would jiggle up and down. He liked the next lines, too.

Ain't life lovely? Ain't life grand?
Here come spring butterflies! Bzzz here! Bzzz there.
Teasing this flower. Teasing that. Bzzz! Bzzz! Bzzz!

Instead, President Syngman Rhee's voice sputtered out.

"Our new Navy will drive Communist guerillas into the Taedong River!"

"Damned epileptic fit," Noodle Leg called such talk. The president's voice always shook a little, but it held strong.

"Our thirty million will rise up!" he said, "We'll drive Communists out of North Korea and fight China, our enemy to the west, and Japan to the south!"

"Damn North Korea, China, and Japan," Noodle Leg had

said, and Phone Pole had agreed. Gui-yong didn't know history or any other educated subjects. If China and Japan hadn't messed with their country, they said, it'd be feeding everyone. Instead, everyone's belly stuck to their back. He could tell that from the lepers and beggars he saw more and more of. Petty thieves stole gasoline from the trucks parked for the driver's run to the outhouse. Right out of the tank. They stuck in a foot of hose, sucked on it, and when gasoline squirted out, they shoved the hose into their can. He caught a seventeen-year-old at it last month. He swatted him twice and let him go. What else could he do? The boy probably had no father. He twisted the radio knob.

Farm women who'd been out feeding their menfolk in the fields walked on the dikes. They balanced the baskets set on their heads with one hand. With the other, they carried a heavy sack or held a baby's butt in a piggyback sling. They wore their skirts the way he liked—hitched up above their ankles. That kept them from tripping but also made their buttocks round and their waists slender, like an ant's. When they strode on narrow dikes, their hips wriggled, teasing him to fantasize making love to his wife in what he dubbed their dragon dance.

He'd take his clothes off and slide into the bedding spread on the warmed floor. Just before she'd turn the light off to undress, he'd ask, "*Yeobo*, how about a walk-away?" He'd lie on his side, facing her, his head on his propped-up elbow.

Eum-chun would pull out her belt from a drawer, gather up her skirt, and sling the belt around her waist, flashing a smile like the famous *gisaeng* Nongae—who'd gone down in history after she threw herself overboard from a pleasure boat. She took the top Japanese general with her by locking him in her embrace. The ten rings she wore on her fingers kept the two stuck together in death.

He'd twirl his finger for Eum-chun to turn. She'd take lazy steps. He would eye her buttocks, and after a few moments, he'd leap and pull her to him. He'd flick the light switch off, and they'd fall to lovemaking. He'd stick his fingers in boiling bean sauce if any man had a better time with his woman than that.

Eum-chun

The gate opened, and Eum-chun's younger brother, Chang-gil, ran in. Out of breath, he whispered.

"Come quick." He breathed hard, open mouthed. "Jin-i is . . ." He gulped more air. "Mother told me to get you." Sweat grayed his high school uniform shirt collar.

Mrs. Rhee looked out. When he saw her, he bowed and asked, "Are you in good health?"

Eum-chun slid onto the tile step and dropped her head

into her hands. Her nightmare came true. Did she have a divination *shin* spirit, as her sorceress Aunt Hong did? Gui-yong and others around her thought her temperament was high-strung, but that's different from a shaman's power. What she had was nerves. But when a dream turned real like this, she felt a chill.

That swine Kim! She cursed under her breath. *My poor Jin-i. Why couldn't he let Jin-i keep the baby at least until school age?* Blood thump-thumped in her temples.

"Something happened to Jin-i?" Mrs. Rhee asked.

"She is . . ." Chang-gil stammered, "upset. Mother said my sister might help."

Eum-chun straightened herself. She bit her lips in order not to press Chang-gil for details in front of Mrs. Rhee.

"May I go to my sister's? I'll rush back and finish the floor."

"Go, then." Mrs. Rhee turned and picked up a sheet of the flooring paper. "I'll get Mi-na if you're not back in time. Go!"

Eum-chun and Chang-gil hurried out the gate.

"Where are you rushing to?" Ah, there by the gate stood Mrs. Choi, the woman Buddha, who could pour spiritual strength down on her by the bucket. Mrs. Choi held a gourd dipper in her hand, as though she had come out to fill a monk's begging sack.

"Have to rush to my sister's." Flinging those words was all

she had the time for.

Across the Munwha-dong main street, the path narrowed, and they passed tile-roofed houses with thatched ones mixed in. The one-bedroom apartment Kim had rented for Jin-i was tucked beyond the Sigumun Gate near Aunt Hong's.

Once there, Eum-chun dropped to the floor, where Jin-i lay in her bedding. Their mother was already there. Eum-chun cast her arm around her sister and the three wept.

"I'll call the police!" Chang-gil shouted from above them. "I'll get 'em to find the baby!"

The women looked up.

"Chang-gil!" Eum-chun said, feeling annoyed. "Don't be dumb. Your job's doing your schoolwork. Go read your books. Even if you've got only the tail lights of fireflies to read by! Go. Now!"

He was a silly boy, too young to know the world. What police would arrest a rich company boss for taking his flesh-and-blood son to his lawful wife? Chang-gil's face turned worm-red. He banged his head against the wall he and Eum-chun had covered with fresh plaster last year right after Jin-i became pregnant. *Thud, thud, thud, thud, thud.* He slowed.

"I've tried to pump Jin-i's breasts," Mrs. Pak said through her handkerchief. "But I couldn't get all the milk out, and she's been hurting. I gave her some herbal medicine, but it's not helping."

"Let me look at you, Jin-i." Eum-chun raised her to a sitting position. Jin-i's maroon blouse popped open. Chang-gil turned away and slipped out. Mrs. Pak moved in with a bowl to catch the milk. Even the famous Chinese beauty, Yang Guifei, didn't have as large and beautiful eyes or a widow's peak hairline as shapely as Jin-i's. Now, from crying, her eyes domed.

Eum-chun massaged the breasts, which were hard as fists. She went from the outer rings to the nipples. In all fairness, she couldn't fault only Kim. How many men would resist doing their peacock dance before a woman like Jin-i and getting her into trouble?

"Where's Li-ho? Who's taking care of her, Mother?"

"Your father," Mrs. Pak said as she slid the bowl under Jin-i's right breast. As always, the thought of Li-ho, Jin-i's older child by another man, sprouted a new sore in Eum-chun's heart.

Eum-chun drummed her fingers on Jin-i's breast, and then switched to gentle squeezing. Milk arrowed out into the china bowl. Eum-chun's own breasts tingled. If she hadn't had a miscarriage, her milk would have squirted into the warm mouth of a boy. Jin-i hissed through her teeth as Eum-chun squeezed her breasts. When finished, Eum-chun helped her lie down.

"Chang-gil shouldn't have brought you," Jin-i said. "You're

ten fathoms deep in your own troubles, and you've got cooking to do."

Eum-chun patted Jin-i's hand. "Don't let your breasts puff up like that again. The fever and pus will make you wish you had died like a malarial dog. Eat everything Mother gives you. Let's wait a while before we try to get Joon-ho back."

Bringing him back would take a miracle. Even if they could, Jin-i would have to part with him sooner or later. Since Jin-i was not Kim's live-in mistress, her chance of retrieving the boy was not great. Besides, if Jin-i didn't let her son go to his father's house sometime and go to school as his child appearing on his family record, she'd do to the boy's future what people did to a cockroach. *Splattt!* Gone. Dead. Still, everyone on Jin-i's side would cut off an arm if that would bring back the boy for at least his toddler years.

On the way back, Eum-chun squinted into the sun and remembered the week in the dead of last winter. Her mother-in-law was considering having a seed-bearer woman live with her son in their house. But out of kindness to Eum-chun, her mother-in-law offered, "If you object, we will get her a rental room. Your husband can go see her there. Will you let me know which way you prefer?" How unnecessary and loving of her mother-in-law to ask for her opinion. "Sweetheart, let's not do what we cannot live with," Gui-yong said that night, holding her with her back against him. His chest knocked against her. The next day, with her mother-in-law's permission, Eum-chun rushed to her parent's home, where she holed herself up. She ripped out her hair and refused food. On the fifth day, her mother laid a bowl of water before her and held out her hands piled with pills.

"Want to kill yourself?" her mother asked. "All right, then. Let's do it. You take these in my right hand and I'll take these in the other." Saying nothing, Eum-chun grabbed the bowl of red bean porridge she had left uneaten in a corner of her room and began stuffing her mouth with it. When finished swallowing, she said, "Put those pills away, Mother."

That night the Moon God that Aunt Hong, her father's sister and a shaman, worshipped appeared before Eum-chun and laid a bamboo stalk, bushy with leaves, on her chest. White steam puffed out of each of the knobs of the branch and blew moist fog into Eum-chun's face. *Sshuuu shhuu mmmeee ummmmee*, the Moon God whispered in her ears. With that sound and the feeling of the bamboo branch tickling her face, Eum-chun rose the next morning, went home, and announced, "Let's bring the woman into the house."

"Sweetheart, are you out of your mind?" Gui-yong's eyes bulged with disbelief.

Now, looking into the sun on the way home from Jin-i's,

she gave herself a sharp nod of you-made-the-right-choice. Keeping one less woman from getting whacked on the head with an unfair deal, like had happened to Jin-i, had to be worth the mountain of pain. When Gui-yong's woman bore him sons, the three of them would raise them. During that time, if his affection for the new woman grew deep, Eum-chun's first-wife status could turn into an empty shell. She and Mi-na might get pushed around like acorns in a dog dish. Well, so be it. Plain and simple. For now, they must try to live peacefully, just as Mrs. Choi, her husband, and his other woman did.

Gui-yong

To his right, rice fields changed to a pine grove. He then saw someone sitting by the side of the road, wearing the gray hemp outfit of a Buddhist monk. Because he didn't want to choke the monk with dust, he stopped a few meters before reaching him.

"Need a ride?" When he got close, he saw she was a nun. "Sorry, I thought you were a monk. Where you going?"

The nun rose and bowed. "Deoksansa Temple. A day's walk. But I've got all day. No need to bother you." She had a sack sitting on the ground.

The nun had a blue birthmark shaped like a baby's hand. It crept from her cheek down around her earlobe to her neck, as if a god had stamped his hand on her. He opened the door. The nun lingered as if checking with Buddha whether to take the offer before climbing into the seat.

He cranked the truck back into the road. "Is your Deoksansa big?"

"Oh, not big. Just fourteen of us."

The nun closed her eyes, her fingers sliding over her prayer beads. He'd heard that monks and nuns who spent their lives in meditation could tell the future of the country. He wondered if the nun foresaw a war between the North and South. Would the South win? Of course it would. In that case, a war might not be a bad idea, as his Uncle Park had said.

"We should make powdered beans out of those Red dogs before they get us," his uncle had said. "President Rhee's been itching to attack the North for two years and begging for tanks and mortars from America, but President Truman refuses! He stands and watches Russian tanks roll into North Korea! Unless the South can grab some of those iron and steel factories in the North and the North can have our rice and beans, everyone on both sides will have their ribs sticking out."

As a boy, his uncle had gone to a private Confucian school and learned all the classics. After that, he went to a Japanese school. He had many friends who were lawyers, government ministers, and bankers. Ideas about how to run the country dangled from every strand of his hair.

"Clouds. Black clouds," the nun said, her eyes still closed. He craned his neck out the window and scanned the sky. Not a single cloud and the sky as blue as the nun's birthmark. Could she have read his mind? Was she predicting a war?

"You see clouds?"

"Your hairline narrows at the temple."

When did she see him closely enough to see that? People saw his nose first. At the shop, Noodle Leg teased him about it. "What's the matter with that big nose of yours? Your other thing not as big, eh? Is that why your wife can't give you no son? Need a stand-in?"

"That narrowing's pulling in clouds." The nun drew a sigh and followed it with a *namu amitabul*. Buddha, have mercy. He learned that prayer from his wife.

"What do you mean by clouds?"

The nun ignored his question. He was itching to know what she meant, but he didn't ask again. Such talk sounded like superstition to him.

The Mt. Jirisan poked out west and tapered down like the tail of a wild boar. The waves of green looked too pretty to hold Communist guerillas dug in there like lice in long johns. If a war really burst open, all healthy men younger than fifty would be dragged away to fight. That would be the only time he'd be glad to be an only son in his family line for three generations in a row: he'd probably be exempted.

What did the nun mean by clouds? Could she be talking about Soo-yang's coming? What would happen to him, his wife, or Soo-yang? Had his seeds already dried up, so he'd not produce a son with Soo-yang either? That wouldn't be just clouds; it'd be like him and his truck going off a cliff.

Where the road turned steep, he switched gears. The engine whined. Stones and broken branches jumped from the ground. Pines thickened on both sides, their fresh smell a nice change. When they got to a clearing, the nun said, "I'll get off here." They were at the knee of the peak.

"Up there? That's where your temple is?" He looked as high as his eye could reach and saw nothing but pine. There'd be more than a few tigers and lots of Reds. He'd have to tease Mi-na with a story of a tiger nipping at his heels. "Here's his hair," he'd say. Where would he get that? An herbal doc might have some.

"Yes. Thank you for the ride." The nun bowed.

Wait—tell me about the clouds, he was about to say. But before he did, the nun said, "I see someone dying, intestines turning to charcoal, burning and burning, but Buddha's merciful." She then turned into the woods.

He stepped on the gas. Die? Who would? Not Eum-chun! Not Soo-yang? Not Mi-na? He didn't believe in superstition, but the nun's birthmark got him shaking.

He might be wrong about Eum-chun's charm and steel pulling her through tomorrow and the days ahead. *You thought that to ease your own mind, didn't you, you ball-less bastard.*

He braked lightly and went down hill.

Eum-chun

In her room, Eum-chun took water into her mouth from a bowl and sprayed it onto Gui-yong's trousers. She was ironing the trousers, shirt, and vest he'd wear tomorrow. The evening grew quieter, with Mi-na asleep in Mrs. Rhee's room. Her mother-in-law was having her bedtime smoke in the hallway, where Gui-yong was fanning himself. Eum-chun had sewn his light blue pants and shirt and the navy blue vest for last New Year's Day. How could she have known the outfit would be worn to welcome a woman into his bed?

She slid the palm-sized iron down the leg of his trousers. Heat from the hot charcoal in the iron's belly warmed her hand.

Earlier in the afternoon, when she'd returned from her sister's house, her mother-in-law and Mi-na were finishing their lunch. When Mi-na skipped out to play with Kwang-ho, she and Mrs. Rhee laid the flooring paper in the new woman's room, and Eum-chun told her about Kim snatching Joon-ho away.

"Our ancestors were right," Mrs. Rhee said. "Life *is* like the intestines of a sheep, folded nine times with impossible bends. Everyone's lives are like that, but Jin-i's seems to hold more painful curves than others'."

Eum-chun folded Gui-yong's trousers and ankle ties and laid them on her dresser top. She ironed his shirt. Through the open door, she could hear Gui-yong's fan swishing back and forth. He cleared his throat. That lovely sound. He had a slightly husky voice people described as "spoiled" for the bit of drag and tiredness in it, but it brought his whole body right up against hers, neither of them wearing anything. When they were alone and cozy on their floor mat, she often asked him, "Clear your throat for me, *yeobo*. I'll give you something you'll like."

"Good night, son." Mrs. Rhee's voice came in from the hallway.

"Good night, Mother."

Gui-yong came into the room, looking cool in the hemp shirt and shorts he'd changed into when he came home. Eum-chun slid the door shut, pulled out a futon, and spread out the green summer coverlet bordered with ruby, the wedding colors. Gui-yong undressed, lay down, and slung his right arm across his forehead. A shadow fell over his eyes, but she could tell they followed her.

"What's wrong, *yeobo*?" he said. He noticed her eyelids pulling tight, which she did when upset.

"Sun-ja nearly killed all of us today. Told Mi-na she was a throwaway child."

"What!" Gui-yong bolted up. "How did that happen? How did Mi-na take it? Is she all right? Why didn't you tell me that the minute I got home?"

"And make Mi-na cry her eyes out all over again?"

"If you and Mother can't keep a lid on this, *yeobo*, you know we'll have to move. We'll have to live somewhere where nobody knows us."

"Shhhhhh. I know. I'm sorry. It'll never happen again. Mother took it hard, too. She gave Sun-ja a good spanking and got an apology out of Mrs. Bang. She lay down with a headache band until just before you came home."

Gui-yong let out a groan and slumped back down on the mat.

"And Jin-i? She's coming tomorrow with her baby and your mother, right?"

She pushed the iron aside, sat down, and snuggled her face against his collarbone. Between the adoption leak scare and what happened to Jin-i's baby, she couldn't hold it in anymore. She let tears fall quietly. He held her. She didn't have to tell him what happened to Jin-i. After a while, she blew her nose into a handkerchief. He looked into her face.

"*Yeobo*, feel like having some of that Namwon wine I brought you?"

"If you'll have a sip, too," she said, and left for the kitchen.

When she brought the wine and two small bowls, he sat up, cross-legged. She poured less than half a bowl for him but filled hers. Lost as to a cheerful toast to make, she froze, her cup in the air.

He raised his cup. "To our Mi-na, ours, always. And . . . to us . . . ten years from now."

Ten years? Long before that, her heart might have turned to soot.

With three gulps of the wine, her stomach smoothed. With another, images of tomorrow, the next few days, Mi-na's crisis, and what happened to Jin-i all became old, yellowed pictures.

"*Yeobo*," he said. She loved the way he said that ordinary word for "spouse." He made his voice serious, and the difference between that and the teasing in his eyes usually got her to giggle. Today, her chest felt too clogged for her to smile.

"Try not to get yourself too heartsick about Jin-i's son," he said. "He'll cry and keep them up all night, and then they'll bring him right back to Jin-i. Want to bet? If I'm wrong, I'll change my last name. But do be extra careful about Mi-na."

She sighed. "Don't joke about your last name, *yeobo*. The

ghosts of your ancestors will hear you." She stopped. Then she added, "Soon, I'll become like cold porridge to you, just as Jin-i did to Kim."

Wine had already spattered pink blotches on his face. "You'll just have to wait to find out, won't you, *yeobo*?" His teasing grin returned to his lips as he clicked off the light switch. Then he closed his mouth upon hers.

The wedding day

Eum-chun

After breakfast, Gui-yong put on the light blue outfit Eum-chun had ironed the night before to head to the woman's house. From behind him, Eum-chun brushed his dark blue vest across his shoulders, as if she saw lint. Down his spine, she lingered. Warmth came through his shirt.

Didn't he want to turn around and say words like "I love you, *yeobo*"? No, he wouldn't say that; men didn't. Couldn't he keep her in his eyes for a little longer? She'd know its meaning. But he'd done that and more last night. How much more did she need?

He opened the gate and left.

She returned to the kitchen, mixed flour, egg, water, and salt for the noodles, and kneaded the dough. After spreading the noodles on a tray and setting them on the side ledge to air, she blanched spinach, carrots, and zucchini.

"Did Mi-na calm down? Are you all right?" Mrs. Bang stood outside the kitchen door. Eum-chun was so steeped in her own thoughts and in cooking that she didn't hear Mrs. Bang entering.

"It was a shock. To Mi-na and to us all." Eum-chun stopped beating the egg, took a drink from her bowl of cold water, and sat down on the straw seat on the dirt floor of her kitchen. "We were all shaken, Mrs. Bang."

"I'm very sorry. I'll make sure Sun-ja will never blabber like that again. I swear."

After a few minutes of silence, Mrs. Bang untucked the *Dong-A Ilbo* from under her arm. Every so often, she brought the newspaper after she and her husband had finished reading it. They both graduated from high schools in Pyongyang, their hometown. But although they had lived in Seoul for twenty years, they spoke with a North Korean accent. Their tone went up and down more than Seoul people's. They also pronounced the "n" as an "r," calling the cold noodle dish, *naengmyeon, raengmyeon.*

"Let me give you a hand. Here, let me wash the watercress and chop it." She set the newspaper on the ledge and rolled up her sleeves.

"Thanks. I could use the help."

"Are you getting a hideout put in? The Lees got theirs

done. I suppose you can't think about anything else except the woman who's coming. We're scared enough to start digging, too. The Workers' Party getting so organized, it's not funny. They'll stir up serious trouble."

"We're over our heads with plenty to worry about, that's for sure."

"Pak Hon-yong's whipping the Workers' Party of Korea into shape for some big Commie scheme. The question is, what's he up to?" Mrs. Bang *tak tak takked* with her knife on the board and arranged watercress strips on a platter in neat rows like soldiers. "If North's going to blast the South to bits, I wish they'd do it *now.* Don't tell anyone I said this! I'll end up in jail! But the tension's driving me wild—I can't stand not being able to open my mouth about anything just because we came from the North. It doesn't matter how long ago we did it."

Eum-chun got up from her seat and beat the eggs.

"If the North wipes us out," Eum-chun said, "there may be any number of us who may not be too heartbroken. At least we'll be dead and done with this life."

After Mrs. Bang left, Eum-chun sat back on the seat and rested her legs.

At noon, her mother and Aunt Hong arrived. They brought eggs and skeins of cotton threads, the usual gifts for setting a wedding table. Even though they wouldn't prepare a formal feast, the presents reflected their good wishes for the couple's long life and plentiful children. By the kitchen door, her mother gave Eum-chun's hand a squeeze. Aunt Hong threw a stern glance at Eum-chun as if to say, "My Moon and Sun Gods are watching you. Be good. Be strong."

Mrs. Rhee's younger sister, the aunt from Suwon, arrived with her husband, too. Suwon Aunt was a sweet woman with a plump, smiley face. Today, as she held Eum-chun's hands, her lips smiled, but her eyes teared.

"My poor little niece-in-law," Suwon Aunt whispered.

To hide her own eyes, which were also welling up, Eum-chun turned her face away and said, "Aunt, go on in. Mother's waiting."

After that, Gae-sun and Mrs. Hahn from next door came. Gae-sun joined Eum-chun in the kitchen.

Even after they boiled the noodles and decorated each bowl with the yellow egg strips, red pepper, and green spinach, Gui-yong and the woman didn't show. Gae-sun seasoned the watercress that Mrs. Bang had cleaned and chopped.

"Why aren't they here yet?" Mrs. Rhee paced and wrung her hands. "The noodles will get soggy! Let's serve. They can join us when they get here."

Mi-na

At least it was a sunny day. Grandma was right. She said that if a drop of dew hung on a spiderweb, the next day would be clear. Grandma was right about the ants, too. Mi-na sat on the floor of the hallway sitting room, her legs dangling off the edge of the wood floor. She didn't want to go out to play. No, not after what happened yesterday. Even if Sun-ja's words were lies as red as a monkey's butt, she still didn't feel like going outside.

"If ants crawl in a line and come into the house, it'll rain," Grandma had said. Mi-na didn't see any yesterday. Last night, the frogs by their shed had stayed quiet, too. So the blue sky didn't surprise Mi-na. She was glad, because she wanted it to be nice for Daddy. If it rained, it'd be crummy for Mommy, too. Noodles would stick to the drying tray.

She looked at the china bowls and small sauce jars sitting on a tray by Mommy's cupboard in the hallway sitting room. Daddy had given Mommy the Japanese china set, which she used only on special days

Close to lunch, everything crawled like a centipede. Even Mommy moved slowly, slicing, mixing, sprinkling sesame seeds, tasting, and hopping in and out of the kitchen. Mommy would get sore legs. Tonight she'd ask Mi-na, "Will you give my legs a little massage?" She'd do it for Mommy, if it would make her less sad. Where were Daddy and the

Little House woman? Grandma stuffed the floor rag mop into the bowl of her pipe, put the fire out, and before going into the kitchen, asked Mi-na, "Aren't you going out to play?"

"No!" Did Grandma forget what happened yesterday?

Besides, she didn't want to miss seeing Daddy and the Little Mommy woman arrive.

As Mrs. Bang and everyone else besides Mrs. Lee said, that woman's coming was her fault. Nobody had to tell her that over and over. She pinched the top of her left hand. *Bad, bad. For not being a boy.* She was as horrid as the wart-faced Kongjui in her story book. Ouch. She'd pinched herself harder than she'd meant to.

She put her shoes on at the stone step and skipped to the kitchen.

"Mommy?"

Mommy stopped her hands, wiped them on her apron, and stretched them out to her. Grandma was standing by the ledge, slicing dough into noodle strands.

"Come sit with me," Mommy said. Together, they sat on her straw seat and looked at the fire.

"Mommy," Mi-na asked, "before I was born, did you tell me how to get born with a penis, but I didn't listen to you?"

"No, Jade Leaf, that's not what happened. Samsin Fertility Spirit makes children into boys or girls. I asked you to be born healthy and beautiful, and you listened! And look at your forehead sticking out! A big brain there! You get tickled for that!" She came at her ribs, making her giggle. Mommy wrapped her arms around her, and they rocked. She felt good all over. Still, there must have been something she could've done to have been born a boy. Lately, something had made Kwang-ho go crazy, too.

"Come here," he said a few days ago, sliding behind his shed, "Want to see what you should've gotten born with?"

Mi-na felt like the rice cake she'd eaten was coming up. Why would she want to see a thing that looked like a worm that had grown too fat? She ran back into her house but didn't tell Mommy.

"Want to see if Kwang-ho wants to kick wrapped coins with you?" Mommy sounded like she needed to get busy with cooking.

"No!" Her answer came out like the sound of a piece of cloth being torn in half by hand when Mommy didn't feel like using scissors. Grandma turned and looked from the faucet in the yard.

"Mi-na!" Mommy looked into her face. "What was that?"

"Nothing, Mommy. I was just teasing. I'll go swing."

Mi-na went to the hallway between Mommy's room and the other one, where the woman would sleep. She shook her shoes off and sat on the swing hanging from the ceiling beam Daddy had made for her. Mi-na hated the snake poop smell coming from the oil Grandma and Mommy had used on the new floor paper in the woman's room. She'd never smelled snake poop, but she could imagine how bad it smelled. The sun warmed her bare feet.

She lifted her blouse front. A thumb-sized red pouch Mommy pinned was there. Mommy's shaman Aunt Hong had given it to her.

"It should keep you healthy," Mommy had said. Was there a red pouch Mommy could have gotten to make Mi-na be born a boy? If there was, it clearly hadn't worked. So why should this one do the job and keep her healthy? She unpinned it and let it fly across the yard. It landed by the mouth of the concrete cellar.

"What are you doing!" Grandma said, pulling her hands out of the water in the basin.

Mi-na got off the swing, ran to her, and covered Grandma's mouth. "Shhhh. Don't tell Mommy, Grandma. I was just playing a game. See, I'm picking it up." She pinned it back on to the underside of her blouse.

She went back to the swing. She wondered what Daddy's new woman looked like. Was she pretty like a poppy flower? What if Daddy liked her better than Mommy? What if Mommy cried every day?

Her favorite game was cooking rice in her seashell. It sat where she left it—on the small ledge by Mommy's room. Every day, after making a tiny fire with matchsticks on the concrete step in the yard, she dropped a few grains of rice and a little water into the shell and set it over the fire—carefully so as not to spill the water. She looked at the seashell. Should she make the rice? No, she didn't feel like doing anything.

"Got a piece of bean sprout stuck in your throat?" her kindergarten teacher asked any glum-looking child. Between what happened yesterday and what was about to happen today, she felt a lot worse than when an unchewed bean sprout didn't go down her throat.

Soo-yang

It was a half hour's walk from her parents' house on Euljiro Road to Gui-yong's home. After washing her face at the faucet, Soo-yang looked up at the sky. The June sun poured down, leaving nowhere to hide. The bright light would bare the hairline creases by her mouth and the nick at her temple from falling off a seesaw board when she was little. More frightfully, the daylight would reveal her as a man's mistress in the neighbors' eyes.

The smell of peonies and wild roses drifted in from her mother's flower bed. *Tschack, tschack, tschack*, magpies' jabbered. A good sign, but what was good about today? *I am taking another woman's husband.* The thought, bitter as sow thistle, left a vinegary taste between her teeth. *What will my life be like? What if I give birth to a boy and they keep him but throw me out? When I jump into a well, how cold will the water feel? How long before I quit breathing?*

She sat before her folding vanity, and as she slid a comb through her hair, an image of a cliff nagged at her.

"Close your eyes and plunge," the cliff said. "If you don't die from this fall, your liver will grow strong, and you'll survive any knife thrown at you." With those words in her ears, she put on her skirt and blouse, the light-green shade of newly sprouted willows. If she were a first-time bride, she'd wear a blouse with rainbow-striped sleeves, a balsam-red skirt, and a green tunic with a broad ruby sash around the waist. A black silk crown with a hundred beads of rainbow colors would adorn her hairdo.

But such fanciness was not for this marriage, a quiet blending into Gui-yong's household. Still, it was a special day for her and his family, and a spring-colored outfit seemed right.

She patted more Coty powder around her eyes. At least this time, Gui-yong had seen her; her father had even told him about her "deformity," the gouged leg.

Before her father had brought Gui-yong, she'd prepared herself to die a virgin. If she did that, her ghost would've waited for a man to urinate on her grave—one way she could free herself from hell and have a chance at entering heaven.

"*Jangmonim*, here I am." Gui-yong's voice greeted her

mother. Her happiest laughter rolled out. She sounded as though she might swoon because she'd been called "mother-in-law."

Soo-yang went out to the hallway and bowed to Gui-yong while her father rushed to the yard and grasped his hands. Soo-yang and her mother followed them into her parents' room. There, he knelt before her parents and lowered his head to the floor with his clasped hands brushing against his forehead.

A lunch of the fattest chicken her father could buy was served. Her father suggested Gui-yong and Soo-yang head back to his home later, close to sundown, to avoid prying neighbors' eyes. Soo-yang could tell Gui-yong was worried about his mother and guests waiting with food prepared and about not having a phone to use to let them know. But he agreed, and so they did not leave until dusk.

When she finally stepped inside his house, a briar patch lay underfoot, and her feet felt thorns piercing her green rubber shoes and white padded socks. She bit her lower lip and held back a groan. Gui-yong turned and looked at her. When his eyes met hers, she looked down and saw blue and white tiles, not thorns. She walked faster then, keeping her eyes on his broad back. The *fffsss fffsss* of her skirt at her every step amplified in her ears. She passed the kitchen, and, out of the corner of her eye, saw a woman in the shadows. Soo-yang's insides jerked back, as though she'd stumbled upon a snake hole. The woman must be his wife. She turned and saw a girl sitting on a swing in the hallway. That must be Mi-na. When their eyes met, the girl stood up and bowed. Her eyes were enormous, lips so clearly outlined they looked painted. Amazingly, her forehead rounded nicely, as Gui-yong's did. She could now understand how strangers never suspected she was not his flesh and blood.

The house was quiet. The guests must have left. Beyond the faucet, the crape myrtles, the red-for-a-hundred-days flowers, stood like guards. The sauce jars on top of the concrete cellar were lined up neatly, covered for the evening. Not one scrap lay scattered anywhere. No mop was flung against the side of the storage shed. The house smelled of order and shine. Mrs. Rhee and two other women sat in the sitting room and watched them approach. They took their shoes off and stepped up.

"Welcome home," Mrs. Rhee said, and introduced the women next to her as Eum-chun's mother and Eum-chun's Aunt Hong. Eum-chun's mother had a graceful, oval face, her eyes as level as a Buddhist nun's and kind toward everyone, even toward a woman like Soo-yang who came to sleep with her daughter's husband.

Hands cupped against her skirt below her waist, Soo-yang bent her knees, squatted, and dipped her head in a bride's bow. Under their gaze, the pores on her face opened with sweat. Gui-yong made a man's bow and sat beside her.

"Bear many sons." Eum-chun's mother wished Soo-yang luck.

"Be rich in children," Aunt Hong said.

"Forgive me for coming late in the day." Soo-yang couldn't make her voice loud. Soo-yang and Gui-yong rose, and he led her across the yard to her room. She again saw Mi-na, her eyes looking whipped. When they came close to Mi-na, Gui-yong knelt on one knee and whispered into Mi-na's ear. A smile came to Mi-na's lips. He then opened the door of the room next to the swing and let Soo-yang in. Without lingering or even saying, "Rest a bit," he turned around and left the house, taking Mi-na with him. Earlier, during their walk, he had said his neighbor Mr. Lee had invited him for celebratory wine.

Soon after Eum-chun's mother and Aunt Hong left, Gui-yong and Mi-na returned from Mr. Lee's, his face flushed. In a while, the dinner hour arrived. After setting the table and carrying it to the sitting room, Soo-yang hung back in the kitchen, planning to eat there by herself, as her mother had instructed her to. *How humiliating, cowering like a servant. Is this a rule men made for women, or one women like her mother made to please men? Either way, what are you going to do about it? Cry like a moron? Go ahead, cry. Just remember, thousands of women have been in your shoes for hundreds of years. Had they all wept like cats getting rained on?*

"What are you doing there?" Mrs. Rhee asked from the doorway. "Come. We're waiting for you."

Tears came to her eyes while following her to the table.

They ate wedding noodles in silence. The toppings were left over from lunch, but the noodles had been cooked fresh.

"Mommy!" Mi-na said, "I hate noodles! I want rice."

"Mi-na," Eum-chun said, wrapping her arm around her, "this is a special day. We eat this. Isn't the topping pretty with the yellow egg, green onion, and red pepper? I'll put your favorite fried anchovies on your spoon, all right?"

"I'll bring rice." Soo-yang got up, but with a tug at her skirt, Mrs. Rhee stopped her. Mi-na looked to her father for help. When he whispered something to her, wrinkling up her nose for fun, she moved into his lap.

Noodles should slide down easily, but they stuck to Soo-yang's throat. She had to pick up her bowl and drink the whiting-flavored soup. Gui-yong, too, didn't eat with his usual appetite. He leaned his head against Mi-na's for a moment and shared his spoon with her, giving her a piece of the anchovies and taking watercress salad for himself.

"Eat plenty," Eum-chun said to Soo-yang. They were simple words, as plain as water, but they carried the power of a bomb. *Make yourself at home*, they implied. *This is your home*. She used the *u* verb ending, too, not too formal and not too familiar. The voice, weighing a ton, spoke of the effort Eum-chun put into it.

"Yes, Big Sister," she answered. *What? I called her Big Sister already?* She hadn't planned to do that despite her mother's advice to do so from the first day. But that was how her heart responded to the words, "Eat plenty."

After the meal, Soo-yang picked up dishes to take to the kitchen, but Mrs. Rhee stopped her. "Not today. Go to your room and get ready for the night." Mrs. Rhee then struck a match to her pipe and puffed at it. Orange specks sputtered from the bowl.

Soo-yang sat in her room, listening to the dishes clinking in the kitchen. She should be helping Eum-chun, but her mother-in-law's words were the law. The sound of plates and brass rice bowls came muffled—Eum-chun was cushioning them. Loud clangs would be interpreted as a sign of jealousy—one of the seven deadly sins for which in-laws could disown women. Did other countries have such rules? Her country had had them for at least the five hundred years of the Joseon Dynasty. Then with the coming of the Japanese in 1910, the dynasty collapsed, but unfortunately the laws didn't. No wonder Gui-yong loved his wife. If Soo-yang could show him over and over how she could obey rules and be big-hearted like his wife, he would come to love her, too, at least a little. Since no tree could stand after being axed ten times, if she worked like a possessed woman at winning him over, wouldn't he soften?

Gui-yong

While Eum-chun cleaned up in the kitchen, he told the Simcheong story to Mi-na in his mother's room. She especially loved the ending, where Simcheong's father, cured of his blindness, saw his daughter for the first time in nineteen years. "Daddy," Mi-na often said, "tell me the story again tomorrow." But today, she fell asleep before he got to the end.

In the hallway sitting room, he and Soo-yang went down on their knees and made a goodnight bow to his mother.

"Have a good dream," his mother said.

Soo-yang blushed at its message: *Conceive a boy tonight.*

They rose, put their shoes back on, and began the walk toward the honeymoon room. Should he just go in there as expected and have sex? If you're going to pull the bull's horns, do it quickly, people said. He liked her well enough. So far, what stayed with him were small, odd features. Even when she smiled, which wasn't often, he couldn't tell whether she was smiling or smirking. Her sincere eyes made it a smile. He liked the tufts of short hair that fanned out from one side of her hairline. He liked her quiet ways of walking, sitting, and keeping her head down as though she were bowing to everyone. He could sow his seed in her, as any man would want to. After all, he was a large-testicled boar, as Noodle Leg called him.

He hung back and let Soo-yang step ahead of him.

But how could he go into the room without passing Eum-chun standing by the kitchen door and looking at her one last time? What should he say with his eyes? I'm sorry, Sweetheart? As you say, it's our fate and karma? My heart's with you, even if my body isn't? I'll lie with her, but it won't be like our lovemaking?

He passed Eum-chun, saying nothing.

He felt her eyes on his back. Just as Soo-yang reached her room and bent down to take her shoes off, a cry erupted. It shot through his spine.

Kkkkkaaaw, kkkkaaaw. Swallows. The same sound he'd heard the day he saw Eum-chun for the first time before their wedding. At this hour, birds should be nestled somewhere, sleeping. He glanced at the night sky—smooth black. No clouds. No flying creatures. Could the noise have come from the cloud the nun mentioned? Where was it? *Kkkkaaaw. Kkkkaaaw.*

He looked at Eum-chun—the moon face that possessed him, the pouty mouth that tingled his, the phoenix eyes that smeared happiness across his face. The thought of last night's lovemaking awakened his groin.

Kkkkaaaw. Kkkkaaw. Then, he knew. He ran after Soo-yang, wheeled her around, and prodded her into his wife's room. Eum-chun let out a choking sound, *uggh, uggh*, her hand over her mouth. He tore to her and threw his arm around her.

"Let's the three of us sleep in your room tonight," he said. He cleared his throat as if that would make what he uttered sound less thunderously sick. But he loved the idea. What a half-balled idiot not to have thought of it before. The thought of not having to abandon his wife, at least for one more night, made him feel as though he had come back to life in his coffin and sat up. But what good would delaying the honeymoon night for a day do? Sooner or later he would have to pull the bull's horns. What he blurted out was like telling a man to piss on his own frozen feet in order to warm them; they'd simply freeze again. But he didn't care. He didn't care if three generations of his ancestors rose from the dead and beat him with bush clover brooms.

"Help me," he whispered. His mouth brushing against his wife's earlobe made his heart knock against his ribs. "A rabbit lobe," he'd called it in bed as he licked it. She looked too stunned to resist him as he picked her up, whisked her into her room, and set her down. Out of the corner of his eye, he saw his mother, her eyes bulging as though a person sick with tuberculosis had coughed blood on her face. Her bamboo pipe crashed down toward his back. He slammed the door shut.

He flung bedding onto the floor. He had Eum-chun lie to his left, the side she always slept on, and Soo-yang to his right, all of them in their clothes. He felt Soo-yang's elbow against his, shaking like a sick dog's. Her lips turned the color of a dry leaf—lips that had expected to be kissed tonight.

He snapped the light off and slumped down. His head felt as if it had been spun around. He stared at the latticework of the door. The darkness turned to gray smudge. He breathed like he'd run from Gyeongju to Seoul, the distance of a day's train ride. He didn't know how long he stayed that way, not turning toward either woman.

No one had better find out about this. Noodle Leg would want to tear down Gui-yong's trousers and check his balls. Or, laughing silly, he might slap him on his back and say, "I knew you were a lucky boar, but not how sly you were. Two women at the same time? Wooooooeeee!" Gui-yong's mother would want to shave his hair and lock him up in the storage shed, his ankles roped together. What other heart-stopping idea would he think of tomorrow to put off the inevitable again?

Maybe he rolled into sleep. Maybe he slept half the night. A noise awoke him, the same choking sound he'd heard his wife make earlier. This time, it kept coming. *Uuuunnhhh, uuuunnnhhh, uuunnhhh.*

The nun's cloud! He bolted up and flipped on the light. Eum-chun was balled up, the corner of the comforter stuffed into her mouth. Blood from her lips had made a half moon on the cover over the heads of the embroidered mandarin ducks. Her legs twitched as if someone had jabbed them with a hot iron. He pried her folded arms apart, slowly so as not to tug the comforter and break her teeth. He folded the cover back enough to put his head on her chest.

Eum-chun

She remembered Gui-yong's voice. His breath blew into her ear. "Let's the three of us sleep in your room. Help me," he had said. Did she hear him right? She knew enough men who lived with two or more wives to fill City Hall Plaza, but she'd never heard of a man who'd slept with two women at the same time. Even a steamed pig would laugh.

Gui-yong pushed her down to the floor in her room. He had brought the other woman in, too, and turned the light off. He spread a cover over Eum-chun. She felt faint—her ghost was trying to flit out of her. When her teeth chattered, she stuffed a piece of the comforter into her mouth. She held her breath and waited. What was she waiting for, and how long would she wait? As long as it would take a bird to eat all the mustard seeds that filled a castle if it pecked one seed every hundred years? Now, a mountain of mustard seeds buried her. She couldn't breathe. She clawed her way out from under the mound and whooshed out of the house. She was the bird with one seed in its beak. She swept above the roof and through the black air. Roofs dwindled to the size of crab backs. She wriggled her legs and pushed up through the sky over a river, pine trees, and craggy rocks. The top of a mountain and the trees covering it brushed her belly. She came down on her feet. A Buddhist temple stood white in moonlight, the monks asleep in dark rooms.

She tiptoed to the pool of drinking water in the courtyard. A stream flowed down a trough into the large basin. Moonlight made rings on the water, the outer one growing larger while a new one sprang from the center. A gourd scoop perched on the stone ledge. To the left stood a pine tree, and under it squatted an earthenware tub filled with water.

On its rim stood double swords, blades up, blue and sharp. A thin thread of light piped along the blades, her shaman Aunt Hong's blades. When Hong's General God took possession of her, her aunt danced on the knives. In bare feet. If she felt fear, had no faith in her gods, and wore shoes and socks, the blades would bleed her feet, and the General God would spit in her face and never return.

Eum-chun spread her arms, just as Hong did. They grew long green and red tassels, the same colors of her wedding dress. She circled around the tub in a dance, fast, faster, like a ghost, like pain. She panted. Her feet lifted in the air. She swirled, toes not touching the ground. Her skirt spun and her hair did, too. At once, she jumped on top of the blades. Her bare feet landed on them hard. If she'd been her aunt, if the Old General God had possessed her, Eum-chun wouldn't bleed. Even in the dream-sleep, she knew that.

The blades moved into her flesh as easily as into tofu. She slumped into a red pool.

Gui-yong

"Bring cold water," he shouted to Soo-yang. "Quick!"

She stood in the hallway, her hands twisting as if wringing wet socks. She rushed to the kitchen. Mi-na clung to her grandmother's leg, her lost puppy eyes darting from her mother to Gui-yong and back.

His mother stepped in, making Mi-na fall on her knees, and massaged Eum-chun's legs, then arms, then legs again. Gui-yong filled his mouth with the water Soo-yang brought and sprayed it onto his wife's face.

Last year, when his wife had embroidered the ducks on the comforter that was now stained with blood from her mouth, she'd said, "Isn't it amazing? Where did they learn to mate for life? How do they recognize each other? They all look the same!" She had laughed.

He dried his wife's eyes with the towel Soo-yang handed him. He pressed his ear on her chest again. Her heart was beating, thank the House God!

Soon, Eum-chun turned on her side and faced the wall, away from him. Her maroon-bloused back seemed to say, *I'll never forgive you.*

The next day, his neighbor Lee brought the news. Kim Koo, the man who'd pushed for cooperation with Kim Il-sung and who'd knocked his head against the President Rhee government by calling for a unified election for the North and South, had been assassinated, right in his own home. An army officer and Ahn Doo-hee had done it. Lee said Ahn was a member of the Korean Independence Party. There were so many parties—Gui-yong thought Lee was a genius, if only for being able to tell at least a few of them apart. A rumor that President Rhee had ordered the assassination swept through the city. Another said a group called White Clothes Society had made Ahn do it. Others said the American CIA had set him up. One thing was for sure—no one could unite the North and South by killing off their own people. As bad as this spelled doom for his country, Gui-yong couldn't dwell on it.

In his mother's words, Eum-chun was "wandering in and out of the doors of death," moaning and unable to rise from her bedding for a week. The doctor came and went. The herbal medicine his mother set to brew over the stove in Eum-chun's room sent steam flying through the paper cover of the clay pot. Every other hour, he and his mother took turns spooning rice porridge and black herbal brew into Eum-chun's mouth.

"Her mind and body got bruised to pulp," the doctor had said.

Gui-yong felt like he was losing his mind. He wondered why he'd never known any other woman to fall apart like this when faced with their husband's other woman. Neither he nor his mother nor Soo-yang had ever heard of any calamity like this.

He sat by the stove to make sure the herbal mix would not boil over. Mi-na came out of the kitchen, where she'd been sitting with Soo-yang. When he waved her over to him, she sunk into his lap. He wrapped his arms around her and smelled the leaf scent of her hair. His lips pressed on the top of her head, and they rocked and stared at Eum-chun's back heaving slightly. *Uuuuhhh, uuuhhh* came from her.

The North Koreans hadn't swooped down on the South yet. But his house looked like a battlefield, with Eum-chun lying like a crushed soldier waiting for a rescue.

Mi-na

After the night the Little House woman came, Mommy stayed in bed all day, every day. Black medicine boiled in the stove and made her room smell funny—cinnamony and bitter. She didn't like the smell of Grandmother's room either, with her tobacco, but now that was less stinky. Still, every day when she came home from kindergarten, she stayed in Mommy's room, her bottom warm from the heated floor. Mommy didn't open her eyes or talk to her. She only made sounds like Grandma's when she had one of her body aches. *Euu-uu-hoo, euu-uu-hoo.* It seemed like a long time, a hundred days, since Mommy had stopped speaking. Would she die? Even if Mrs. Bang and Kwang-ho changed their minds, which they didn't, and said Little Mommy's coming and Mommy's getting sick were not because of the fat, wormy penis Mi-na didn't have, she now knew it was. She was killing Mommy. How could she skip outside and play?

Today, when she felt sick of looking at Mommy's yellowed and puffy closed eyes, she decided to look at her books. *The Sun and Moon Gods; Heungbu and Nolbu: the Poor and Rich Brothers*; and *How Many Legs on an Octopus?* She couldn't read all the words, but she knew the stories by heart.

"Mi-na! Come out and play!" Kwang-ho's voice.

"Mi-na," Little Mommy said from the yard, "your friend's calling you. Don't you want to see who it is?"

Mi-na now called her Little Mommy. Not because grown-ups said she should, but because she felt a little like a mommy to her. She did most things Mommy had done for her, like brushing her hair and fixing up spinach salad with lots of red pepper paste. She had also taken her to her own parents' house for visits. Their house was a Japanese-style one, with bedrooms on the second floor. Little Mommy's mother had a cucumber-shaped face like Little Mommy's. She kept a flower garden with the usual balsams and sunflowers, but with dahlias and moss roses, too. Mommy never grew moss rose. Mommy liked the *baegilhong*, the red-for-one-hundred-days flower.

"Mi-na, did you hear me?" Little Mommy called.

Even if Mommy didn't talk to her, she wanted to stay with her. She might die while she was gone.

"I did, but I don't want to."

She looked at the hopscotch pattern on the floor made by the latticework of the rice-paper door. She spread out a summer blanket so as not to make too much noise with her pebbles. She threw the five of them up in the air and tried to catch some as they came down. She caught two. Holding one in her palm, she tossed the other one up and grabbed the other three on the floor before catching the one that was falling down. Playing the game alone was no fun, but she sat by Mommy, fingering the pebbles and wondering what she'd do if Mommy died.

Who'd call her "Jade Leaf"? Who'd squeeze her so tightly she had to say, "Not so hard, Mommy. I can't breathe"?

Gui-yong

The nightmare his first night with Soo-yang had turned into was no one's fault but his own. Soon, on the ninth lunar day of the ninth lunar month, the swallows would fly back to the south, but Eum-chun stayed bruised to pulp in her bed. Why? Did it mean Eum-chun loved him more than other women loved their men? Or did Eum-chun have more sensitive nerves, the kind people called *shin* spirit? Shamans had it: a mind so tuned it could hear the voices of heaven.

Eum-chun did have a spirited side to her. The way she jiggled her shoulders to lively tunes, the kisses that stopped his breath, the madness with which she ground her body against his. Her love for him broke her. His eyes misted over. But then, he'd not heard of a man suggesting to sleep with both of his women on the first night, either. Did he have a touch of the shaman spirit, too? He and Eum-chun made the oddest pair, perfectly matched in finding the most outlandish ways of reacting to situations. The writer who wrote the Chunhyang love story should write about them.

After Gui-yong washed up by the faucet, he looked in on Eum-chun before sitting down for dinner. These days, she did swallow the spoonfuls of porridge he slid into her mouth. Today, because he came home late, his mother had already fed Eum-chun. He slid his hand under his wife's and squeezed it. He gulped his disappointment at seeing no improvement.

Once again, his heart withered at the thought—he should've chosen Peach, or even set up Soo-yang in a rental somewhere. They could've made a boy baby hidden from the sight of others. Then, Eum-chun might not have collapsed. He'd have had to wrest the baby away from his mother, but the boy would grow up believing Eum-chun was his birth mother and become a man of legitimacy and position.

"*Yeobo*? You awake?"

No answer.

"Want to hear about my drive to Gangneung?"

The two thin lines for her eyes were enough to drive him to drink.

"I caught a boy stealing gas out of my truck today, *yeobo*. The second one in a month! He was only twelve years old. I whacked him on his back."

Her eyes didn't open. He rubbed her boney hands, so unlike Soo-yang's plump and smooth ones. He smelled his wife's knuckles, as she'd done his.

"I'm glad you didn't scrub all the gasoline smell off," she used to say.

After his one-way rambling, he ate in the sitting room and went into Soo-yang's room, asking her to bring him rice wine. He drank and glanced at Soo-yang's quiet, lowered face and the tiny tuft of hair at the front end of her part. Her closed mouth kept her worry in, but he could guess her thoughts. *Do you think I made your wife sick? Is that why you won't touch me? How long before you do? How do I get pregnant with a boy?* He wished he knew how long it would be before Eum-chun recovered so that he could turn his attention to Soo-yang.

"Sorry I can't sleep with you, yet," he should say to Soo-yang, but he couldn't. Her face let him know she understood; he was grateful. When Eum-chun returned to normal, he'd not ruin Soo-yang's life again by conjuring up another bastardly idea.

Eum-chun

A long time passed. Maybe the seasons changed. It was cold now. She could tell by the rattling of her window, the whistling of the rice paper on her door. She remembered the bitter taste of Chinese medicine and saw her own face, a peeled-millet color, and swollen eyes in the black water in the bowl. *Why? Have I been crying?* She recalled the voice of her mother-in-law ("Come on, swallow. You must swallow." *What am I swallowing?*). Gui-yong's hand pressing hers, simply pressing without words (*It's his hand, fingers thick, palm rough, and that sexy gasoline smell*), someone else, coming and disappearing, a woman in spring green, her closed mouth afraid to speak or smile (*the color shatters something thin like glass in the back of my eyes*). Mi-na? Mi-na! Who's taking care of her? Jin-i was here. Her breasts were hard as brass bowls. What happened to her son, Joon-ho, Superior Tiger? Mother came, too. Gae-sun fed her. What was it? Someone took her wrist and put cold fingers on the vein. Warmth on her back. Someone shoved wood into the hearth under the floor of her room, under her bed. Snow one night, she felt snow on the roof, its cold sliding down her ribs. A bowl of black water again and again, a strange face there, long straight hair, eyes deep holes, no pupils, just black, Gui-yong's voice, the lovely voice, ("I saw you in my dream," he said. "A spirit woman pulled out of an ocean, very blue, very green. Her necklace was strung with chunks of raw chicken meat. Can you believe that, Sweetheart, a raw chicken meat necklace? She put *that* around *your* neck. I yelled, lunged, and tried to wrest the sick chicken string off of you. I couldn't stand the meat juice sliming your pretty skin. The spirit woman told you it would keep you safe from sharks. Sharks? I've no idea what this dream means, do you? You're good at interpreting dreams. What does the chicken meat mean? You listening, Sweetheart?") *Yes,* yeobo. *I hear you. I saw them, the sharks. Their mouths, blue-veined, red-tongued. I saw their teeth in the water.*

Soo-yang

"A penis! Why didn't Buddha bless you with that, Mi-na?" Mrs. Bang's voice came from Eum-chun's room between the clucking of neighbor women's tongues. *Would that woman ever shut up about Mi-na?* Soo-yang wanted to know. The tongue of a woman like her should be cut off.

In the kitchen, Soo-yang sniffed her clothes. The smell of dead beetles and deer horns in Eum-chun's herbal medicine brewing in her room on the brass stove burrowed into Soo-yang's green blouse.

Did she really hope for Eum-chun's recovery? Did she mean it? Confucius had better not find out about it if she didn't mean it. Gui-yong was waiting for his wife to heal before he would get Soo-yang pregnant.

As if this wasn't enough to sicken her, she worried about Mi-na, too. The girl was in her mother's room listening to the grown-ups every day.

"Mi-na, come sit with me," Soo-yang had asked her. "Wouldn't you like to come into my room? I have pretty things to show you. Face powder. Lipstick. Want me to read you *How Many Legs on an Octopus*?"

But Mi-na shook her head and listened to the women, gabbing and fooling themselves into believing they were comforting Eum-chun.

Soo-yang didn't know how to let the girl know her mother's collapse wasn't her fault—without telling her the adoption secret. God forbid she ever find out she was thrown away by her parents. If she did, surely she'd lose her mind. Wouldn't any child in her shoes? Her blood family, Soo-yang heard, had kept their sons. If Mi-na survived the shock of discovery and grew to teen years, she'd flunk out of school. Later, no family would give their son to her in marriage. Who'd take her, not knowing her blood heritage? Leprosy or insanity could run in the family. If Eum-chun discovered Mi-na knew about her adoption, Eum-chun might jump into a well, too. Soo-yang bit her tongue. Karma hung around the necks of women and girls like a string of dead mice. They had to live with them. What else could they do? Jump into a well? Run out into the street and laugh silly?

The neighbors jabbered away.

"Don't get yourself sick worrying," said a voice. It sounded like Mrs. Choi's.

"After Soo-yang gives you and your husband a son, he'll send her back to her parents and be finished with her." Mrs. Bang's voice.

"Like Mr. Song's little mistress," said another woman. "Mrs. Song sent her off to Gangwon-do to eat potatoes for the rest of her life."

"Well, that's how things should turn out," a fourth said. "You don't have to memorize all *Four Book and Five Classics* to know that. Just try to get your strength back. Think of the son you and your husband will raise!"

"Let me help you," urged Mrs. Choi. "You have to drink this before it gets over-brewed."

These days, with help, Eum-chun was sitting up and swallowing soft foods. Soo-yang held her breath, waiting to hear what Eum-chun would say, but she didn't say anything. It figured. What right did an unlucky woman like herself have to expect good news to end her nail-biting so soon?

She reached for a bowl in the cupboard, took out a paper packet of medicine, and swallowed it with a cup of water. The oatmeal-colored powder soothed her sour stomach. It bothered her more and more often now. Since she had no chance of getting pregnant anytime soon, she didn't worry at all about the effects on an unborn child.

Mi-na

During the first snow of the year, Mommy sat up by herself, had Mi-na sit by her, and squeezed her. She did it softly, with a sad smile.

"Are you finished with lying in bed every day, now, Mommy?"

She nodded.

"Can I sleep with you again then?"

"Maybe, after a while. Grandma likes to tell you stories until you fall asleep. So how about staying there a little longer?"

Mi-na dropped her head on Mommy's chest.

"Mommy, I hate the medicine smell on your blouse. But I'm glad you can talk now."

"Me, too, Jade Leaf."

"When you can sit up every day, I'll dance for you, Mommy."

Before Little Mommy came, she'd done that every day.

"You and Daddy look up at me and clap, like you used to. Promise? You'll be like sunflowers, I'll be the sun. All right, Mommy?"

Mommy nodded and combed Mi-na's hair.

Just then, Mrs. Lee and Mrs. Bang came into the room, carrying a basin and soap. They washed Mommy's hair and helped her get dressed. When Mrs. Bang said what she always said about Mi-na's not being a boy, today, Mother spoke.

"But you know what my fortune-tellers told me? They said Mi-na would grow up to be ten times better than a boy."

Ahhhhhaaaahhhhhaaaa. Mi-na's belly button went honey-gooey.

"Oh," Mrs. Bang said and looked at Mi-na, as if she saw her for the first time. Mrs. Lee's eyes were closed, but her lips smiled.

But how could a girl become ten times better than a boy? Would she begin by wearing pants and having her hair scissored almost bald? She wanted to ask but she didn't. Maybe she'd do that after the evil Mrs. Bang left.

Mommy added, "Mi-na'll become like Yim Young-sin, right, Jade Leaf?"

Mi-na asked, "What did she do, Mommy?"

"She was a National Assemblywoman."

"What's a National Assembly?"

The grown-ups laughed.

"They make laws. Make decisions for us. Only the smartest people get to be members. Or, maybe, you'll become like Park Soon-cheon. She started a newspaper just for women. She'll become a National Assemblywoman, too. Lee Tae-young is studying law to become a judge. Can you believe that? A woman judge? When you become famous and wear a judge's robe and hat, you'll look beautiful, Mi-na."

Mi-na stopped playing with the pebbles and smiled at Mommy.

"Mi-na? Aren't you playing the pebble game? Don't you need five pebbles? Why do you have so many?" Mommy leaned over.

"I have fifteen, Mommy." Last week, she'd picked up ten more. With more stones, she could do adding and take-away. Her kindergarten teacher showed her how to do it.

"Miss Shin said I have to do math because I'll be going to the first grade. It's a new game, Mommy. I'm adding."

"See how smart she is, Mrs. Bang, Mrs. Lee?"

After they went home, Mommy lay back in her bed.

Mommy seemed to grow sleepy and closed her eyes. Mi-na poked at her blouse front where her red talisman pouch was pinned, the one for health and long life. When Mommy got better, she must ask Mommy to get her a new one from Great Aunt Hong—one to help her become a lawyer and a judge.

She'll stop cooking rice in a seashell. Who ever saw boys do that?

Soo-yang

Soo-yang sank to the kitchen dirt floor. One of the logs in the hearth crackled and sprayed up sparks. She envied the flames; they looked beautiful, dancing wildly, the peaks turning blue, purple, or green. When they finished, they puffed into gray ashes and into comforting Nothingness.

She pushed the poker into the fire and prodded the half-charred log pieces into a new pile. Brighter flames leapt up. Her life needed to come alive like the logs; it had fallen through the crack between Gui-yong and his wife. He slept in Soo-yang's room, but didn't touch her. He wasn't a drinker, but now he drank rice wine every night until he passed out. The funny stories his eyes had once held were gone. When he flopped onto his bedding, he pulled his legs up to his chest. He snored, the strands of hair over his eyes straight like pine needles. He was not the man Soo-yang had hung a nib of hope on.

Last night, she spent a long time staring at his back as he lay in his bedding, wearing the shirt and pants he slipped into after coming home from work.

I underestimated your love for your wife, she told his back silently. *Even if you can never love me, I wish you'd at least not blame me for your wife's condition. If I hadn't come, another woman would have.* These thoughts circling in her mind drove her mad. Why didn't she blurt them out to him? Even if she didn't get satisfactory answers, throwing the questions at him would at least open a hole down her blocked intestines. But what woman would dare do such an ungodly thing? If her mother heard about it, she'd slap a headache band around her head and collapse onto her bedding.

"Soo-yang," her mother had said after Soo-yang was cast out by her groom, "we didn't name you Weeping Willow so that you could weep your way through life. That tree has a beautiful nature. It dips with each storm that lashes it, but it never snaps." Maybe the willow wouldn't, but she felt as though she would any day.

It was quiet with the visitors gone. Eum-chun napped; Mrs. Rhee took Mi-na with her to Grandma Hahn's next door. A gray chunk of lye peeked out from its newspaper wrapping on the kitchen ledge. Once a week, she mixed it in water and boiled laundry in it. Sheets came out teeth-white. But every year, it also killed the many who swallowed it.

The gods of the Nine Layers of Heaven knew she shouldn't mope. True. She came to this house to save herself, Gui-yong, and his family. But she'd turned life into a heap of dung for all. Perhaps her luck would change, as in the case of an old man and his son in the Sae-ongjima story. How could the old man have predicted his good luck when his horse ran away? It returned, bringing with it another horse.

How could he have predicted his lucky lot when his son broke his leg riding the new horse? When a war overran the country, his son's broken leg got him exempted from going to war. But she didn't think such luck would fall on her. At least doing what her mother had taught her to do—waiting on everyone and satisfying their "stomachs and spleens"—hadn't been difficult so far. No one seemed displeased with her cooking and cleaning. Even if life was a field of dog droppings, wasn't it better to lie there than die? Weren't tears like medicine? The more she kept them inside, the healthier and happier she'd become?

She took out her sour stomach medicine from the cupboard, tossed the powder into her mouth, and gulped it down with water. Lucky she still wasn't pregnant. No need to worry about hurting an unborn child. As for harming herself, why should she care?

"Death," she called out in her head. She heard a cheery whistle. She looked around. It came from the lye.

"Need me?" it said. "I love to see you bear so much pain, but I can wipe it out."

"As you did for my cousin when her husband took a mistress?"

"Yes."

"Does it hurt?"

"Only for a few blinks, if you do it right."

"How do I do it right?"

"Make sure you'll be alone for at least half a day. You don't want to get caught in the middle. Smash a big chunk of me to fine grain. Add water. Let your mind feast on scrumptious things, as men do when they rub a watercolor stick on an ink stand. What do you suppose they think of? Peace? Compassion for every man? Ha! Pussies! You can think of whatever you like. Sunlight, running brooks, little fish, their orange and gold fins. More likely, Gui-yong's balls squirting a dozen babies up your pussy. Eum-chun's neck you want to wring."

"Shame on you. How long before I feel no pain?"

"How much nerve you got? You'd better not try it if you don't have a whole outhouseful. You have to take big gulps. One full cup. Cowards with pea-sized livers shake all over and spill a lousy half sip into their mouth, and where does that get them? Their esophagus gets chewed up like a rat's gut dangling from a cat's teeth. Believe me, you don't want to live with a ragged hole in your throat for the rest of your life."

She wrapped her hands around her neck.

March 1950

Eum-chun

Eum-chun sat on her bedding and looked up at the pine rafter. A light was on. Shame pricked her. Her prayers and good intentions had blown into the four winds. How could a thirty-four-year-old woman with a grand name like the Voice of Heaven have fallen apart like a whiting? Bearing no son was one kind of a shame, but behaving badly was unacceptable. Who would forgive her? How would she be able to look at Gui-yong and her mother-in-law in the eye? Where was he? Where was Mi-na? She turned. Gui-yong sat by her, her hand in his like a tea cup.

She looked at his face, and there she saw what she'd seen before—their love.

"Oh, *yeobo*." She slipped her hand out, lifted his to her nose, and sniffed. The same gasoline smell she craved the whole time she was ill mint-leafed up her nose.

"Will you be all right now?" he asked.

"Where's Mi-na?"

"Soo-yang's been taking care of her. She's with Mother now."

"What happened to Jin-i? Joon-ho, Superior Tiger, her baby?"

"She's back in Busan, working. Your mother was here

every week, fed you, gave you a wet-towel bath. Kim, his wife, and Joon-ho moved away. Disappeared."

He squeezed her hand. They both sighed.

"Looks like the Reds didn't bomb us. We're alive."

"Yes, we are, but five of our neighbors have dug bomb shelters."

"Did you dig one, too?"

"With you looking like you'd die any day? No. Now I can start to think about it. Lee's going to help."

"I was a drooling fool. Behaved like the worst crybaby." She leaned her head on his shoulder.

"Expect me to say you weren't? I won't, because you were foolish. More than I was." He slid his hand down her hair and held her.

Soo-yang

"What're you doing? Didn't you hear me?" Gui-yong loomed at the doorway. Soo-yang jumped to her feet and spun away from the lye and the flames. She'd forgotten it was Saturday and he'd be home early. She ran to the faucet, took the hose, and filled the concrete entryway inside the gate, turning the box-shaped area into a tub. Since it was not warm enough for a cold bath yet, she added hot water from the pot. After he took off his coverall, shirt, and undershorts and slid into the water, she ran a dried gourd sponge across his back, rinsed him, and held out a towel for him.

That evening, for the first time, Eum-chun ate with them in the sitting room.

"Eat a little more, *yeobo*," he said to Eum-chun, and before she put a spoon into her mouth, he set a piece of roasted seaweed on her rice. He boned the saury fish and piled that onto her spoon, too. When picking out the bones, his calloused fingers moved as nimbly as a seamstress's. His mother gave him a sideways glance, and a wrinkle of disapproval formed a crescent moon on her forehead. Only an idiot paraded his affection for his woman. A man bragging on his child was a half idiot; a man making a show of his pleasure with his wife was a whole one. He didn't notice his mother's frown, or he ignored it. Mi-na slid into his lap, and he boned fish for her, too.

"Taste better because Daddy fed you?" Eum-chun asked Mi-na, her eyes wilting with love for her husband and child.

Mi-na smiled, showing a piece of the fish between her teeth.

After Eum-chun, his mother, and Mi-na went to their rooms, Soo-yang followed Gui-yong into hers, carrying wine. She used both hands and watched him raise the white ceramic bowl. Gui-yong took sips from it, his eyes on somewhere between the door and floor. When he finished one bowl, he gestured for another, his face already red. His eyes looked puffy and serious, not like when he had tried to think of funny stories at her father's house. When his eyelids drooped more, she laid out the red-and-green mat and summer-weight comforter, which her mother had hand-sewn for their honeymoon. The embroidered dragon made of gold scales and green eyes on his pillowcase were Soo-yang's work. She set the bedding to face the east.

"Always the east," her mother had said, "where the sun pushes up, where life springs forth."

Soo-yang didn't put down her own pillow next to his. He might not welcome it. She'd spread out her own bedding later.

After the second helping of the wine, he filled the bowl halfway and, for the first time, offered it to her. He even looked into her face, a faint smile on his lips. She took the bowl, sipped a little, and handed it back to him. He finished it and slumped onto his mat. After he closed his eyes, Soo-yang turned the light off, readied her own bedding and pillow, changed into her white long-sleeved undershirt and full-length slip, and got under the covers. She sighed.

Gui-yong

In the mornings, Eum-chun would roll up her mat and covers, stack them in her bedding wardrobe, help Soo-yang in the kitchen, and read stories to Mi-na. But in the afternoons she would lie down. One Sunday, from the hallway sitting room, Gui-yong watched her and Mi-na squatting over the flower bed and dropping seeds.

"Let's do the balsam seeds first," Eum-chun said. "Then marigolds and the red-for-one-hundred-days flower."

Mi-na nodded her head like a yo-yo. "You'll color my nails when the balsam flowers get big, right, Mommy? Last summer, Little Mommy did."

"That was nice of Little Mommy. What do I get if I color your nails?"

"Little Mommy didn't ask for anything!"

"That's because she's nice. I'm not."

"Daddy!" Mi-na turned to him. "Mommy's bad!"

"Come here, I'll tell you something."

She skipped over and held out her ear to his mouth, her dirt-covered hands out like wings. He whispered to her. She ran back to her mother and whispered to her.

"All right, then." Eum-chun said and smiled, showing her corn-row teeth.

That night, he drank wine in Soo-yang's room and slipped

under his covers while Soo-yang turned off the light. He looked toward Eum-chun's room, which was dark. He waited a long time, fearing the light would come on and she'd make a trip to the outhouse.

Should he betray his wife tonight and sow his seed in Soo-yang? All he could see and feel were Eum-chun's moon face, her pouty mouth, her belly against his, and the moisture from her eyes that dampened his face during their lovemaking.

When Eum-chun's room continued to remain dark, he pulled Soo-yang toward him and rolled over her. He moved slowly, as though movements would make piercing sounds. Every few moments, he held his breath. The feeling that he was losing control and giving in to an explosion of pleasure annoyed him. It'd been so ghastly long since his dragon dance, his lovemaking, with Eum-chun. At this point, his body could've found satisfaction with a toothless woman. When the first groan tore into his throat, he swallowed it. He couldn't hold the second one in as well. He did better with the third, but not completely. He cowered. Did he wake Eum-chun?

Even crickets didn't give him cover with their chirps. He slid onto his mat and flattened his back muscles. Did the fireworks go off in lightning bolt colors because of his pent-up energy? Or did they have to do with Soo-yang, feelings for her he'd been unaware of? How did this set it apart from his time with Eum-chun?

His body felt too much like spilled honey to think clearly. The only clarity in his head was that he felt like a mountain horse thief in ten different ways.

Late March 1950

Eum-chun

She rose early, though not as early as before she'd fallen apart. This morning, she put a bowl of clear water on the sauce jar stand in the yard and bowed to Buddha and her aunt's gods. She didn't pray; her prayers had dried up. Besides, they hadn't done her any good. How else could she have stayed bedridden so long? She sat on a straw mat for the length of time it would take to do a round of prayers on the Buddhist beads made of one hundred and eight Job's tears. Her bows would send a message to the gods. *Forgive me.*

After the ritual, she took the bowl into the kitchen. Soo-yang was cooking breakfast.

When Soo-yang saw Eum-chun, she asked, "Slept well, Big Sister?"

Sleep well? He has planted his child in you, hasn't he? I've seen sharks' teeth in my dreams. Like the ones Gui-yong said he saw.

"Yes, I slept well."

"Rice'll be ready in no time." Soo-yang bent over the steam rising from the white pearls in the pot. Through the door, the sun poured a tub of light onto Soo-yang's back. As though too weak to bear the weight, her back curved.

Like Jin-i's back. Like mine. We're all in it together, working through our sins from previous lives. Must help one another to straighten our backs. Eum-chun stood sunstruck.

"Young Sister, would you like to learn to make radish kimchi the way Gui-yong likes?"

There. She called Soo-yang "Young Sister." What a mopping-rag of a person she'd been to refuse to say it for this long. Did she think not saying those words would make Soo-yang go *poof* into the air? Even a boiled pig's face would laugh.

"Yes."

"All right then. We'll begin after I take Mi-na to school."

By the Seongdong-gu District Office, as usual, men read newspapers on the board. Lately, rumors about possible attacks from the North had gotten worse. Some fliers dropped by North Korean spies in Seoul and other cities had been confiscated by the police. The leaflets said the North "will rescue the South Korean brothers from their misery and American imperialism." In January, when she was still not well enough to get out of bed, an

American official, Dean Acheson, declared South Korea to be "outside the perimeter of American defense." No wonder Communist guerillas stepped up their killing in the mountains down south. She tightened her grip on Mi-na's hand.

"We can all die, but Dean Acheson and his Americans don't care!" Grandma Hahn had said. She tied a headache band and didn't eat for a whole day and a half. How could the Americans do that to thirty million South Koreans? She'd have to begin another hundred-day prayer so that Americans would give tanks and mortars to President Rhee to attack the North with before Kim Il-sung bombed the South.

After she returned from school and Mrs. Rhee left for Mrs. Hahn's next door, she and Soo-yang made the kimchi. Soo-yang had set the radish, green onions, and red pepper flakes on the ledge.

"Mix the radish and leaves," Eum-chun said, "in a bowl with the green onion, garlic, sugar, and red pepper flakes. Put some water into the bowl, add a little salt and sugar, taste it, pour it into a pan, and simmer it. Throw in a pinch or two of flour to thicken the sauce. Cool it and pour it over the kimchi. If the sauce is not made right, the kimchi will taste like wet rags."

"Yes."

"He likes it a bit sweet," Eum-chun said. "So toss in an

extra pinch of sugar." Soo-yang's face looked serious, like a student's, and smelled of Coty.

While Soo-yang was busy, Eum-chun dabbed her forehead with the towel Soo-yang had laid out for her. When Soo-yang finished mixing, she put a cover on the jar. Eum-chun had given away a secret recipe for making Gui-yong happy. Her innards felt as though red pepper flakes had gotten into their folds.

She looked at the sun. The sheets Soo-yang had hung on the line earlier blocked the mid-morning light. How many days, weeks, or months did they have to do things like make kimchi and cook rice under this roof before Communists stormed into Seoul?

That night, Gui-yong came back safely from a run to the province of Jeolla-do. He looked beaten. He had smudges on his nose from unloading coal. Soo-yang scrubbed his back by the faucet. Eum-chun watched them from the sitting room. He bent over a basin while Soo-yang rubbed his naked back and then poured a gourd of water over him. Eum-chun got up and went into her room. Seeing Soo-yang's hands on his skin felt wrong.

Her mother-in-law's room turned dark. Mi-na was sleeping there.

She spread out her bedding, turned the light off, and slid in. She stayed awake, not like other nights when she'd fallen asleep before he came home, and listened to the sounds of

Gui-yong's footsteps *tep tepping* into Soo-yang's room and of dishes clinking. Soo-yang was setting his table. Did Soo-yang pick up the roasted seaweed squares and put them one at a time on his spoonful of rice as she used to? Was he moving his lips in a hungry, happy way? Did she know to put a raw egg on the table? Halfway through his meal, he mixed his rice with a little of each vegetable, dropped a spoonful of red bean paste on it, cracked the egg, and mixed them all together vigorously.

After a while, she heard Soo-yang cleaning up in the kitchen. Her footsteps padded back to her room, and the door closed softly. The light went out. Eum-chun's room turned a shade grayer. She drew in a long breath and pictured the faces of the Gwaneum Bodhisattva of Mercy and Mrs. Choi. She breathed out and pictured a green-blue sky, the color of the backs of mackerels jumping in the ocean. *Go ahead*, she ordered herself, *slide into sleep and stay as closed to the world as a sack of borrowed potatoes. Don't fret over him and Soo-yang. Easy. Peaceful. Like a green-black sky.*

From far away, the flute music of a blind masseuse crept toward her like silk worms munching mulberry leaves. The tune neared until it sounded as though the massage man was on the other side of her wall. Then came his cry, "*Anmayo! Anma!* Gentle massage! Massage!" He sang this several times in his best *pansori* gut-sawing style. Then the flute took over. His voice and the flute took turns flying high and plunging down the hill, thinning to a thread.

Another sound, suddenly, dovetailed.

A gruff moan, Gui-yong's throat sound, the familiar teeth-together noise coming in lumps, saying nothing, but everything. Her scalp shrank. The cold feel of a wet rag wiping the inside of her belly slithered through her. She bolted up in her bed. Without turning the light on, she yanked her blouse and skirt off the wall hook. Her hands, shaking, tore the fabric. She flinched, waited, and threw the clothes on. She opened the door and slunk across the sitting room.

She put one foot down on the floor. Then the other. She slipped into her shoes. One step. Another. Past the kitchen. At the gate, she fumbled for the wooden crossbar, thick, worn shiny from their hands. Where was she going? Why? Hadn't she expected him to make love to Soo-yang? How else would they produce a son? *Go back to your room and stay quiet.*

The wood squeaked. She cringed. Ice shot into her toes. She slid the latch open. *Krrrkk.* Something shuffled in Soo-yang's room, lights came on, and the door flung open. Without stopping to put his shoes on, Gui-yong, bare-chested and in his underwear, lunged across the yard and grabbed her arm. He slammed the rod back in place with his free hand. He picked her up, carried her into her room, and put her down. In the dark, he stood over her, panting.

She whispered into her lap. "Please." Please what? What did she want?

She felt his arm, brushing against her hair on its way to somewhere. *Ttthhhwwaaakk!*

Glass shattered. He turned the light on. Pieces of her wardrobe mirror were scattered on the floor. One large shard lay by his naked foot. She swept it away from him and reached for his hand to check for cuts. Blood beaded out from the knuckles of his middle and ring fingers. She sprang to her knees to get clean cloth from her dresser, but he stopped her with his elbow.

He nudged her away and, with a rag mop she kept in the room, cleared the wedge shapes to the far corner. He opened a drawer, pulled out a handkerchief, and wrapped it around his knuckles. Breathing more quietly now, he sat and looked at her. He cupped her face with both hands and tilted it toward him.

His eyes looked angry but also soft. He ran his thumbs below her eyes and down her cheeks, drying the tear tracks on them. He then lowered his head next to hers and spoke, his voice coming out rusty. "Sweetheart, don't do this. Please."

He brushed her bedding, made sure it held no glass, and then turned the light off. He pulled her down next to him. In his still swollen voice, he said, "Sweetheart, do me a favor."

She didn't respond.

"Don't leave me. Please."

Soo-yang

Soo-yang straightened from squatting and salting cabbage by the faucet, bowing her belly out, her hand supporting her back. Her mother-in-law's sharp eyes saw the signs. Mrs. Rhee jumped up and, knocking the basin of water, burst out, "Little Daughter-in-Law! Come here. Let me look at you!" Mrs. Rhee took Soo-yang's wrist and swept over Soo-yang's stomach with her other hand.

"Thank you, Samsin Fertility Spirit! Why didn't you tell us! You're two, maybe three months along!"

Soo-yang's palms became sweaty.

"I have to tell my son. I have to tell Big Daughter-in-Law. But they aren't here! What happy news! I'm going to Grandma Hahn's. I have to tell somebody." She swept up her skirt and rushed out.

Once Soo-yang began to show more plainly, Mrs. Rhee said the same thing every day.

"It's a boy. Look how that belly sticks out! Cone-shaped like a persimmon. If it's not a boy, I'll stick my fingers into boiling bean sauce. My belly stuck out like that with my son." Mrs. Rhee didn't stop talking and laughing.

After that, Gui-yong didn't ask for wine and slept with his hand on Soo-yang's stomach. Did she win at least a pebble-sized piece of his heart? Shortly, it would be a year since she'd arrived. Through the small shoulder-height window she had left a crack open, she smelled wisteria blossoms.

Each night he snored, sounding like hundred-year-old roots ripping from dirt and rocks. She wondered if the sound kept Eum-chun awake in her room. She moved his hand from her belly to her breast.

"Have many sons," Eum-chun had said on her first day in the house. Her voice had shaken. Since the brushing of a stranger's sleeve against one's own means you'd had a relationship in previous lives, what had she been to Eum-chun? Had they been sisters who fought over one man? Whatever fateful connection they had, now her baby joined it. A destined link never died. It connected people in one way or another from one life cycle to the next.

One night the next week, she lay with Gui-yong, listening to crickets. He had not yet begun to snore when the gate creaked. She raised her head, but Gui-yong threw his hand over her mouth. Crickets stopped chirping. Soft footsteps, a woman's, padded over the tiles, up into the sitting room and Eum-chun's room. Low voices murmured. Gui-yong eased his hand. In a while, the visitor tiptoed out. After the crickets started up again, Gui-yong whispered.

"Eum-chun's sister, Jin-i, came up from Busan for a visit. Now she's going back. She came by to say goodbye. Jin-i gave up trying to find her son. She's too ashamed to come by in the daytime. She wanted to see only Eum-chun."

"What happened to her son?" Soo-yang asked.

What she knew about Jin-i was a thimbleful. Jin-i had visited Eum-chun twice while she was bedridden but didn't stay long and said little after greeting Soo-yang and Mrs. Rhee.

"I didn't tell you because Eum-chun wanted to keep it quiet." He sat up and gulped from the bowl of boiled rice drink Soo-yang kept by the bed. He lay back down, his mouth close to her again. "Her last lover, Kim. A boss of a construction company. He'd set up a place for her. They had a son. Joon-ho, Superior Tiger. Just before you came. But the swine took him away! Gave him to his wife. They moved. Jin-i can't find them."

"Poor woman. Poor baby." No wonder Jin-i's large and beautiful eyes had looked so sad. "What's she going to do?"

"For months, her brothers and mother took turns watching her to keep her from jumping into a well or swallowing lye. Or hanging herself from the ceiling beam. She finally gave up hope of getting Joon-ho back."

Soo-yang imagined Jin-i weeping into a white handkerchief, her widow's peak exquisite over a crocheted edging.

"If you're worried about your baby being taken away from you, don't be." He cleared his throat and went on. "I won't make a Jin-i out of you. If I was going to do that, there were plenty of other women I could have taken. Peach, for one."

"Peach? You had a woman other than your wife?"

"Ask Eum-chun to tell you about Peach sometime."

She fell quiet. She didn't want to spoil her happiness with more words. Most people who struck luck of this scale would burst out, "Who left this rice cake out for me?" She'd caught the largest rice cake of her life.

For the first time under his roof, Soo-yang slept with her legs not folded but stretched out.

Gui-yong

It felt good to come home early for a change. He drove in from Yeosu Port, clear down south. It must be ten. Every time he made it back from the Yeosu area in Jeolla-do he felt lucky. He'd dodged the guerrillas. More South Korean Communists were hunkered down there, too, than in other places, except maybe on Jejudo Island. Two years ago, forty Communists broke into the Yeosu police station and gunned down the police. They took over the whole town and rode trains up to Suncheon and killed citizens there, too. Men at his shop talked about nothing else for weeks. They told stories about the hundreds of policemen who were lined up and shot. They woke ordinary people in the middle of the night and killed them, too. In just two or three days, five hundred people died. Funny, Suncheon meant "peaceful heaven." Luckily, an army general crushed the Reds in both areas. Since then, every time he drove there Gui-yong got local news from Mr. Huh at his gas station first.

Today, he stopped there around lunchtime. As usual, while his helper filled his truck and washed down the windows, Mr. Huh sat on his tree stump, smoking his Hwarang, Noble Pioneer Soldier, cigarette. He handed Gui-yong a steamed corn on the cob.

"Been quiet around here, Uncle?" He could've called him "Grandpa" instead of "Uncle," since he looked much older than his own Uncle Park.

After blowing out the smoke, Mr. Huh made his deathbed face wrinkle into one giant frown.

"Don't you like smoking? Does it make you sick?" Gui-yong asked him.

"Why you ask? Do I look unhappy? This is my happy face."

They laughed.

"A few quiet days are bad news around here," Mr. Huh said. "Never know what'll jump up and put a bullet through my neck." Mr. Huh flicked his head toward a mountain ridge sloping down from Mt. Jirisan. "Can't get much sleep these days. Never know when those Red bastards will get us. Heard up North they got some hundred fifty thousand troops. Russians are training them. They got hundreds of Russian tanks and fighter planes, too. What do *we* have? If we got more than one third of the troops they have, I'll boil two of my fingers. And tanks? We got none! Americans won't give them to us! And no fighter planes, either! One day, I'll wake up to the *tung tung tung* of the Reds' tanks and the *wang wang wang* of their planes! And where will General MacArthur be? In Japan, throwing a geisha party."

"He said he'd help us if the Red bastards got us."

"He talks with ten mouths. He said he'd save us like he'd save his own country. But how fast can he get here? By then, we'll all be lying on the ground with our mouths open and flies going in and out."

It's time he dug a hideout for his family. But where? Lee got it done in a small space behind his house. Bang, Hahn, and the rest of the neighbors constructed theirs under their hallway sitting room.

His mother's room was dark. Mi-na would be sleeping there. Low light seeped out from the rice paper of Eum-chun's door. Soo-yang brought his dinner to the sitting room. Eum-chun slid her door open and greeted him with a smile and a nod.

He'd hoped she'd be awake. Would they ever get back to

the old times? His bones felt weary from the drive. He'd missed her. How could he begin making love to her?

After dinner and washing up, he stepped into Eumchun's room. Something smelled new. A faint trace of herbs. But along with that, face powder? She looked up from her bedding. A wrinkle line of surprise appeared on her forehead. Her hair, undone from her daytime bun style, fluffed down the front of her white slip. The cover with embroidered mandarin ducks lay on top of her futon. The blood stain from the night she collapsed had turned to gray from several washings.

"Why do you use *this* cover, *yeobo*? You've got others."

She pulled his blue cushion out from a pile for him. He sat on it.

"A good drive from Yeosu?"

"Uumm."

Her voice came out round and clean like *yeot* candy, as if the last few months hadn't happened.

"Should I ask Soo-yang to bring you some cinnamon and persimmon drink?"

"No, I had some already." That wasn't true. The words tumbled out, the quickest way to move their conversation away from Soo-yang.

He reached for the light switch, turned it off, lifted her cover, and slid in. He wrapped his arm around her head. She rolled toward him, moved his hand up to her nose, and sniffed.

"Smells good."

When he pulled her slip off, her legs came at him at an awkward angle. How he'd missed that odd way of hers. Her fingertips on his wrist, her nails there, his left hand on the back of her head, her hair seaweedy between his fingers, her stomach a bit to the left, and he chasing after it. The deep paralyzing sweetening—here, all over, back here. He never thought a man could do it while weeping.

Noodle Leg would laugh and say such a pleasure paralysis was hogwash. A wife of fifteen years was as washed out as a rag mop. She'd smell like unwashed hair. *Pull your pants down*, he'd say, *what's wrong with you? And you did it while doing what? Crying?*

It had to be that "inner flesh fit" he'd heard of. What else could such a head-to-toe sweetache be? Confucian gentlemen had known about such a meltdown addiction. They had a name for it. They might have called what he had with Soo-yang an "outer flesh fit"—good enough.

The taste of Eum-chun's mouth wasn't there. The *kkkaaawww kkkaaawww* of the swallows in his head from the first time he saw her wasn't there. The moisture from her eyes against his cheek during their peak wasn't there.

Noodle Leg had been right after all. Gui-yong was Treasured Dragon, a spike-haired boar, and a lucky one at that. If it wasn't for the damn bit about needing a son, he'd be like Americans and Christians. Happy with one wife and one daughter.

His throat hurt with what he wanted to tell his wife. *Thank you for coming back to life. Our love isn't like anything else I've known. Will you believe me?*

Instead he said, "*Yeobo*, we're stuck together. Is that all right?"

She lifted his hand, the one cut by the mirror, and planted her lips there.

He couldn't imagine his feelings for Eum-chun ever changing. But would they, when Soo-yang gave birth to his son? Having a boy formed out of his own loins would be a whole new world, and he didn't know how that would change him.

Soo-yang

The sun shot through the red balsams. To Soo-yang, they looked bloody. Eum-chun began doing more housework. Her help was welcome, as Soo-yang grew tired in the afternoons.

Last night, Gui-yong went into Eum-chun's room and slept there. Soo-yang pulled a cover over her head and kept her back to that room all night. One minute she felt free of guilt. Eum-chun was no longer sick, and Gui-yong was sleeping with her again. Then the next minute, she felt jealous. The arms she came to love were holding Eum-chun now. *Why don't you get sick again, Eum-chun?* The nasty wish startled her. *What if the evil wish causes a miscarriage?*

Soon, Gui-yong went to Eum-chun three times a week. When he came back, he slept as though he'd exhausted himself. Soo-yang wasn't sure which was worse: guilt or jealousy. At times she thought the baby would drop right out of her. She couldn't wait for Gui-yong to come back to her, even if he did nothing but snore.

This morning, Eum-chun's face wasn't that dried turnip color. Her eyes opened with a shine. Gui-yong had slept with her last night. When an image of them together flashed across Soo-yang's eyes, her stomach felt as though straw had been rubbed across it. She kneaded her knuckles on it.

"Let's smooth wrinkles from the sheets," Eum-chun said.

Soo-yang stopped massaging her stomach and took down the sheets she'd hung on the clothesline earlier. They folded a sheet into a rectangle, lining up the corners and gathering them. Eum-chun set the table-shaped smoothing stone between them. When Soo-yang laid the sheet on the stone, they picked up two pine mallets each.

"You know what people say." Eum-chun ran her palms over the cotton. "If two people get along, their mallets make music. Ready?"

Eum-chun hit down hard and started the rhythm. Soo-yang followed. She pounded lightly at first and then harder. *Dtoo dtahk, dtoo dtahk, dtoo dtahk, dtahk, dtahk.* Soo-yang couldn't figure out Eum-chun's rhythm. The mallets went up and down in a mixed bag of beats. *Dtoo, dtahk, dtoo dtahk, tu tu, dahk, dahk, dahk.* Even if their sticks clopped worse than a horse and a pig running together, pounding felt good. Before she knew it, she hit the seam, and her mallet exploded out of her grip, pistoled across the floor, and clanged against Mrs. Rhee's brass chamber pot.

Soo-yang giggled first, then Eum-chun. It was as though little bells rang inside Soo-yang. She bent over, holding her stomach, laughing, and squeezed her legs together to keep from wetting herself. She dried her cheeks with her blouse tie.

"Good thing Mother's at Mrs. Hahn's." Eum-chun pulled up her skirt and dabbed its hem at her eyes.

"Stifle your laughs," her mother had said to Soo-yang. Too late to worry about that. She sniffled and blinked. Just then, Eum-chun took their mother-in-law's pipe lying across her ashtray, grabbed a match, and lit the leftover tobacco in the bowl. She took puffs to get the fire to catch, sucking in her cheeks. No woman who was not yet a grandmother could smoke without disapproval from others, much less smoke her mother-in-law's pipe. When did Eum-chun begin smoking anyway? What would happen if Mrs. Rhee walked in?

Eum-chun blew smoke toward the balsams across the yard, squinting her eyes.

When the tobacco ran out, Eum-chun stuffed a corner of the rag mop into the pipe bowl and snuffed the fire. She picked up her mallets. "Try again?"

This time, Soo-yang caught the rhythm. Sunlight skidded off the jumping mallets.

Eum-chun

Two weeks after Gui-yong broke the mirror, Eum-chun cut rice paper into plum blossom shapes and dropped them into a ceramic bowl in her lap. Even after several evenings' work, dozens of more cutouts were needed to patch the mirror. She spread rice glue on the backs of the blossoms and tamped them down along the cracks. Mi-na was stretched out on her stomach, practicing her handwriting on ruled work sheets. Eum-chun tilted her head and surveyed the finished branches. They showed a rough outline of a tree. Right now, with more spots to fill, it looked badly mauled.

"Mommy, I want to cut some, too." Mi-na looked pretty in the red top Eum-chun had crocheted for her.

Two days ago, when Gui-yong saw Eum-chun cutting and

gluing, he said, "You'll hurt your back bent over like that. I'll get you a new mirror."

She gave him a pretend scolding look.

The sound of the gate opening and closing came. Then Gui-yong's footsteps.

"Daddy's home. Let's do this later." Eum-chun shoved the bowl aside. Mi-na dropped her scissors and ran out to the sitting room. Soo-yang brought his food and when he began to eat, Mi-na jumped into his lap and waited for him to feed her from his spoon. Afterwards, Eum-chun took Mi-na into her mother-in-law's room, lay down on Mi-na's bedding, and told her the story of good-hearted Heungbu, who found gold in a pumpkin he grew from a seed that a swallow had dropped into his hand.

"When can I sleep with you again, Mommy?"

"You like sleeping with Grandma, don't you?"

"I do, but I want to sleep in your room, too."

How could she tell her six-year-old the truth? That she was older now, and it was time she left her mother's room private, because her father might decide to sleep there?

After Mi-na fell asleep, Eum-chun passed Gui-yong sitting in the hallway, waiting for his mother to finish her pipe and turn in for the night. He smiled at her. Did that mean he'd come to her tonight?

For weeks he had taken turns sleeping with her and then with Soo-yang. It was about time Eum-chun became used to anticipating his decision on whom he'd sleep with. But as though each night was a brand new adventure, waiting for his choice took Eum-chun's breath away.

Back in her room, she took deep breaths and reached for the glue and the blossoms.

"Good night, son." Mrs. Rhee's door closed.

"Good night, Mother." Then came his footsteps. She planted her hand over her heart; it helped keep her heart from thrashing.

The *fst, fst* of his rubber slippers grew quieter as they moved away.

She felt like a cucumber being sliced and falling into thin little moons.

From down Munhwa-dong Street came the rumbling of American and Korean military jeeps and trucks moving in convoys. *At least I'm alive. The South is still alive. The Han River isn't running red. Gui-yong breathes under the same roof with me. Mi-na knows me as her Mommy. Some day, Mi-na'll make me a prouder mother than those with ten sons.*

She cocked her head at her handiwork. After a few more evenings' work, the tree might not look so hail slashed.

She felt grateful for her life, but she stared at the peanut-colored wood ceiling beam and wondered, *How it would feel to hang from there?*

Azalea Wine

Mid-June 1950

Eum-chun

"Want to die. Kill me. Will you do that for me?" Eum-chun said to Gae-sun, who was standing in her kitchen, washing rice in a gourd dipper. When she heard Eum-chun's words, her wrist went limp, making water and rice spill out.

"Ballooning and ballooning! That woman's stomach's getting larger than a winnow. With my husband's child!" Eum-chun went on. "Do I have to look at it day in and day out? For the whole nine months? Oh, Buddha, have mercy. Just kill me, will you?"

Eum-chun plunked down on a straw seat on the dirt floor of the kitchen. "Your mother-in-law's not home, right?" She lowered her voice and said, "Can I have some rice wine?"

With each bowl she drank, she poured her heart out. "I need to go somewhere. I need to go where I don't have to see that belly. But where can I go? Not to my parents. I want to whip myself with willow tree switches. Her belly growing big is what I expected to happen, isn't it? I prayed for that, didn't I? We all want it, like rain after a five-year drought, don't we? But I can't stand it! More wine! More wine, please."

That's when Gae-sun told her about the mung bean pancake stall. She stuttered more than usual, her eyes staying shut longer.

"My husband's cousin . . . she got a stomach ulcer . . . can't run her pancake shop . . . a widow, got no one to . . . keep it open for her . . . Want to try running it, if I helped?" Gae-sun asked. "For two weeks? It could be longer, like six months? But we don't have to tell our husbands that. They'll want to chop our hair and lock us up. Especially Gui-yong. He'll blame me for getting you into trouble."

Run a pancake stand every day and in the evening, too? That would get Soo-yang and her belly out of her sight. Was Gae-sun's cousin a genius? A psychic? An angel from Aunt Hong's Moon God? How did she know to fall ill and to need someone to take over her shop at such a perfect time?

"My mother-in-law," Gae-sun kept on, "and my girls can get meals together . . . even with me gone a few hours every day, and I can help you. Want to try it?"

Gae-sun was stretching her neck out for Eum-chun's sake. She needed to sell pancakes as badly as she wished for a snake to scare her in the shower shed. And here she stood, offering to flip pancakes with her neighbor. What had Eum-chun done in her previous life to deserve such a friend?

"Yes, of course I do. But you're right. Gui-yong will want to do more than punch his fist into a mirror." She squatted, closing her eyes. A moment later, she sprang up and said, "Let's do it!"

At predawn the next day, she bowed before the azalea wine set on the lid of a water jar in her yard. Except for a few stars, the sky was black all over. She lit the candles flanking the wine bowl. Everyone was sleeping. Soo-yang's room was dark with Gui-yong there, his forearm likely taken as her pillow. Maybe he was rubbing her belly.

Today, she used wine instead of cold spring water—her prayer called for a special offering. Several months before Soo-yang came, she had helped her mother make the wine. Pine wine would've soured by now, but azalea stayed fragrant.

Extra money would help Gui-yong, too. How would he feed the babies if Soo-yang kept having them? Gui-yong's testicles would split, Eum-chun's father had said, feeding his family on his cheap noodle salary. But Gui-yong would rather have that happen than allow his woman to work outside and be ogled by other men. After all, as the saying went, the two things a man should never leave outside were his drinking bowl and his women. But with money, one could buy anything in this world, even something as nonexistent as virgin's balls.

Soo-yang

After Eum-chun drank the rice drink, she left for her parents' house. No sooner had she stepped out of the gate than Soo-yang heard a groan bursting from her mother-in-law's room.

"Mother!" Soo-yang ran into Mrs. Rhee's room, much too fast. She heaved. The spinach soup she ate bubbled up to her throat. Mrs. Rhee's brass chamber pot lay open by her side, the air too nauseating to breathe. Soo-yang slammed the lid back on the pot, letting out a clang.

"Sorry, Mother. Didn't mean to be clumsy. Where does it hurt?"

Her skirt pulled up, her bottom showed. Mrs. Rhee waved her away.

"Mother, can I massage you? Did you hurt your back?"

Mrs. Rhee kept motioning her away. Soo-yang stepped backwards out of the room and wondered if she would have let Eum-chun help her. Mrs. Rhee was excited about the baby, but that didn't make the relationship between her and Soo-yang any closer, while Mrs. Rhee and Eum-chun seemed as tight as ever. For one, Soo-yang sat on her legs around Mrs. Rhee to show the highest respect, but Eum-chun didn't need to.

Soo-yang waddled back to the kitchen. She might never be able to catch up with Eum-chun in winning their mother-in-law's affection. If Eum-chun was like a stork, she was a titmouse. If a titmouse tried to run as fast as a stork, its crotch would split. Should she try anyway, even if it killed her? No, not when she finally got what she came to Gui-yong's house for—his baby growing in her. She repeated wise sayings to herself instead.

"Stay where you are, and you'll find yourself halfway there."

"Keep your head down; then yours will be a house of peace, not of beans frying and stinging words flying."

"There comes a day when the sun shines into a den of mice."

Eum-chun

In the evening, Eum-chun kneaded Mrs. Rhee's lumpy calf muscles while she lay on her stomach.

"Mother, Gae-sun told me her husband's cousin ran a mung bean pancake shop. Have you heard about that?" Eum-chun's voice shook.

"No, I haven't. Something happened to her?"

"Stomach ulcer. Gae-sun'll work at the shop instead. She asked if I could help her. May I, Mother?"

Mrs. Rhee turned her head toward Eum-chun and took her hand.

"Thank Seongju House God," Mrs. Rhee said, "for this medicine hand." Mrs. Rhee called her hand that from the time Eum-chun was a newlywed. When her mother-in-law had the worst case of hemorrhoids, instead of turning away Eum-chun had gotten a clean rag, dipped it in cool water, and did the cleaning, dabbing, and easing of the flesh.

Mrs. Rhee's eyes and the warmth between their hands communicated to Eum-chun that her mother-in-law was sorry she had nagged her son to get another woman. But she wouldn't apologize—forcing her son to produce a son was her duty to Heaven.

"Tell me," Mrs. Rhee said, "Where's the place?"

"Sigumun Market. Office people stop for snacks."

"Gae-sun's mother-in-law and husband are letting her work there?"

"Until they find someone else. Just for a few days, maybe a week or so."

"Did you say the woman was a widow? If a woman alone

ran it all this time, it must be a nice, safe spot. But men drink and throw up even in broad daylight at those stalls! I can't offer you up to such a vile place."

"Mother, we'll serve mung bean pancakes. Even people asking for wine are office people wearing ties, Mother. That's what Gae-sun said."

"Men drinking wine can end up behaving like mutts, tie or no tie." Mrs. Rhee stopped Eum-chun's hands, sat, and picked up her pipe. Eum-chun lit it for her.

"Mother, please."

"I'll go see Gae-sun's mother-in-law. I'll get to the bottom of this."

Gui-yong

Gui-yong finished digging a bomb shelter under the hallway wood floor. Lee helped.

"What has gotten into the head of that President Truman?" Lee began his harangue against the withdrawal of the Americans. He wheezed as he squeezed his potbelly through the hole Gui-yong had cut into the floor. Once he got into the hole, he kept on.

"How could he yank his troops out of here? Did he really think our side could fight off the Commies with our bare hands?" Lee slapped the back of a hoe against the dirt wall and packed it.

"If Truman kept the soldiers here for another ten years, would we be digging this hole? No, sir!" Lee wiped sweat from his brows with the back of his hand.

The June heat was made worse by the candles and a flashlight steamed them alive.

Gui-yong handed him a towel.

"This is going be tight for all of you to fit," Lee said.

"I know, and Soo-yang's not getting any smaller."

"Think it's a boy?" Lee whacked at the dirt wall where it bowed out with an axe. Dust shot out. Gui-yong shoved his face into the crook of his arm. When his coughing slowed, he tamped the wall with his hands, then picked up the burlap.

"Better be. I don't want to drive myself into the Han River." Gui-yong measured the fabric against the width of the dugout.

"Isn't it a kick to feel your flesh and blood jump around in your woman's belly?"

"Melts my heart. Beats sex!"

"Nothing beats that!" They both chuckled.

The warmth he felt toward his unborn spread to his mother. He now understood what people said about children binding their parents tighter than boiled-horse-bone glue could any two things. He'd seen men who'd fooled around suddenly settle down with the woman who bore them babies. But then he'd seen men who kept messing with women even after their wives had borne sons. Life was like five grains mixed and steamed; it's hard to tell what's what.

"Hold that end up, will you?" Gui-yong asked Lee, nailing the fabric to the wood joist.

"The puss-head Reds." Lee's face turned a tomato color. "*Ssipalnomdeul.*" Motherfuckers.

Eum-chun

"I asked Gae-sun's mother-in-law yesterday about the pancake shop," Mrs. Rhee said during dinner. "She said it's a safe place. Her niece made a nice bundle of money there. I've got half a mind to let Eum-chun help out. It'll be for only a short while."

Gui-yong kept eating.

That night, he slept in Eum-chun's room and bombarded her with questions.

"How long before Gae-sun's relative comes back? When I get back from Jinju on Saturday, I'll see the place myself. Don't work later than nine in the evening, promise? Long before the midnight curfew. If Gae-sun can't be there with you, take Mu-ja or somebody else with you, hear me? When men come in, stay behind the counter, understand, *yeobo*? You sure Gae-sun can't find another friend or relative to help?"

"So, other men ogling me. Is that what you're really worried about? What if they do? Once your baby's born, your eyes will fill with nobody but him and his mother. So why should you care which men will squeeze my butt?"

Eum-chun! The Voice of Heaven! How dare you speak to your husband like that! He looked as though an A-frame porter had run his stick through his face, his throat too smashed for words to escape. She cringed. He was about to drive his fist through the wardrobe mirror again. She threw her arm around her forehead and ducked. Instead, he snapped the light off and slapped her body against his.

They made fierce love. It felt lovely and terrible at the same time. Even after months of taking turns with Soo-yang and sharing him, unruly thoughts plagued her.

You don't love me the way you used to, do you? She nursed the question. His tongue tasted like chestnuts.

Our secrets are not ours any more, are they? She pulled away.

What're you doing differently with me from what you do with her? He came after her, bitterly, sweetly; how could he make it feel like new every time?

Do you hold the back of her head with your left palm while you . . . Ahhhh. Ahhhh.

The first day at the shop brought Gae-sun and Eum-chun more than what two porters with A-frames strapped to their backs could earn. As soon as Eum-chun collected some paper money, she moved it from her apron pocket to the one sewn into her underskirt. With each step, the money thumped against her thigh, giving it friendly pats.

And how sweet not to see the belly of that *ssipal* woman. *Ssipal? Eum-chun, the Voice of Heaven! How vulgar!* But saying it felt as tasty as pickled octopus.

Customers streamed in, keeping her on her toes through late afternoon. She only had time to wet her lips with roasted barley tea. Now she truly understood the meaning of an old saying about stress making the bottom of one's feet break out in sweat like the paws of a dog. Only just before the dinner rush did she and Gae-sun eat a mung bean pancake. Then they flipped more pancakes, poured more wine, and made more money.

"Sisters! Another plate here!" Men flattered them by calling them sisters, not aunts. Only a few porters turned either quiet or gruff. Women and children took pancakes home. Eum-chun could keep going without eating or resting. The gold in a shark's mouth that she saw in her dream two nights ago piled in her pocket. And not seeing Soo-yang's stomach all day felt as though a tunnel had opened inside of her, allowing air to breeze in and out of her body. *Aunt Hong, thank you and your gods!*

She'd give much of the first day's earnings to Mrs. Rhee. Even if she gave her all she made for weeks, it still wouldn't equal the heart Mrs. Rhee had poured into brewing herbs for Eum-chun for years. She had recited while brewing the sage, "Bear a son, bear a son."

What would Gui-yong do if he found out she worked this late? No time to worry about that now. She hoped Gae-sun's relative would still need her even if she recovered and returned to the shop. If she could work like this, she could endure Soo-yang's pregnancies five times over. Even if Gui-yong's affection for Soo-yang grew thick, perhaps she could bear it without losing her mind completely. Work, work, work. That would save her life. And if she made money like this for the next ten years, sending Mi-na to Seoul National University Law School would not be a pipe dream. Picturing Mi-na in a judge's robe and the mouths of women with ten sons twisting with envy made her swing her hips in a dance to the tune of "Taepyeongga" playing in her head.

"What're you so happy about?" Gae-sun asked, pouring rice wine, white like milk, into a kettle.

"Not being cooped up at home and making money." Eum-chun whispered into her friend's ear. Both laughed.

That night, Eum-chun handed Mrs. Rhee all the money she had made.

"Money's good," Mrs. Rhee said, smiling, "but look at my arms. Rash from worrying about how upset Gui-yong will get."

Eum-chun didn't sit and comfort her; she needed to go wash and get some sleep.

"Were there many ordering wine?"

"Yes, but they were all gentlemanly."

"Oh, the ghosts of my ancestors! Wait until Gui-yong sees the men."

"Mother, nobody, not one man, fussed about anything. Some talked politics. One man said his next door neighbor got caught trying to cross the border to the North. The North, Mother! They took him to the main Seoul police station and beat him to death. His body was rolled into a straw rice sack for his family to pick up."

"His eyes must have gotten rolled backwards. How could he not see Commies are worse than what's in the outhouse hole? But for every crazy like him, we have a hundred dying to come to the South. Shows our side's better, doesn't it? Go get some sleep. Don't work yourself sick. That'll really drive Gui-yong mad."

The fifth day was Saturday, the busiest day so far. Eum-chun didn't get the time to admire the red cloth banner fluttering across the doorway that advertised her "Flat-as-a-cockroach" pancakes.

"So, this is the shop we've heard about!" three men

arriving together said. "Prove the rumors right, aunts! If not, we won't pay. Deal?"

"No!" Gae-sun laughed. "If you don't pay, we won't call the police. We'll just make you eat until you do!"

Two of the earlier customers lingered and drank three whole kettles of rice wine. One of them began to sing "The Camellia Maiden," slurring the words.

The tear-shiny camellia maiden's face
Weary of loneliness and longing for him,
Weary of weeping, oh, camellia maiden
Fallen in a heap in a restless sleep.

Eum-chun asked the one man who wasn't banging chopsticks what time it was. Ten thirty, he said. In an hour and a half, the curfew sirens would wail. The last thing she wanted was to get caught in the street, dragged to the police station, and spend the night there. That would certainly make Gui-yong's heart burst.

But every man joined the singing, picking up aluminum chopsticks and clanging them against the tables. It was getting close to eleven.

"We must close now," Gae-sun braved. Some fished out money, but others kept blaring. This crowd and yesterday's were like night and day. One customer grabbed Eum-chun's arm and pulled. She tipped and bumped her shoulder against his.

That instant, in burst Mr. Lee and Gui-yong. They must've been watching from across the alley. "Get up, men! Time to close!" Gui-yong shouted, driving one of the door boards into the grooves. A few men scrambled to their feet, paid, and staggered out. A man shot up, took Gui-yong by his collar, and shouted into his face, spraying spittle. "Hey, hey!"

Mr. Lee tore them apart. A wine kettle clanged onto the cement floor. Gae-sun rushed around in circles with soy sauce in her hand.

"Forget the money," Mr. Lee yelled. "Just leave! It's curfew time!"

Gui-yong slammed another clapboard door into place. Eum-chun grabbed his arm, but he shook her off. She sprinkled water on the coal briquette stove and covered it with a metal lid. But before she and Gae-sun could gather up the leftover food and the next day's supplies, Gui-yong pulled Eum-chun out the door and clicked the padlock he'd found on a shelf behind them. While the women trudged behind the men on dirt paths snaking around houses dark in sleep, dogs barked from behind fences and high walls.

Even before Gui-yong got to the gate, Soo-yang opened it. They passed her without a word. He ignored his mother, too, who rushed out of her room to the hallway. Gui-yong pulled Eum-chun into her room and slid the door shut. He turned the light on and pulled her down to sit. He sat, too, and faced her, their knees touching. His nose looked larger and redder than usual. His hands planted on his knees, he hunched forward, panting. Strangely, she felt calm. Her punishment was coming. She'd bucked against common wisdom—a caterpillar must eat pine needles, not something else. Likewise, women should stay home. That was the Obedient Way, the command from Heaven.

Slowly, his breathing quieted, but his eyes burned like double-wicked candles.

"Sweetheart, that's the end of that," he said, "Or I'll have to quit work and make sure you don't leave the house."

She stared at the floor.

He suddenly turned, took a pillow out of her bedding pile, and lay on his side, his back toward her.

She watched his shoulder heave.

She wanted to believe that what had bothered him the most was the attention other men gave her. That it had troubled him more than his losing face because she was working. Did that prove he loved her as much as before? Would he have gotten as upset if other men had paid attention to Soo-yang? Eum-chun felt like lying down and throwing her arms around him, but she needed to wash up first. She got up and slid the door open.

"Ouch!" Mrs. Rhee crumpled to the floor. Eum-chun had stepped on her toes, making her lose her balance and crash against Soo-yang, which sent her teetering. Eum-chun should've known they'd eavesdrop. Soo-yang let out an embarrassed giggle.

"Mother, you all right? Let me see." Eum-chun fumbled for Mrs. Rhee's foot, but Mrs. Rhee turned, mumbled she was all right, and hobbled into her dark room. Eum-chun bowed to Mrs. Rhee's back and called out, "Good night, Mother." Soo-yang whispered a "Good night" to Eum-chun and disappeared into her room.

By the faucet, she poured water into the brass basin and splashed it on her face. Seven, twelve, thirty times. When her arms got tired, she added water and dropped her forehead into the basin. How would she survive each day watching Soo-yang's stomach rising like ten moons?

The curfew siren wailed.

The next day, Eum-chun showed Soo-yang how to marinate raw beef the way Mrs. Rhee liked. They were yoked together for life in this house and kitchen, Eum-chun as the Big Sister and Soo-yang as the Young Sister. Neither would venture to work outside the home again. They'd become like the *nang* and *pae*, two animals in old storybooks handed down from olden times. One was without hind legs, and the other without front ones. Though they quarreled often, they had to move as one body—without each other, they couldn't hunt. Thus, *nangpae*, the two together, came down to this day as a most difficult situation.

Despair gnawed at Eum-chun. Even if she could survive Soo-yang's pregnancy, how would she eventually afford Mi-na's law school education? How could she show off her daughter to women with sons?

The midmorning sunlight hit the dirt bumps on the kitchen floor. The lumps made a neat crisscross pattern, as though a handyman had aligned them. The design moved her as though she'd never seen it before. As every family needed all the tiles in their roofs, every member also must keep their posts that worked for the best for the whole family—the Obedient Way. It had been spelled out by the design on the kitchen floor all these sixteen years of her marriage, her life before that, and her life before her birth.

How long would it take before her thoughts about Gui-yong's relationship with Soo-yang and her belly growing fat fell into place like the dirt bumps?

While watching Soo-yang slice the beef and chop the green onion and garlic, Eum-chun sipped azalea wine from a white sake cup.

"Did Mrs. Bang bring this newspaper yesterday?"

"Yes," Soo-yang said.

She glanced at the front page and skipped the news about the upcoming National Assembly election. She'd heard predictions the parties opposed to the President Rhee's

Freedom Party would win the majority. She had no idea whether that was good or bad for the country. But she did know that whoever won needed to show leadership so that the South could produce what everyone needed, like electricity. There had been blackouts because the Reds cut off the electricity supply to the South. Those Red dogs! They deserved to have the word "thieves" branded onto their foreheads with a hot iron. But instead of uniting to stamp out the Northern dogs, Southern politicians foamed at the mouth against their fellow politicians and split into new factions every month.

"What're you reading?"

"Politics. You'd better not hear about them. Your stomach's already weak. But here's some good news. Kim Hwal-lan, the president of Ewha Womans University, is establishing a graduate school! Isn't that stunning? She has a doctoral degree from an American university, too." She let out a sigh heavy enough to drill a hole in the floor.

"Some women get to go all the way to America and study and come back and set up a university," Eum-chun said, "when I can't even run a pancake stand! But girls like Mi-na will go to schools like this! Imagine Mi-na getting a PhD! Since I can't work and make money, maybe Mi-na can get the PhD first, get a job, and earn money for her law school."

When a picture of her daughter in a judge's robe fluttered before her eyes, she slapped the paper down and stood up.

Her hope for Mi-na's success stirred her spirit. She thrust her arms out, jiggled her shoulders up and down in a dance, and belted out the refrain of "Taepyeongga."

Nilririya, nilririya, ninanoooo!

Soo-yang laughed.

"Should I start seasoning the beef, Big Sister?"

Big Sister! Big Sister! What a sickening title! The ruined pancake business cut across her heart again, and Eum-chun plunked back down on the straw seat hard enough for *ssssss* to steam out from between her teeth. "Put in lots of garlic," she said, "and plenty of black pepper. With the raw beef dish, you can't spice it too much."

"I soaked some sowthistle roots for a salad for you," Soo-yang said.

"Well, isn't that nice of you." She was the only one in the family who loved its bitter taste.

A low groan came from Mrs. Rhee's room. As though a bomb shelter siren had gone off, which happened regularly these days, Eum-chun shot up, snatched a clean rag, poured water into a basin, and rushed out of the kitchen.

"I'm here, Mother." Eum-chun bent over Mrs. Rhee's half bare buttocks.

When she was finished, she reshaped her mother-in-law's millet-filled pillow and guided her head to it. Mrs. Rhee's eyes filled up.

"I'm sorry you had to give up the shop," Mrs. Rhee said.

"Rest a bit, Mother. You'll feel good enough to visit Grandma Hahn in no time. We're making the raw beef you like for dinner."

Eum-chun closed the lid of the brass chamber pot and carried it out. She emptied it into the outhouse and sat by the faucet with it. She dipped a fistful of straw into the heap of ash saved in a bucket and scrubbed the inside. After washing her hands, she went back to the kitchen and poured herself another cup of wine.

"Didn't you say the wine was for an ancestral rite?" Soo-yang kneaded the seasonings into the beef. "What'll happen if our mother-in-law catches you with wine?"

"Will you pour me a little? Wine tastes better when someone pours it for you. You know what azalea wine can do?"

Soo-yang sat on another straw seat next to Eum-chun and waited.

"It stops bleeding."

"You're bleeding? Where?" Soo-yang's forehead wrinkled in worry, but she poured.

Even when agitated, Soo-yang's face looked happy like a pumpkin rolling in the autumn sun. The look of a pregnant woman. Eum-chun would've given up her wine and nirvana for that. Wine burst through her chest and head. Did Gui-yong make real love to Soo-yang or did he just mix flesh with her? How much did he love it?

Eum-chun took a sip.

"Shouldn't you see a doctor? When did the bleeding begin? Where?"

"Nowhere," Eum-chun said.

She meant everywhere.

PART II

THE WAR

(1950–1953)

June 25, 1950

Mi-na

What a surprise. The Commies really showed up and bombed her whole town. Not her neighborhood, though, but close to it and all around it. What would this mean for her? Her parents? Little Mommy? Would she go live with her parents?

"Heard that popping? Sounds like laundry pounding sticks dragging over rocks." That was Mommy's voice. Mommy had the ears of a rabbit. Mi-na kicked her covers off, pulled on her skirt and blouse, and skipped outside. Men milled around by Mr. Lee's house at the dead end. Women clustered by Mi-na's house, Grandma and Mommy among them, whispering and looking like they'd seen a snake bellying across their rafter, which was the worst thing Mi-na could think of. She caught the words, "Communists," "tanks," "North Korea," and "Dongdaemun Gate." The last one was not too far from her neighborhood. She and Mommy had walked there to catch the trolley past the Sports Stadium. When she slunk around to Mommy's side and gripped her hand, Mommy's eyelids pulled tight, which meant trouble. Lots of it.

"Bastards! Criminals to die by *yuksi*!" Grandma Hahn said.

"Mommy, what's a *yuksi*?"

"*Shhhhhhh.*"

Later, she asked Kwang-ho. He wasn't bright, but he was a fourth grader and knew what a *yuksi* meant. A long time ago, when a man did something very bad, his arms and legs were tied to four horsecarts and pulled in different directions.

"You know what *yuk* means," he asked.

"I know. It means six."

"His head is one, his body two, and his arms and legs three, four, five, six." Picturing them tearing apart, Mi-na felt like a bear had slapped its paw on her back.

A few days later, Mommy didn't shush her any more. Every child heard about or saw North Korean tanks move into Seoul like monster beasts with no eyes.

"They're burning everything down!" a shout came from the street.

That was after Father had left to get Little Mommy from

her parent's house on Eulji-ro Road where she was visiting.

"Get out!" someone shouted from outside.

Get out to where? It was near dinnertime.

Mommy and Grandma yanked their wardrobes open. *Drrruuuk, drruuuk*, the drawers went. They took out money and gold rings. They lifted their skirts and dropped them into their secret pockets. They filled cloth sacks with things she couldn't see because they moved too fast and tied them around their waists. Finally, they each put one sack on their heads. Mommy pulled Mi-na's hand and they ran out the gate.

"Where we going? Aren't we waiting for Daddy?"

"We're only going up the hill over there. To take a look."

Then why did Mommy pack the bundles? They scrambled up the dirt road winding around the houses behind theirs. Dozens of other people were climbing, their bags on their heads and backs. The pathway narrowed, and people's elbows and sacks bumped into Mi-na's face. The matted grass turned a mustard color from the setting sun. She stumbled over a fist-sized stone, which made her sweaty hand slip from Mommy's. Mommy wadded a part of her long skirt and said, "Hold onto this."

Crackling came from behind them, making everyone turn. Puffs of smoke flew up from buildings; red and orange flames burst, too. Someone cried. "*Aigu, aigu*," some people wailed. When they got to the top, they dropped their loads and looked down. Flames popped up.

"That's near Dongdaemun Gate! The Gate's hit?"

"There! The Sigumun Gate too!" That was a fifteen-minute walk from their neighborhood. Five different flames blossomed below the hill where they stood. Was her house burning? Mr. Lee's? Grandma Hahn's? Where was Daddy? Was he looking for her? What if one of those Communist bullets hit Little Mommy? Mi-na should feel sad, but she didn't. Not as much as she should. If they didn't have Little Mommy, they could go back to being by themselves and being happy again.

For what felt like an hour, grown-ups didn't budge. Some women dried tears and pinched their noses and threw snot into the dirt. Men spit into the ground. A few boys and girls her age, in the first grade, stood all eyes and ears, taking in the *tu tu tu tu* of the guns and the *weeng weeng ppppccchhooo* of the monster airplanes.

A boy at the end of Mi-na's row turned around. He had a shaven spot around a sore on his head. He skipped away and down a slope. She wondered where he went. Were flames popping up on that side too? She followed the boy. When she got there, boys and girls stood in a soybean field, slashing pods off the plants.

"Let's cook 'em!" Shaved Head said.

"Yeah!" another boy in a homemade cotton shirt and school pants shouted. Poor children wore school pants during vacation.

Soon, the group had a fire going and ate roasted beans right out of the pods. Mi-na did, too. She'd never dreamed plain beans could taste so good. She kept eating until she heard Mommy call, "Mi-na!"

When she climbed back, the grown-ups still pointed at places, watched, and wept. So this was the war they said would break out. What did it mean? Would they be driven into an ocean and drown, as Simcheong did when sailors bought her and threw her overboard to make the sea gods calm the waters for them? She buried her face in Mommy's skirt.

They didn't return to their homes until the stars began nodding and blinking. Mi-na's house and neighborhood remained as they'd left them. Little Mommy didn't get killed. She and Daddy waited for them. So even after the Commie war she'd heard about all year actually came, with Reds shooting at them and burning Seoul, Mi-na's life didn't change. She was still the girl who had made Little Mommy's coming necessary, which had made Mommy stay in bed like she was glued to it.

That night in her bedding in Grandma's room, she thought about the day. Even though her stomach felt stuffy and she farted a lot, she hadn't thought about how to become ten times better than a boy while roasting and eating beans with the kids. Grown-ups were busy watching fires and buildings shoot smoke into the sky. And Mrs. Bang didn't throw fart-stink words at Mi-na. Would the war make everyone forget about her not being a boy? If that's true, the war started by the criminals sentenced to die by *yuksi* might be the best thing that ever happened to her.

One day, North Korean soldiers stomped around her neighborhood. Some of them camped in schools. They did that at Mi-na's, too. The Communist soldiers' long guns, brown uniforms with red stars on the shoulders, and squinty faces scared her, and she didn't go near them.

"If a Communist soldier asks you what you ate," Mommy told her days ago, "say you ate bean sprout soup with barley. Don't say rice. If you do, he'll come and take it. He might shoot us."

Last night, Mrs. Lee stopped Mi-na and asked, "What did you eat for dinner, Mi-na?"

Did she have to lie to Mrs. Lee, too? Mrs. Lee had never said Mi-na should have been a boy. Would a nice person like her squeal to the Communists?

"Barley and bean sprouts," Mi-na said. She didn't want to take a chance a Commie might overhear them.

"That's a smart girl," Mrs. Lee said and smiled.

But boys weren't scared of Red soldiers and followed them, calling them "uncle." Kwang-ho was among them. Mi-na hung back and watched the boys skip around the soldiers and laugh. They carried on like a circus had come into town.

"Uncle! That house is the section chief's," the boys shouted.

"Good boys." A soldier ruffled a boy's hair and let him touch his gun. The boys pressed against the soldier and rubbed the gun. After a minute, the soldier shouted, "Step back."

"Why do you have tree branches stuck in the band around your hat, uncle?" a boy asked. But the soldiers stomped ahead.

"That's Mr. Hong's house," a third boy said. "He runs the rice shop."

One soldier wrote in his notes. From then on, Mi-na didn't see neighborhood boys kick their wrapped coins or play the horse-rider game. Tagging along with Commie soldiers was their new game. Once, the Commies broke out in a song.

"Our Glorious National Song," one said.

"Do it again, uncle. We want to learn," the boys said.

So the soldiers sang more slowly, and the boys followed. Mi-na did, too, but only in her head.

... the brave Jangbaek Mountain ...
streaked red with blood ...
the Amrok River stretches to no end ...

our General Kim Il-sung . . . far
into our bright future . . . .

One night that fall, Mi-na woke to the sound of her gate crashing open. Then lights stung her eyes. She was sleeping in Mommy's room; Father was hiding in the dugout under the hallway floor. When she opened her eyes, a puppy's wet nose was in front of her face. When she blinked and looked at it again, it was the tip of a long gun. A soldier aimed it at her and Mommy. Two other solders, the "uncles," stood behind him.

"Rice!" the Gun Man yelled. "Brass! Turn them over! Quick, or I'll shoot!"

Mommy fumbled with her skirt and blouse to put them on quickly over her nightshirt and panties. Beyond the door, Mi-na saw another soldier. He yanked open the grain bin in the hallway. She didn't worry about rice being taken away; the bin was empty. She worried about Father. What if he coughed? He would've heard the soldiers not to do that, but she still held her breath. Mi-na had been in the hideout; it smelled like a dead mouse.

Mommy went out to the sitting room, wobbling. Mi-na followed. Grandma stood at her door, her lips paler than her brownish skin. The soldiers let Mommy through. She crossed the yard, forgetting to put on her shoes. Little Mommy's room stayed dark.

"If Communists raid our house," Father had said to Little Mommy a few days ago, "stay in your room and keep it dark. Don't turn the light on, no matter what. Even if they find me in the dugout, beat me, drag me away, and you hear me scream. Understand?"

Father wanted the baby in her belly to be safe. How about Mi-na and Mommy? Was it all right for them to get dragged away? Father didn't mean that. What did he mean then?

Mommy went up the ten steps to the roof of the cellar where jars were lined up. Some were bean sauce jars, but one held rice and another had barley. She took the lids off. The soldiers looked up at Mommy, who stood higher than their shoulders.

"See? We have no more rice," Mommy said, her voice cracking. Her face turned whiter than the socks she forgot to wear. Mi-na didn't know Mommy could lie.

"Your comrades already searched our house. Like they were looking for lice in long johns," she said. "Yesterday they took all we had!"

What would happen if they went up and saw she was lying? Mi-na felt tingly all over, as if she had to pee.

"Come up and see for yourselves," Mommy said. Did she think this was a game? How did she become so bold? Grown-ups said brave people's livers grew large. Did Mommy's liver grow so big she was begging to be shot?

"They took all our brass bowls, too" Mommy said. "Even

my mother-in-law's ash tray and chamber pot."

The Gun Man flicked his head toward the gate. Others turned and marched out. Then came banging from the Hahns' door.

Mi-na couldn't hold it any longer; warm water flew down her thighs.

No one got killed that night, and even though the Commies scared the ghosts out of her, Mi-na's life still stayed the same. She still had one father, one grandmother, two mothers, and a brother on the way. What if the baby was a sister? Would Grandmother send Little Mommy and the girl away? That's what Mrs. Bang said she should do. For once, she liked Mrs. Bang's idea.

November 1950

Eum-chun

"Sweetheart, hurry." Gui-yong burst through the clapboard gate of her parents' one-room rental. She and Mi-na were visiting them.

"You and Mi-na, go, go!" he said, his face red. "The dog-faced Commies! They're bombing the bridges!"

Mi-na darted to him and wrapped her arm around his waist. He thrust a bag at Eum-chun and put his hand on Mi-na's head. For five months, they nearly went deaf from the roars of the fighter jets, both the UN's and North Korea's.

"Sweetheart! The Chinese are coming down to kill us all!" Gui-yong said, "Three hundred thousand Chinese! Two times more than the North Korean army! Hurry and leave!"

Eum-chun pulled at the tie of the bag Gui-yong had thrust at her.

"Your clothes. I got only a few things. And Mi-na's, too."

Eum-chun's mother, weak as a willow branch, stood by the faucet, her wrists ringed with foam from the wash she had been doing. She looked about to faint. Eum-chun had always hated her own second toe; it was longer than her big toe, a sign she'd lose her mother before losing her father. Her mother wiped her hands on her apron and hugged Mi-na. Then she shooed Eum-chun and Mi-na toward the gate, her eyes reddening.

"Move! Go! You heard him!" Eum-chun's mother said.

"Mother! I can't leave without you! Or Father, or Li-ho!" Eum-chun then turned to Gui-yong. "And you? Aren't you going with me? Isn't Mother?" She didn't mention Soo-yang.

"I broke through roadblocks even to get here! The bastards are all over! You've got to go the other way, cross the river! Mother's bundling their things. Soo-yang, too. The minute I get back, we'll follow you. I want you to get a head start."

Mi-na wailed. Eum-chun grabbed her and tucked her under her arm.

"Then you shouldn't go back either!" Eum-chun said.

"You're scaring her, Sweetheart. Come here, Mi-na." Gui-yong plopped on the hallway floor and swept her into his lap.

"I'll find you, Mi-na," he said. "I'll bring Grandma and Little Mommy. We may get on the same train! It'll take us to the countryside. When we get there, we'll catch crawfish. Will you be my brave girl? My grape eyes?" He held his pinky out to her. Her lips stuck way out in her best pouting form, but she wrapped her finger around his.

"What kind of a weak promise is that? Make it tighter." He locked their fingers, his smile disappearing from his eyes.

"Sweetheart," he said. "Move like lightning. Get on the first train heading south. The *first* one. You hear, *yeobo*? Go as far south as Masan. I'll find you." He pressed money into her hand, squeezed Mi-na once more, and rushed out the gate.

Eum-chun grabbed Mi-na and joined the people herding across the Han River Bridge. Her legs wobbled from the fear that the bridge might fly up and shower down in pieces along with her limbs. Bombs popped out of North Korean planes. Then the *kkkkkrrrrrfccchhhhh*.

"Mommy, Mommy. Why isn't Daddy coming? Where's Grandma?"

Eum-chun tightened her grip on Mi-na's hand. Mi-na didn't ask about Little Mommy, either.

"He's coming. He promised. He's getting Grandma. And Little Mommy. Hold tight and keep walking."

Mi-na's hands were ice. November wind shouldn't be this cold. When it didn't rain much in the fall, Eum-chun knew they'd pay for it through the winter.

"Keep your other hand in your pocket." She shoved Mi-na's hand into her own. Mud-colored planes swooped down, and their roars plugged up her ears. She covered Mi-na's eyes and ears.

"Mommy, don't cover my eyes! I can't see!"

"You don't need to see. Just hold onto me and walk." By shielding her eyes, she kept her from seeing the man by the hillside crumple onto the snow, his blood blooming into peonies. Some people trudged along with mattresses over their heads. Why hadn't she thought of that? She kept looking back to spot her husband, but all she saw was a thousand faces. They lugged bags on their heads and backs and in carts. Even if she tried to sidestep the crowd and wait for Gui-yong, she couldn't have. If she tried, she'd be trampled.

She should've gone home with him. They should've stayed together dead or alive. But that would've meant risking Mi-na's life. Even if she and Gui-yong died, Mi-na must live.

As she expected, her parents refused to leave Seoul.

"At our age, we want to die here, not become strange-land ghosts." Neither did they let Eum-chun take Li-ho.

"Jin-i'll come for her," they insisted.

"*Aigu, aigu,*" old women and some young ones wailed. The most pitiful crying came from toddlers sitting by the side of the road. They were lost or had been abandoned by families who couldn't carry them. Many were girl babies, with short bangs across their foreheads or braids sticking out from under their hats.

If you, Seongju House God, help Gui-yong make it out of Seoul alive, I'll never mope about my life again. I will even force myself to look at Soo-yang's pregnant belly and like it.

Soo-yang

A man cleared his throat. Soo-yang freed her nipple from her baby's mouth, lowered her blouse, and yanked her door open. Mrs. Rhee, who'd been smoking, dropped her pipe on the ashtray and rose to her feet. And there stood Gui-yong, in broad daylight, too. He'd squeezed in four quick visits so far in the eight months since Soo-yang and Mrs. Rhee began living in Masan, all just before the night curfew.

Every time she saw his khaki uniform, it looked odd. Who would've thought the only son for three generations in a row would become a soldier? The gasoline smell from his army truck blew into the room.

"Can't stay," he said, not undoing his boots. "Have only a minute." He looked down at Kyung-jin in Soo-yang's lap and then at his Mother.

"Mother, heard anything about Eum-chun and Mi-na? Did the section chief know anything? Policemen? Pickled baby octopus sellers in the markets around here? Have you asked them if they saw Eum-chun? Octopus sellers, Mother. They'll be the first Eum-chun will try to find. You know that, Mother."

Soo-yang cringed at his loud voice. Her landlady, Mrs. Shin, sat outside Soo-yang's one-room rental. Mrs. Shin ran a hole-in-the-wall store, and her chair leaned against the mud wall of Soo-yang's room. Every uttered word, unless whispered, could be heard by anyone outside. Mrs. Shin didn't know Soo-yang was a second wife, but she might have gotten a hunch. How true that even if one wore ten layers of clothing, people would see what one tried to hide. Now, thanks to Gui-yong, the secret was out. Her neighbors would have fun with that. How could he be so inconsiderate?

In the eight months of living without Eum-chun, Soo-yang's stomach felt better. She didn't need her powdered medicine. Now, Mrs. Shin would surely ask, "Who's Eum-chun? Who's Mi-na?"

She already felt vinegary fluids dripping into her innards.

"No, son," Mrs. Rhee said. "People looking for their wives, husbands, and children fill the market! Easier to find a needle in a rice paddy. Seongju House God knows how many policemen I have talked to. How many *dong* chiefs I have talked to. But I haven't seen any pickled octopus women around here. The weather's been too hot for that. Imagine how fast seafood would spoil, even if pickled! Stay and eat rice and pork before you go. A bite of meat will keep you alive!"

"Gotta go, Mother. Convoy's pushing north all night. We took Cheorwon, Geumhwa, and Seoul back. Keep looking for Eum-chun, Mother." He crawled on his belly toward Soo-yang, leaving his boots laced, and stroked the baby's cheek. Then he was gone.

Kyung-jin whimpered. Soo-yang pulled up her blouse and let his mouth close on her nipple. Didn't the mother of his son deserve to have him look into her face?

Soo-yang's temples throbbed at the thought of having to face Mrs. Shin. Later, after she put Kyung-jin down for a nap, she went out. Mrs. Shin fanned herself, staring out into the alley. It was midafternoon, the slowest time of the day, and she usually let Soo-yang watch her store while she ran to the outhouse.

"I can watch the . . ." Soo-yang offered.

Even before Soo-yang finished, Mrs. Shin snapped.

"No, thanks." She turned away and worked her feather duster fiercely over the box of hairpins and combs, as if dirt were caked on them.

Soo-yang slipped into her cooking shed, opened the jar she kept to the back of the dish shelf, and took out a folded packet of her sour stomach medicine. She tossed the powder into her mouth, scooped up water with a gourd dipper, and gulped.

Eum-chun

Where was Gui-yong? Eum-chun spent months looking for him in streets, left his photo in neighborhood offices, and asked the chiefs to let her know if they saw him. But no leads for eight months. She shuttled the short bridge between heaven and hell every day. Heaven when she realized she wasn't looking at Soo-yang's mounding belly. Hell when she imagined smelling gun smoke and watching blood noodle down Gui-yong's face. The need to stay alive in order to see him come running toward her was what kept her muscling through her days.

Eum-chun found the cheapest rental in Old Masan,

a neighborhood of a few dozen thatch-roofed huts surrounded by rice fields. Rooms went for more than she could afford in downtown New Masan. Buses, old discards from America, came here twice a day. Gaping holes on the floorboard showed dirt roads flashing by as buses bumped along. But she was grateful. If she missed them, it took forty-five minutes to walk to town through winding rice paddies and across a railroad track. Luckily, Mi-na and Li-ho's elementary school was only a fifteen-minute walk away. Eum-chun had taken her niece under her wing. Jin-i lived in Busan, a few hours' bus ride away, and after visiting her rental room in a house full of wine house women sleeping with their lovers until noon, she took Li-ho off Jin-i's hands.

An hour before the girls would come home from school, she headed to her neighbor from Sangju's house for a drink of the rice wine she had brewed. The two of them had become close in these months, comforting each other about Mrs. Sangju's dead husband and Eum-chun's missing one. Mrs. Sangju lost her husband to typhoid when he was only seventeen. She never remarried, as was customary, and had lived with her mother-in-law for the next forty years, until she died.

"Senile, a real bad case," Mrs. Sangju had said of her mother-in-law. "Drew pictures on the wall with her poop," Mrs. Sangju had said.

They ate *gaetteok*, lumps of cooked barley dough specked

with sage, and washed it down with a round of rice wine. Humidity from the South Sea blew in, too, and made sleeping at night a sweat bath. She could hear the sound of Mrs. Sangju's thatch roof frying under the sun. War or not, Gui-yong and thousands of other men dead or alive, it was perfect weather for Mrs. Sangju's rice in her paddies to ripen to gold.

"No news about your hubby, huh? Lonely nights, huh?"

A lopsided smile jumped from Mrs. Sangju's lips up her triangular face to her ordinarily placid eyes. She pushed something wrapped in a handkerchief across the table to Eum-chun. When she closed her fingers around it, it felt like a zucchini, but it was an Asian eggplant. It was dried but felt like fine leather.

"A little gift for you," Mrs. Sangju said. "The best woman warmer. You won't be able to tell it from the real thing."

Eum-chun's hand went the way of snowflakes. The eggplant rolled out of the wrap and tipped her bowl. Wine splashed.

Mrs. Sangju giggled so hard her breath squeezed out in puffs of wheezing. Eum-chun jumped up, grabbed a towel from the kitchen, and dabbed at her blouse and wiped the table.

"Careful, now," Mrs. Sangju said when she caught her breath. She lifted her blouse tie and dried her eyes. "Any idea how hard it was to make it soft and firm at the same time? How long it took? If you did, you'd give it the respect it deserves. Lots of it."

Eum-chun's heart felt as though air was leaking into it in little bubbles. She'd overheard her widowed aunts talk of their lonely nights and what they used, but she was not allowed a peek at them.

"I picked it early in the morning two weeks ago," Mrs. Sangju said, "and dried it in the sun only one hour each day. The rest of the time I let it dry slowly on the hearth ledge. You dry it too fast, it'll take skin off you! Better to have sex with a laundry pounding stick. I dipped it in sesame seed oil and rubbed it into the skin. I used satin, my dear. The folds, creases, and the rounding didn't just happen. I don't make a gift like that for just anybody." She rewrapped it and put it in Eum-chun's hand, closing Eum-chun's fingers around it. "Don't drop it again, dear."

Eum-chun's belly went soft from the heft in her hand.

"Look at me," Eum-chun stood up and said. "My girls! They'll be home. Thank you for the wine . . . and the gift."

Mrs. Sangju smiled her lopsided grin. Mrs. Sangju's odd way of smiling seemed connected to the sorrow that must have grown like fungus inside her. Eum-chun rushed through Mrs. Sangju's bush clover gate and then stumbled across her own landlord's yard and into her room, keeping the eggplant in the fold of her skirt. She made it without running into her landlady or Mrs. Yum, a fellow renter. Where should she hide it?

Eum-chun understood Mrs. Sangju's loneliness and her need for whatever could make her nights more bearable.

"No one," Mrs. Sangju had said, "was as unlucky as me. If a lucky widow fell on a chamber pot, she'd land on the cover, its knob sliding nicely up her pussy. Not me."

Eum-chun herself had difficult nights these eight months without Gui-yong. In sleep, she fantasized about loving him. Often, in the middle of the night, she recalled her third-grade textbook story of the three thousand palace maidens of the Baekje Kingdom. How would it have felt twelve hundred years ago to hit the water when they flung themselves off a cliff rather than be raped by Tang soldiers? She shuddered to think she might be unable to pull out her chastity knife from her slip pocket fast enough, if something happened. Would she be able to use it on herself, as expected, or the attacker?

Who really knew? Maybe those palace maidens had eggplants, too. She'd heard jokes about Chinese palace ladies' ceramic pottery pieces shaped like rabbits. She also knew about pin cushions. At least one of her aunts' pins doubled as her weapon against the weakness of her flesh. She'd seen her washing her sheets at dawn before others awoke, scrubbing to get the bloodstain out of the cotton.

Kkkkkkkktttttttrrrrrr sssshhhiiiiinnnnngggg. Six B-29s appeared from the east and tore across the sky, waking her up to the reality of the war and her empty rice jar. If it hadn't been for General MacArthur's Incheon Landing last September trapping the Reds between Seoul and Busan like rats, she wouldn't be breathing. One day, when the war was over, and if the general survived and she was alive, she would ask Aunt Hong to offer a special prayer of gratitude—*Thank you, Moon and Sun Gods, for General MacArthur. May he live a long and prosperous life! May President Truman also live a long life for sending the general and American troops.*

For now, she had one fistful of barley to cook for dinner and no money for bean sprouts. Was this the proper time to give an eggplant penis "respect"?

"Mommy! Mommy!" Mi-na and Li-ho skipped through the gate. She thrust the eggplant under the kindling in her cooking shed and outstretched her arms to them.

"Mi-na! Li-ho! What are those sacks on your heads? Rice? Let me see. From Americans, aren't they?"

"But American rice doesn't taste good, it falls off chopsticks, and it stinks, Mommy." Mi-na took her sack off her head and a smaller one off Li-ho's.

"What's in the smaller bag?"

"Powdered milk."

"Did you tell your teachers 'Thank you' and bow to them? Good taste or no, stink or no, these will keep us alive this week." Eum-chun squatted and hugged her girls.

"I'm not eating it, Momma," Li-ho said. "Powdered milk

gives me runny poop."

"Me, too," Mi-na said, sitting on the wood floor by their room.

"Well, I'll have to work some magic and turn them into delicacies, won't I?"

Eum-chun had sold her rings, gifts from her mother-in-law and her own parents, and paid for food and tuition for the girls so far. She earned some money by knitting sweaters for her neighbors through the winter. She cooked for them at special ceremonies like a baby's one-hundredth-day party, someone's sixtieth birthday, or ancestor worship rituals. Sometimes she was paid in cash; other times in food or both.

Would she really have to consider she might never reunite with Gui-yong? She'd caught the first train out of Seoul, which had brought her to this city Gui-yong had told her to come to. But she found no trace of Gui-yong. The train had been a freight train and had no windows, no bathrooms. When the train stopped, everyone who could ran to the woods to pee. People's belongings had gotten tumbled into shoulder-high piles in the box cars. They sat on top of the heaps or draped themselves over them. Eum-chun couldn't find the sacks that her mother had thrown rice cakes into. When the train stopped, without knowing whether she'd make it back in time, she ran to the nearest farmhouse and bought whatever the villagers could spare—cooked barley smeared with red pepper sauce.

The police stations and neighborhood unit offices where she had stopped and asked whether they heard of a man named Gui-yong looking for Eum-chun or Mi-na brought no results. One day, the response she received was a yell.

"Over there!" a policeman said, shoving her away. "Maybe he's among the corpses rotting under the straw sacks. Help yourself. Go lift the covers and take him." Women and children plopped on the ground and wailed by the bodies. One woman dug her fingers into the ground and flung dirt on herself.

Eum-chun had run to an azalea bush nearby and thrown up. He couldn't be among those rotting in the sun.

Could he have been dragged up north? Forced to join the North Korean army? That happened to thousands of South Korean men. Separated brothers bombed one another from opposite camps. In smoke, tears, and screams of smashing machetes into skulls, they killed one another without recognizing them as their own.

If Eum-chun didn't think of a way to earn some money, spiders would soon spin webs in her girls' throats. She would open a roadside stand and sell cigarettes, gum, apples, and squids. Even if Gui-yong were with her, he wouldn't be able to stop her this time.

Luckily, a week ago, she'd run into Ok-hee, her grade school friend from Seoul. She ran a dried seafood wholesale business. Eum-chun would ask for a loan of two dozen squids.

So, she set out to visit Ok-hee as the burning sun poured down heat on her. She passed the market in New Masan. Lost children with dried tears on their cheeks lined the streets.

Announcements blared from the radio shops staying open along the main street by the market.

"Three hundred soldiers," the radio said, "bravely gave up their lives for our country yesterday. The number of UN and American fatalities has not been confirmed."

She climbed the stairs to Ok-hee's flat on the third floor.

Gui-yong had to be alive and looking for her. For one, they hadn't made love enough times yet. Each man was allotted only so many times of the mixing of their flesh. That's why some men, even if young, couldn't have sex any more; they'd used up their share. Wherever Gui-yong might be, did he break out in a heat rash? How she used to spread rash cream around his testicles after his shower and wave a fan back and forth to help cool them. She'd buy him dog soup. That would help him deal with the heat. She never ate it, though; the way dogs were hung from a tree and bludgeoned to death turned her stomach.

She was glad to visit Ok-hee today and get her mind off her worries about Gui-yong, even for a bit. Soo-yang must have had the baby. If it was a boy, Soo-yang would have draped her doorway with a straw rope decked with red peppers to declare the room off-limits and broadcast his birth. Or, if a girl, with pieces of charred wood.

When Eum-chun stepped into Ok-hee's place, the heavenly smell of dried squids blew into her nose, and her mouth watered.

Stacks of squid ringed Ok-hee. An American army blanket hanging from nails was draped over a window. Light leaked in crooked lines at the sides. At the bottom, where Ok-hee had pinned back the cover, the sun formed mustard triangles. During the day, the risk of enemy planes spotting their homes and bombing them was not great, and people opened their curtains. But Ok-hee never did. She wouldn't have pinned back the blanket either, except to save electricity for the bulb in the ceiling.

"I swear you won't die from opening the curtains," she said as she sat down on the floor next to Ok-hee. "How about pulling them apart a bit? Getting some fresh air?"

"A dark window keeps burglars away! I'll bet a dozen squids on that."

"True. Thieves are everywhere. It's the war that's doing it. Driving them into begging and robbing. If I can't find Gui-yong and feed my girls, I may have to do that, too!"

"Keeps spies away, too," Ok-hee said.

They slinked down from the North. Eum-chun heard about them on her neighbor's radio every day.

"You owe it to your country to report suspicious characters," the announcer said. "Anyone who doesn't know what three-year-olds know, like bus fares, and who speak with the funny North Korean accent." So the refugees from the North, like Mr. Shin, her neighbor, made a show of calling Communists "dog crap."

"I'll wring the Commies' necks!" he mumbled, even while walking alone. The South sent spies to the North, too, but that was not broadcast.

"Need some help?" Eum-chun took a handful of squids from a pile, dropped them into her lap, and ripped the extra long tentacles off. Ok-hee sold them separately. They were cheaper, and some people liked their extra chewiness and stronger taste.

Ok-hee's transistor radio by her bedding in a corner belted "The Soldiers' Song."

Stepping, stepping over our dead pals,
over one and over another,
a one, a two, a three, we march forward, forward,
Go on, Nakdonggang River, do your flowing.
We'll keep marching forward, a one, a two, a three . . . .
Ah, my pal, whose face vanished behind
the Hwarang cigarette smoke . . . .

Ok-hee turned down the volume.

"Thanks," Eum-chun said, shaking. "Nightmares! I get them just thinking of those faces disappearing behind cigarette smoke. I see boot heels crushing Gui-yong's face and grinding it into the mud."

"Still no word from him?" She poured barley tea into a cup and handed it to Eum-chun.

Eum-chun drank it and calmed down. They chatted. Yes, Mi-na and Li-ho were making good grades. Mi-na had gotten over her one-hundred-day cough. Ok-hee's husband's leg wound from the first two months of the war was healing slowly.

"Ok-hee, I have to find a way to feed my girls. What if I opened a roadside stand? Will you loan me some squids? When I make some money, I'll buy you a bowl of fermented baby octopus from the big market across the street from you."

"A roadside stand? You out of your mind? Did the Masan sun fry your brain?" Ok-hee let out her whinnying laugh. Big-boned, she fit her sign, the Horse. Ok-hee finally stopped laughing. "Sell things? You think it's easy, like gobbling cooled porridge? You won't last two days. And as for the fermented octopus, no thanks."

"Why in Buddha's name can't I run a stand? And you would turn down octopus?"

"I crave that slimy stuff as much as you do, woman. But if you set your butt out in the open, full of strangers, who's going to beat away the drunks for you? The pickpockets? The shoulder thugs? You've heard about what those shoulders do to women sitting alone at roadsides, haven't you?"

"But women sell things everywhere! Not all of them have men with them. Women peddle sesame seed oil, red pepper, and Chinaman cakes."

Ok-hee wriggled her mouth, trying not to laugh. Eum-chun knew that look. It made her feel like a rice pot idiot who didn't know how to do anything but eat rice. In a way, Ok-hee did have the right to see her as that. Even before Ok-hee's husband was wounded and couldn't make a living, Ok-hee had pulled through blood-teary years. While Eum-chun ate food off Gui-yong's hands, Ok-hee had peddled everything from bolts of cotton to rice cakes to cosmetics, carrying the loads on her head and trudging on foot until her feet blistered.

"Start a business, like a clumsy bear picking corn? Like a eunuch wishing for in-laws to visit? Ha!" Ok-hee said.

Eum-chun had expected some objections, but not such harsh words.

"I have a better idea." Ok-hee changed her tone. "I know a Mr. Bae. I met him through his sister, Mrs. Yang, a customer. He has a job. Good-looking, too. You know what they say about good looks: 'Even with rice cakes, the good-looking ones taste better and go down more smoothly.' Why don't I introduce him to you?"

Eum-chun looked at Ok-hee. Meet a man? She was too

stunned to respond. What did her friend take her for? A woman without a fleck of faithfulness to one husband, dead or alive? A woman with a *gisaeng*'s looseness? A woman who'd peel pumpkin seeds with her pussy?

Some women did take lovers or remarry before making sure their husbands had died. But who could judge them? They more than likely had children to feed who needed a father. But more women hung onto their one-husband-for-life rule handed down for centuries. She pulled in her mouth tightly. She didn't mean to think demeaning thoughts about loose women. She'd never do that to Jin-i. Their mother's words to Eum-chun and Jin-i as little girls—"Don't let any man touch the twenty-nine buttons on your dungarees"—must *not* go down the outhouse hole with Eum-chun as they had with Jin-i. One daughter going bad was enough of a blow to their parents to last a lifetime.

Eum-chun kept pulling apart the tentacles. Ok-hee was a good friend. She wouldn't deliberately insult Eum-chun. She tied the squid legs with hemp twine and gave it an extra yank.

Ok-hee babbled away about Mr. Bae.

He was a native of Pyongyang and had a house there.

"Pyongyang? He's a Commie?" Eum-chun yelled out so sharply she scared herself.

"Shhhhh! You out of your mind, woman? Listen to me! He's a 100% South Korean business man! He ran specialty tile and brick factories in Seoul *and* right here in Masan. He planned to move his wife and their two sons to Masan, near his sister. Last summer, after he brought his sons here to visit with their aunt, he returned to his factory in Seoul. Then, *cccrrrraassshhhh*, wouldn't you know the war unleashed a thousand bullets around him? He tried to cross to Pyongyang to get his wife, but, merciful god, North Korean bastards' machine guns, popping like beans frying, pelted ammunition around him and a hundred others! *Whoooosh*, his soul shredded into ninety-nine pieces, he scrambled back to Masan and hid in his sister's bomb shelter. He survived eight months there. His factory in Seoul got bombed. His sister sold the one in Masan for him. Finally, he climbed out of the dugout, found a job at a blanket factory. He refuses to remarry, but his sister wants him to." Ok-hee caught her breath.

"'If he doesn't want a wife, his business,'" Ok-hee quoted his sister, Mrs. Yang, "'but finding a mother for his sons, my business.'"

When Ok-hee had happened to tell her about Eum-chun and Gui-yong's second wife, just chatting, without any other intention, Mrs. Yang had wanted to know more. Eum-chun's not having a child of her own and Mi-na's adoption appealed to Mrs. Yang. A woman without her own flesh and blood made the best stepmother. Even if they couldn't or didn't want to officially marry, they could do what others did: live together and make do.

"Don't worry. Do I look like a friend who would get you mixed up with someone who may put your life in danger? Of course, no one knows about people with connections to the North, but I'll bet my squid business he's as good as a South Korean. You think even South Korean men are all safe? There are more South Korean Commies who would turn you and me in before you can say 'Commie,' if it suited them."

True. More South Koreans had turned Red since the Japanese gave up Korea six years ago and left it in chaos and without solid leaders. Even so, she needed to get within miles of anyone with a North Korean connection as badly as she needed Gui-yong and Mi-na to get into danger.

"Just meet him once," Ok-hee said, plopping a bundle of squid on the stack behind her. "If you don't like him, I won't pester you. Nothing lost. But think, my dear. A war is doing a shaman's sword dance over our heads! Men and women drop dead every day! How long before you and I do? What good is saving morals and saving face when you're dead? Here's a moral dead face. Kowtow to it." She laughed.

Eum-chun's fingers shook.

"Ever heard of old faithfulness putting rice into your mouth? My friend, you know old sayings as well as I do. Nothing tops stinky fermented fish for the best taste, and nothing warms your belly like an old hubby can. So get yourself a new one! Whether Gui-yong's dead or alive, he's got a new woman. He's probably got a son, too, by now. Why hang on and starve for him? Bunch of cow turd, I say!"

Ok-hee peered into Eum-chun's face.

"You mad at me, woman?" Ok-hee asked. "Seongju House God strike you dead! I'm trying to get you a man in your arms and rice in your mouth, and you sulk? Want to call me a *hwanyangnyeon*? Go ahead. Call me a royal bitch. Keep your leper's-poop loyalty to one husband, dead or alive. Go ahead and starve. Just don't ask me for squids."

"Did Mrs. Sangju tell you about the eggplant she gave me?" Eum-chun finally spoke. While listening to Ok-hee's barrage, it had dawned on Eum-chun that Mrs. Sangju and Ok-hee might have gossiped about Eum-chun's loneliness without Gui-yong. "Is that why you're pushing this man on me?" Eum-chun pulled up her skirt hem and wiped her nose. "If you are, thank you. But I've got to stuff my mouth with rice first. I've got to feed my girls first. I've got to find Gui-yong first. Will you loan me some squids or not? No. Never mind. I'll find them somewhere else."

A few days later, after eating bean stew for dinner, Eum-chun went to sleep early so as to not waste electricity or candles. She missed the girls. She had sent them on a bus to go visit Jin-i for two weeks of their summer vacation.

Jin-i, behave yourself and keep men away while you have

the girls. Eum-chun sent her silent wish Jin-i's way.

The horrible day at Ok-hee's remained a lump in Eum-chun's chest. The night was quiet for a change—no B-29s swooping down nor bombs nosediving into the dirt. Even as she breathed calmly, North Korean and Chinese soldiers were slinking through the woods somewhere, dividing rivers with their thighs and setting up death traps. The breathing of men facing enemies eyeball to eyeball swelled in her ears. She squeezed her eyes shut: Could Gui-yong possibly be among the fallen? Her spleen turned. Even though he had fathered a child with Soo-yang and his heart might be inching away from her, she loved and needed him. She wanted him to touch her here, fill her there, fire it there until the shock of the sweetness became unbearable and tears spilled from her eyes. He'd lick the moisture. He'd murmur, "I hear the swallows, *yeobo*. They're back from the south."

The eggplant loomed before her eyes as her body grew warm. *No*. She turned on her side. If she stretched out her left hand, she'd find her pin cushion on her nightstand.

She snapped her thoughts toward those who'd died since last June. Already, the number of the dead, North and South Koreans, Americans, and Chinese, had reached a million. The face of General MacArthur that she'd seen in the paper came to her—his pipe, sunglasses, and hat. Our hero. Our savior. Our god! A handsome man, too! The size of his nose must match his liver, grown large and tough through carrying out daring acts, like the Incheon Landing of last September. If he hadn't had the genius and guts to make that landing, braving the thirty-foot high tide, the South would've remained taken by the Reds for good.

Then why wasn't he fighting for her people? Why did Truman fire him? Why did Truman hate Koreans so much he'd watch the Communists slaughter them?

Her landlord said Truman thought General MacArthur's ambition to drive the Commies completely out of the peninsula would turn this war into World War III. He spat into the dirt and said, "What's wrong with World War III? If that's what it takes, why not? Hasn't enough blood been shed? Does Truman want *that* to go to waste?"

Meet Mr. Bae? Oh, Buddha have mercy. Any negative energy loosened from behaving so recklessly would arc through the air and split Gui-yong in half.

Mr. Bae's North Korean connection blazed in her mind. If the military investigators found leftist activities on him, not only he but anyone within miles of him could be rounded up for execution. Sometimes, a person could be as clean as a dinner plate and still get a bullet through his or her head. Both the North and the South made mistakes on who deserved execution. Often, they seemed to be not mistakes but intentional rampage. Eum-chun stared at the ceiling. She'd go back to Ok-hee's tomorrow, apologize, and ask for squids.

The next day, she coughed outside Ok-hee's to let her know she was there. Laughter burst from inside. Ok-hee opened the door and welcomed her with, "We were just talking about you!" Kang-woo, Ok-hee's husband, offered Eum-chun a cushion to sit on. He was the mildest-mannered man, one whom people described as nondescript as water mixed with water and wine mixed with wine.

"Sorry. Didn't know you had a guest."

"We're just having seaweed birthday soup for Kang-woo." Ok-hee set a spoon and chopsticks for Eum-chun. "Oh, meet Mr. Bae."

Eum-chun jumped. He looked freshly released from a prison—gaunt, unshaven. His eight months in his sister's hideout showed. But his white shirt looked clean and ironed. Even in Eum-chun's sidelong glance, his eyes, fixed on the wall, seemed large and warm, his eyebrows dark. And Ok-hee was right; he was good-looking. At the introduction, he lowered his head and eyes slightly in her direction. She also avoided looking directly into his eyes.

After dinner, Ok-hee packed a large bundle of squids and pushed Eum-chun and Mr. Bae out the door together.

"It's dark out there," Ok-hee said. "Mr. Bae, Eum-chun has a long walk through black woods with no houses. Would you walk her home and carry the bundle for her?"

"No, I'll be fine." Eum-chun tried to wrest the bag from

Ok-hee, but she thrust it at Mr. Bae. They started down the stairs.

"Too many horrible things happen to women these days!" Ok-hee yelled out again. "Be careful. Watch your step!"

Light shone from Ok-hee's door on Mr. Bae and his blue summer jacket. It seemed unusually bright, especially for a man, like the blue on a peacock's tail.

Once on the sidewalk, he took the lead. The terrible things Ok-hee mentioned had been on the news. A woman and two girls had been beaten and raped by white-skinned, foreign soldiers. The girls had already hanged themselves. The woman's husband chopped his wife's hair and locked her in a shed. Neighbors shunned her and him. He and his wife would slowly fall apart. But even in the dark, Eum-chun feared someone seeing her with a man from Pyongyang even more.

Once they entered the fields, she relaxed. No one would recognize them. But Gui-yong would not like her to walk with a man. The moonlight made Mr. Bae's shirt collar look whiter and his jacket a darker blue. At their approach, frogs stopped their croaking. The frogs' noise reminded her of the legend of the Blue Frog, which made her laugh a little.

"I thought of the Blue Frog story. Do you have that in the North, too?"

"The frog that never listened to his mother? And always did the opposite of what she asked?" His voice sounded round, his Northern rhythm prominent. She cringed.

"It's a sad story, so I shouldn't have laughed," she said.

"The frog was a scoundrel, but a funny one, too." He made a sound that could've been a low laugh. "What amazes me is . . ." he said, but stopped.

Eum-chun tripped over a pebble and hurriedly corrected her pace to keep him from noticing. He drew a long sigh.

"How's a moment like this, talking about a fable and laughing, possible?" he asked. "With all the dying going on?"

He must feel uncomfortable about their walk, too, and felt guilty about laughing when his wife could be dead.

A roar burst from the rice paddy to the right.

She screamed and shot away from the sound, while he leaped toward it to shield her, which caused them to ram against each other. She landed flat against his chest. Grunts, cursing, the sloshing of water, the sound of the kicking or throwing of stones or mud clots, and more grunts volleyed from the rice field.

A rough shape of a beast on two legs lunged from the ditch that ran alongside the path. Once they saw that it was a drunken man who'd fallen, she pulled away from Mr. Bae. She felt too agitated to utter a word. They walked the rest of the way, listening to the frogs. At her house, she took the bundle from him. They bowed to each other, and she slipped through the low-fenced gate.

Once inside her room, her legs shook too much to go out to the faucet and wash. She threw herself on the floor, lay on her side, and drew up her legs. She forced her mind to turn to Gui-yong. She imagined him looking for her between supply runs to the front line, which kept moving up and down. She pictured him in a uniform. He was dying to see her, too, wasn't he?

She squeezed her eyes shut and saw herself in Gui-yong's arms. Warmth spilled into her. He rubbed his unshaved face against hers, her neck, and her hands. His stubble felt unusually stiff. He wouldn't have had the time or the razor to shave. The prickliness awoke her. She looked around. She was not in her room but in the kitchen, her face buried in the pine kindling, her hands in the belly of the pile, where she'd shoved the eggplant penis. When did she leave her room? She pulled her hands out. Afraid someone might have seen her, she looked around, but the landlord's and another renter's rooms were dark. Holding her head, she ran into the outhouse and squatted over the hole in the black night.

Gui-yong

He had fifteen minutes to look for Eum-chun in the New

Masan market before having to hop on his truck piled with the sacks of rice he and his unit men picked up here. They got fuel, too—tanks of kerosene and boxes of charcoal briquettes—to transport to UN and South Korean camps along the way up to Seoul. His convoy boss, Hook Arm, who'd lost a hand but didn't want to leave the army, kept a radio contact with their unit sergeant, who'd tell the drivers which bunkers to deliver the supplies to.

"Auntie, have you seen this woman? This girl?" He showed a photo of Eum-chun and Mi-na to a woman shouting, "Bracken fern shoots!" Without looking at the picture, she slung her baby to the front from her piggy back blanket and rammed her nipple into the baby's mouth.

"Move! You're blocking my customers from seeing my vegetables!" she said.

He trotted a few feet and stopped.

"Grandpa, have you seen this woman?" Gui-yong asked an old man squatting and weaving a straw egg-holder. "And this girl? She's eight. Very pretty. Large eyes."

The old man turned in the general direction of the picture and smiled.

"You've seen them? Grandpa, you saw them? Where?" Gui-yong dropped to his knees and grabbed the old man's shoulders.

"Grandpa, where?"

The old man's pupils were all white from the little Gui-yong could see under the man's wrinkled eyelids draping over his eyes. How could a blind man weave an egg basket?

Gui-yong struggled up, fished out a few paper notes, and tucked them into the man's tobacco bag hanging down from his shirt. "A little lunch money, Grandpa."

He stopped by an old woman selling rice cakes. "Grandma, is there a fermented octopus seller in this market? Octopus?"

The woman's lips were drawn inward, wrinkles pointing toward the center of her mouth. "No octopus, young man. Maybe when it cools down. Come in October, army man."

Maybe Eum-chun didn't make it across the Han River Bridge to the train. The bridge blew up that day, but she would've had time to get across. She couldn't have died. She survived the black cloud the nun had predicted. If the nun had foreseen Eum-chun's death, either shortly after he met the nun or several years down the road, she would've said so. If Eum-chun and Mi-na didn't cross the river, then where did they go? They probably trudged on frozen ground to another bridge miles away along with the hundreds of others scrambling to get to the south side of the river.

Stay alive, yeobo.

He stopped and asked an egg vendor, a beltfish seller, and stationery store owner before he checked his watch. He didn't have enough time to stop and see Kyung-jin, Soo-yang, and his mother.

Could he live without his wife? His *yeobo*? Even if he now had a son and his life should be perfect, not knowing Eum-chun's whereabouts drove him mad. He couldn't breathe normally; air went out in wisps. His eyes misted over. He was being punished by the gods for putting two women together under the same roof and sleeping with both of them. He didn't care what Noodle Leg said about such things, and he didn't care if other men did it all the time. Life was whipping him.

He hustled over to where his convoy waited.

Eum-chun

Five days after her walk with Mr. Bae, her girls returned from Busan, and not a day too soon. She'd missed them and now needed their help to move from Old Masan to a new rental near Ok-hee's in New Masan. Li-ho's mouth overflowed with stories about what she and Mi-na ate and saw in Busan: swimming at the beach with a Mr. Rim, (*so Jin-i did have men while the girls were there*); the fish market with live crabs, eels, and snakes (*Eeeekk*, the girls yelled out); the one hundred steps they climbed from there to Jin-i's apartment; and the American GIs who tossed chocolates at them (*Yum, yum. Want one, Momma? I saved some for you.*)

Two weeks later, Eum-chun opened her stand on the road across from a large open-air market. Making money to feed herself and staying alive was the only way she could see Gui-yong again. She didn't dare speculate what might have happened to Soo-yang—whether she had died of bullets or bombs or lived and had the baby. She didn't dare wish for a life with Gui-yong without Soo-yang. With or without her, she wanted him back alive. If he was dead, then? Get close to Mr. Bae? His scholar's voice, his blue jacket, the way he kept his face away from hers most of the time and how that made the moments he gazed at her so startling—her face and back broke out in a sweat just thinking about it.

She took the white towel off her head and brushed her face and hair with it. Then she slapped herself with it all over and mumbled, "Shoo, shoo, get away from me!"

On the scrap plywood board, she arranged dried squids, apples, matches, and sesame-seed candies, as well as the Marlboro and Camel cigarettes and Wrigley chewing gum bought in the black market. Gui-yong would have to agree with her this time that she needed to go outside the home and earn money.

A crammed bus roared past her. During rush hour, buses passed every ten minutes. The one that just took off was so full that two men hung out the door as the bus girl muscled them in, her palms flat on their butts. The bus lumbered away after she finally took a toehold on the step herself and signaled the driver with slaps on the side of the bus and yelled, "*Oraii.*"

Eum-chun cocked her head. Did she see something blue on someone? Was it a woman or a man? People who could afford colorful clothes weren't in the streets these days—they'd left the country. Went to Hawaii. Even if one had a bright shirt, it was unpatriotic to wear it. What was there to celebrate? Even children wore drab colors, mostly black or gray. Where did Mr. Bae get such a blue jacket? A gift from his wife? She shook her head so hard she nearly lost her balance off her stool.

She lowered the white towel on her head to her eyebrows. There was no godly reason to look at buses except to spot passengers already off the bus and heading toward her stand. Yellow gingko leaves lay scattered on the sidewalk. Some had fallen into a ditch behind her and decorated the stream already sluggish with garbage. When the wind blew up, the foul odor made her pinch her nose.

Mr. Ku's radio blared from his roasted sweet potato stall next to hers.

"Our ROK soldiers and allied UN troops pushed the front line up twenty-six kilometers today. Hundreds of citizens poured into the streets and welcomed them! The sight of our national flags flapping everywhere moved everyone to tears. *Manse*! Long live the Republic of Korea!"

She didn't know where Mr. Ku was from, but from his habit of always mounting at least three South Korean flags on the poles of his tent and loudly calling Commies *ssipalnom* even when no one was within earshot made her suspect he might have a relative in the North, too.

She riffled through the days-old *Kyunghyang Daily* she used as wraps. President Rhee's doleful face, his one eyelid drooping, occupied the front page. Next to him ran a report about the new American General Ridgeway. He and his troops inched their way up north and crushed the Chinese and Northern Reds. So he hadn't fallen flat on his nose as Koreans thought he would without General MacArthur. But 100,000 South Korean soldiers had already been killed.

She used her teeth to cut the twine around a new bundle of dried squids and began pulling the two longest legs off of each one. The gamy smell she loved suddenly brought back an embarrassing memory. Before the war, at Dongdaemun Market in Seoul, she'd once overheard a drunken man yell, "Give me some squids! That's as close to smelling a woman's bottom as I can get!" Her face burned for having remembered.

She refocused her gaze on the mouth of the market across four lanes of traffic. Was she seeing things? A man wearing peacock-blue clothing blended into the crowd. Ok-hee's words from a few days ago rushed at her.

"Mr. Bae keeps an eye on you. Bless his heart. He takes the

bus this way to work and back. Evenings, he ambles around the market across the street. Seen him?"

Was she being too paranoid? She probably was. Gui-yong could be dead. Was she a fool not to let Mr. Bae into her life?

She stood up and dusted the candy with the duster she'd made with strips of her threadbare dungarees. She moved to the Wrigley gum packages, both the stick and pebble kinds. Then the apples. The fruit turned peacock blue. She blinked. Blue apples? Suddenly, she changed the direction of her duster and leveled it clean across the display board. Candies clattered to the concrete sidewalk. Apples flew up, then thudded and rolled. She lost enough apples to wipe out the day's earnings. She sank to her seat.

"What happened?" Mr. Ku craned his neck into her stand.

"Oh, my knee bumped against the board." Mr. Ku helped her pick up the apples and candies.

The day of her move to a rental in New Masan, before wrapping the kindling, she'd looked for the eggplant to throw away. When she shuffled the branches, the handkerchief dropped out, but not the eggplant. It was somewhere in the tangle, but it was Saturday, and the girls were skipping about, helping her move pots. So she shoved an old newspaper under the stack, tied it with a straw rope, and brought the load to her new rental. The penis came with her.

Soo-yang

"Child, get up and eat this porridge," her mother-in-law said, setting a small tray on the floor. The smell of sesame seed oil wafted from the bowl.

"You have to eat," Mrs. Rhee said. "If you don't, you'll starve our little prince."

Kyung-jin lay napping, his bottom bare. Soo-yang didn't fasten his diaper because of his rash.

"Such a handsome penis." Mrs. Rhee stroked it, her eyes wrinkling into a smile.

Soo-yang took the spoon from Mrs. Rhee. Rice gruel should go down easy.

Since Gui-yong's last stop, when he spoke loudly about whether his mother had found Eum-chun and Mi-na, her neighbors looked at Soo-yang with squinty eyes. No one said anything, but whenever Soo-yang joined the women chatting by the well, they grew quiet. One day, Mrs. Im, her mother-in-law's new neighborhood friend, plainly asked Mrs. Rhee, "Is it true your son has a first wife? That she's alive somewhere? And that he has a daughter, too?" When her mother-in-law nodded, Mrs. Im clicked her tongue. Soo-yang's stomach felt chewed by tiny teeth. What was new? From the day she'd stepped into Gui-yong's house, she'd known people would do this to her.

When she finished eating, she brought the prayer equipment in from the kitchen: a bowl of water and a candle on a tray.

"Praying this late?" Mrs. Rhee asked, then moved closer to the tray and lit the candle. "All right, then. Let's do it together."

If Gui-yong got killed, Soo-yang's life would turn blacker.

Eum-chun

"I brought you a few dumplings. Eat them while they're hot." Eum-chun handed a covered aluminum "Western" pan to Mr. Ku. She'd gone home and cooked dumplings for her girls, eaten a few herself, and brought some to him. He had watched her stand while she was gone. Whether he had links with the North or not, she wouldn't be able to run the stand without him. Lepers came around begging several times a day, drunken handicapped war veterans threatened to knock her down with their crutches, thugs eyed her cigarettes, and child pickpockets circled around her.

"Give me a roasted squid!" a man in army fatigues and leaning on a crutch shouted from behind her kerosene lamp light. The sight of a drunken veteran who'd lost an eye or a limb always sent a chill down her spine. She was thankful for their sacrifice, but they got into street fights.

She pulled a squid from the pile and set it over the stove fire.

"Got a better looking one than that?" he shouted. The stench of rice wine and kimchi blew into her face.

"This is the largest one I have."

"You call that large?"

"Sir, this is the best one."

"Don't you have any respect for a veteran? I lost a leg! Don't care? Bitch!" He wobbled on his good leg as he lifted the crutch and leveled it at the table. He looked like he was about to sweep the cigarettes to the ground. Before he could, he slipped and crashed onto the sidewalk, taking down the apple crate and board. The stove tipped and sprayed red charcoal chunks. The moment she jumped away, one foot missed the sidewalk, which sent her tumbling down the cement slope. Rocks ringed by wet newspaper scraps, leaves, and other trash caught her, but her feet and skirt hem had already gone into the sewage water. She lay on her back. The left side of her head felt as though a stone chip had opened her skull. She felt slashes on her ankle, too. Through the crack of her eyes, she saw fog, and beyond it, Mr. Ku's light.

"Help! Hey, you, young man! Come here!" Mr. Ku's voice.

"Is she dead?" Another voice.

Pebbles crunched. Shoes scraped against cement.

She shut her eyes. She was being lifted. Gui-yong's arms.

He found me??? When I stink like sewage water? How did he find me?

"Do you know where she lives?" he asked. "Show me the way."

It wasn't Gui-yong's voice.

"Follow me," Mr. Ku said.

The arms carrying her weren't Gui-yong's, either. His would've welded her against him in a way she'd struggle to breathe. Then whose arms were these? A stranger who happened to pass by? Someone Mr. Ku flagged down to help?

She kept her eyes closed. She didn't want to know. If she discovered it was anyone other than Gui-yong, she'd have to free herself, even if her head was cracked open.

She jiggled as he picked his way over the footbridge and around the potholes in the ground. Finally, inside her room, he set her down on her floor. She smelled him. Soap. Brown laundry soap.

"Mommy!" Mi-na's voice. Her hand shook her shoulder.

"She's all right. Don't worry."

She recognized the voice—the man with the blue jacket.

"Momma!" Li-ho's sleepy voice.

"Shhhhh."

"Will she be all right?" Mr. Ku's voice.

"I think so. Mi-na, I'll get some warm water. Help your mother into dry clothes."

Mi-na loosened her blouse tie. She wriggled her shoulders

and arms and helped Mi-na get her into her pajamas.

Eum-chun slung her left arm over her forehead and opened her eyes to thin lines. Mr. Bae came in, carrying a basin and a towel. Soon she felt his hand on her ankle and the warm towel on the sole of her foot, the damp cotton working its way between her toes and up her shin. His palm went over the vein on the top of her right foot; then, the tips of his fingers rounded the heel of her left. He pushed her pant leg up to her knee. Shamelessly, her body warmed.

She woke up at dawn. Her ankle hurt. She felt her scalp; a lump rounded into her palm. She touched it and cried out. But there was no gash or dried blood clots on her head. She sat up and lit her kerosene lamp. The girls lay on their floor mat, their eyelids tile-smooth. She left the room, lowered the wick of the lamp, and set it on the dirt floor of her cooking shed. She rummaged through the kindling. One by one, she moved the sticks, some still bushy with needles. Toward the bottom, she felt the eggplant. She tore a piece of newspaper and wrapped it before she pulled it out. It had hardened to a stick. She broke a dried branch, laid the pieces in her stove, and lit a match. When the flames flared up, she dropped the penis.

Bright orange sparks sprayed up. She wanted to move away, back to the Old Masan, to the rice fields. Far from Mr. Bae and temptation. She'd sell fabric in Jinju, a good market. Last year, she'd decided against the idea because Jinju was about a two-hour train ride away, which meant staying nights away from her girls. Now, she must. Her girls, eight and five, would have to be left home alone.

Mi-na

"Who will wake me up?" That's the first thing Mi-na asked when Mommy told her and Li-ho they'd live alone.

"I'll be gone a few days at a time," Mommy said. "I'll make money and buy you new clothes. Shoes, too. If you need help, ask our landlady. All right? Mrs. Shin and Mrs. Sangju said they'd help, too. Waking Mi-na is your job, Li-ho. You also have to help Mi-na cook and clean."

On the first day without Mommy, Mi-na washed rice in a gourd scoop by Mr. Shin's faucet. Li-ho skipped in from outside.

"I got some dandelions. Can we make dandelion stew for dinner?" Li-ho asked.

"All right. Get down and wash them." Mi-na handed her a pan.

"Look! Chol-soo told me to give you this." Li-ho held out a string of grasshoppers and began to do a singsong. "Look-ee-ee, look-ee, somebody's got a boyfriend! Look-ee-ee, look-ee!"

Mi-na shot an evil eye at Li-ho. "Stop that! Drop them on the side ledge."

Li-ho stuck her tongue out and wriggled it before dashing to the ledge. Mi-na half-liked Chol-soo, but she wasn't sure about the other half. He was the boy who'd yanked her away from a snake hiding under persimmon leaves last fall. He'd also plucked a leech from between her toes this summer while they played in a stream with other kids. Don't think about him, she thought to herself. Just think about studying. Reading textbooks and doing homework. There were thirty-seven boys in her class. That meant her grades needed to be the highest among the forty girls' grades and those of the boys.

The dandelion stew turned out yummy with the yellow bean paste, garlic, green onion, green peppers, and a few dried anchovies Mi-na threw in. It tasted almost as good as Mommy's. They ate on the straw mat they had spread by the fire in their cooking shed. When Mi-na finished washing the dishes, the first star popped out. Li-ho roasted four grasshoppers and handed two to Mi-na. Although she was full, she couldn't pass up the half-nutty, half-chicken giblet taste.

"Look what else I got." Li-ho brought something from the kindling. Back on the mat, she leaned into Mi-na and whispered, "Let's smoke."

Mi-na opened Li-ho's fist.

"Hyo-suk showed me how to roll these pumpkin leaves into newspaper," Li-ho said, her dimples puckering. Hyo-suk was the hunchbacked boy who lived across the courtyard. Mi-na and other kids had gone there to pick persimmons from his tree the day Chol-soo saved her from the snake.

Li-ho rolled the bits of pumpkin leaf into a square piece of newspaper, licked the edges, and ran her finger over the seam. Soon they had two cigarettes. They lit them with the cooking fire, slid them between their lips, and puffed. Mi-na choked and coughed, which made Li-ho giggle. Li-ho held her cigarette as if she were a grown-up who'd smoked all her life, her wrist cocked at a stylish angle, like her mother's. Li-ho turned her head and blew smoke toward the evening stars in the sky. She was the queen of no worries. Mi-na took one more puff; the smoke tasted bitter, worse than parasite medicine.

She looked up at the Big Dipper. Stars looked brighter and larger in Masan. Her life here was as beautiful as the Masan stars. She had pretty rice paddies to walk through on her way to school and back. She was like an adult, living alone and taking care of her cousin. She had a friend, a boy, who had pulled a leech from her toe. Her new neighbors had no idea Mi-na had made Little Mommy's coming necessary. They were too worried about the war to say to her, "You should've been a boy."

Other than feeling sick over whether or not Father was dead, war was fun. Her life in Masan was as tasty as a roasted grasshopper.

"Should I fry some more grasshoppers?" Li-ho asked, slurring words from talking with the cigarette in her mouth just like her mother did.

"Why not?" It was a perfect day, and she didn't want to spoil it by being a good girl.

Eum-chun

She came home for two days to be with her girls. They did well living by themselves. Mrs. Sangju said she saw them trot past her home in the morning, bookbags in hand and Li-ho's hair expertly braided, too. "That Mi-na's got some talent. Where did she learn to do the French braid?"

While they were at school, Eum-chun decided to visit Ok-hee, but as she was putting her shoes on, Ok-hee came rushing into her room.

"Shhhhh!" Ok-hee went, her ways as dramatic as ever. "I mean it. This is hot, hot news," she said, her face actually looking drained of blood. "I'm on my way to the stream by the Bull's Horn Hill. The new anti-Reds chief's at it again, having his slaughter-the-Reds party. Mrs. Yang's dashing there, too. Her brother's been missing for a week. I have to go because my brother-in-law may be in trouble. Kang-woo hasn't been able to find him. Got to make sure he's not getting a bullet. Let's go! Hurry!"

"No!" Eum-chun's legs shook already.

"Shhhhh! You want to see us all get it, too?"

"But I don't want to go anywhere near such a thing! Why should I? I have my girls to worry about!"

"Is that right? What about your dear Gui-yong? Isn't he missing? You haven't heard from him in a year, have you? What makes you so sure he won't be among those getting their heads blown away? This new police chief kills, kills, kills! He doesn't care if they *are* Commies or just smell like them. How can you tell without doing a thorough investigation that can take months? He says he doesn't have that kind of time. He'll kill first and then see about whatever. It's a luxury he can't afford, he says. So, if I were you, you'd go with me. If you want to find Gui-yong . . . "

Even before Ok-hee was finished, Eum-chun was running out the gate.

They took the long, windy way through a pine grove and abandoned factories to avoid being seen. Just as they rounded the bombed airport hanger between Old and New Masan, they saw it. They stopped mid-gait and watched a mass of blindfolded forms lined up on sand along the stream, their hands tied in the back. *Ping, ping, ping, ping.* They dropped on their faces weightlessly, like shadows. Eum-chun fell to her knees, plugged her ears, and closed her eyes, but not before she saw someone in blue.

"*Aiiiguuuu* !" Wailing erupted. Others on their knees several meters ahead of them let out their throat-shredding sounds, too. Eum-chun couldn't advance further, but Ok-hee pushed on and sank next to a group that appeared to be Mrs. Yang with her nephews. Several women huddled together, forming a mound of stooped backs.

Only after the shooting stopped and the soldiers and policemen dropped straw sacks on each body did Eum-chun crawl forward to the site of slumped forms. Dark blood spread from them. She must make herself see each of those fallen faces. May none of them be Gui-yong's! She felt possessed, without feeling fear or sick to her stomach.

Men flipped the corpses right side up and flung the sacks back on them. Women followed and lifted the corners of the covers only enough to see what they needed to see. Although the blood made it hard to tell, Eum-chun peeked under each cover. When she came to the body wearing a blue jacket, she dropped to the ground and bent over. *Oh, oh, oh.* What other words were there? What other sound could she make?

What about Gui-yong? She shot up and went mad, flipping and flipping straw sacks, bumping into other women and crying children, falling onto her knees and getting up again.

Perhaps her wish not to see Gui-yong's body had blinded her. Perhaps it was really there. She could not be sure, but she didn't see him.

"*Aiiigguu, aiiigguu*, my poor baby brother! *Aiigu, aigu.*" Near Mr. Bae's corpse, Mrs. Yang threw her head back, her arms flung around the two boys huddled against her.

Eum-chun dropped to her knees next to Ok-hee. Ok-hee turned and, seeing Eum-chun, freed her arm that was wrapped around Mrs. Yang, blew her nose with her handkerchief, and took Eum-chun a few steps away from the others.

"You didn't see your brother-in-law here, did you?" Eum-chun asked.

"No. You didn't see Gui-yong, did you?"

"No."

They hugged and rested their heads on each other's shoulders. Then Ok-hee found her voice again.

"The anti-Reds chief Mr. Ro ought to be gunned down, like these men he killed." Ok-hee wiped her eyes. "Mr. Bae ran his business in Seoul and Masan for thirty years! He was a South Korean, just like you and me."

Eum-chun couldn't believe her own countryman had done this mass slaughtering.

"Patriotism sickness," Ok-hee said. "National security

sickness. Democracy sickness. One Blood One Nation sickness. Reeks worse than diarrhea!"

"What will happen to Mr. Bae's sons?" Eum-chun asked, but she already knew the answer. They'd have Mr. Bae's blood on their records. They'd be under the strictest surveillance. One false move and they'd be lying under empty rice sacks, too. They wouldn't be allowed to leave the country. Never, not for studying, not for anything.

Eum-chun turned her head away from Ok-hee and finally emptied her stomach.

Back at her rental, she spread out her bedding and dropped into it. She could not raise herself again, gather her fabric sacks, get on the train, and head to Jinju. Mi-na brought rice porridge she herself had made. On the third or maybe fourth day, Eum-chun looked at the two drops of soy sauce and one drop of sesame seed oil in the center of the porridge bowl and threw up. She tried to miss the bowl but she didn't. Her bones ached. Her chest rattled. Her tongue felt coated with sawdust.

"Mommy!" Mi-na cried out, which made Li-ho cry. Just then, someone yanked the door open.

"Look who I brought!" Ok-hee stood there beaming, and from behind her, Gui-yong lunged into the room. His uniform's gasoline smell filled the room.

"I found him in the market. Of all things, he was looking for pickled octopus!"

PART III

AFTER THE WAR

(1953–1960)

At the Shaman's

Seoul, October 1953

Gui-yong

Perfect. That's how his life was now. He had found Eum-chun and Mi-na. The whole family lived together again. Their old house had barely been touched by the war. To top it off, he had his son. Three years old and sturdy as a toad. At the ancestor worship ceremonies held several times a year, he now squared his shoulders and informed his ancestors, "I've fulfilled my obligation. You can't keep me out of Heaven."

But he was afraid his happiness was about to end. He might lose Eum-chun and Mi-na again. To cool his head over the problem facing him, he agreed to go away with Noodle Leg to Yeonhui Hill, on the west side of Seoul.

Noodle Leg needed to find his father's remains in the cemetery lot gouged out and gashed by bombs and rebury them somewhere else.

Gggilll gggilll gggilll. Noodle Leg bawled. He sat with his legs splayed by the mound of dirt he and Gui-yong had dug out of what Noodle Leg thought was his father's grave. If a blind man had heard the cry, he might have mistaken it for giggling.

Gui-yong stared at the gray pieces of bone lying by Noodle Leg's feet. That and one palm-sized corner of a tombstone were all they had to show for an afternoon's work, poking around the hillside and shoveling dirt. The stone had been shattered into shards too small for them to read the writing. Telling one grave from another was impossible, the ground disturbed by fires and bombing.

"Those Reds were desperate to break our Marines' front line," Noodle Leg had lectured him earlier while passing through the Yeonhui-dong area. "Our side was freshly supplied and charged up. Right after Gen. MacArthur's Incheon Landing. Our ROK gave the Reds the bloodiest nose!" Noodle Leg had said, punching the air with both fists.

They had passed buildings with missing walls and a statue standing headless. "That's the monument of the American missionary, Mr. Underwood. He founded this university," Noodle Leg had said.

A bulldozer went *kong tutu kong kong*, scooping dirt from the hill to make room for apartment buildings. Men and women groped the ground to find their ancestors' graves. They had a week to move the remains. A woman pounded her fists on the dirt. The fragile shards Noodle Leg retrieved might not be his father's bones, but Gui-yong had no heart to say so. He dug into Noodle Leg's shirt pocket, fished out a cigarette, and lit it for him.

"Have a smoke." Gui-yong wished he smoked, too. No moment felt more right for that. Since the signing of the armistice between the North, China, and the UN forces three months ago, refugees from Seoul, like him and his family, had returned and begun cleaning and rebuilding.

Thank god his neighborhood was spared serious damage. But when he drove through other neighborhoods, he saw charred tanks, jeeps, and buses left where they'd burned in fields of leveled homes, stores, factories, schools, and government buildings. The first day he drove by Namdaemun Gate, with all the buildings leveled and nothing blocking his view, he could see Dongdaemun Gate. A prayer popped out of his mouth: *Buddha save us.*

While Noodle Leg wiped his face with his shirtsleeve and puffed away at his cigarette, Gui-yong took out his handkerchief and wrapped the bones.

"Let's get some rice wine down there," Gui-yong said, flicking his head toward the Yeonhui Ridge and picking up the tombstone piece. He'd never thought he'd suggest drinking before Noodle Leg would.

At a Sinchon wine stall, Noodle Leg vented his fury again.

"I've got another one of those propaganda fliers those dog faces dumped out their planes! The shoeshine boy who comes around Mondays? I bribed him with a bowl of noodles to give it to me. This one said the American troops stationed in the South instigated President Rhee to attack the North! *Instigated*, mind you. Who'd believe that crap except Kim Il-sung's shit-brained suck-ups?"

Gui-yong sipped wine and handed the bowl to his companion and poured. "Calm down. At least we're alive! Look at Phone Pole, already dead."

Noodle Leg poured himself more and gulped that, too, before handing the bowl back.

"So how's living with two women? You still like your old wife? You've probably changed your tune by now, haven't you? 'Fess up. You can tell me."

"I'm just glad we all survived the war and got back together again."

"Come on, pal. Throw me a bone, here. Neither one tried to gouge out your eyes? No scratches on your balls?"

"Not yet."

What Gui-yong had in bed with Soo-yang was good. What Noodle Leg had called him proved true. At first, he'd felt like a thief, stealing pleasure behind Eum-chun's back.

But his time with Soo-yang didn't make him lust after Eum-chun any less. What a boar. His appetite went wild. Maybe the guilt shuffled his insides. Maybe sharing him made the women clamp onto him for dear life, too.

"Hey, drink up and pass the bowl," Noodle Leg said. Gui-yong's ability to hold his liquor had grown during Eum-chun's bedridden days.

"So what's this dog crap about your daughter flunking the Kyunggi High School entrance exam? Wasn't she supposed to be a real brain?"

"Don't know what happened," Gui-yong said, working a toothpick into his teeth. The day of the exam, Eum-chun had returned home with Mi-na, worried sick.

"Mi-na's hands were ice, *yeobo*," she whispered to him. "Children who pass have warm hands."

"So your wife wants to separate from you? Live near the second-ranked school Mi-na will go to? What'll that do to your love life? If you ask me, I think it's only fair you separate from your wife. She had fifteen years. Your new woman deserves a chance to have you all to herself. Make sense?"

Gui-yong spat his toothpick on the floor. "How's your wife?"

Noodle Leg chuckled and winked. It looked like bad news for her.

"I got myself a new pinky."

Eum-chun

Today she'd attend a spirit ceremony at Aunt Hong's. Hong would heal Soo-yang's stomach trouble. How unforgivable would it be if Eum-chun were to wish for Soo-yang's condition to worsen, for her to even die? If that happened, Gui-yong and Kyung-jin, the baby boy, would be all hers to possess and love. Yes, yes, she'd love that.

During her dance, Hong might also give Eum-chun some direction on whether she should separate from Gui-yong again or not. Their lives depended on the words about to pour out of Aunt Hong's mouth and the color of the flag Soo-yang would pick while blindfolded.

Later that afternoon, Eum-chun walked up the steep dead-end path leading to Aunt Hong's house. The sun threw barley gold on the stone chips on the ground. This fall, the root radishes she pulled up to make kimchi with had been unusually long, foretelling an extra-cold winter.

Eum-chun loved Aunt Hong, but she feared her, too. Her gods were powerful, and they could thrash an accident, illness, or even death on anyone. But since childhood, she'd heard stories about Hong, especially about how she'd become a shaman. When Hong was twenty-nine with a husband and three children, she began hemorrhaging for reasons doctors couldn't figure out, the story went.

"A white-bearded man appeared in my dream and told me to climb a mountain at night," Aunt Hong had said. "I was too scared to go alone. I took your mother with me."

"By the time we got to the top, Hong's white socks were filled with blood flown down from her bottom," Eum-chun's mother had said about that night. The bleeding stopped after she decided to become a shaman. "Her family threw her out in the street," her mother had said. "Luckily, a shaman living by Dongdaemun Gate took her in as her spirit daughter."

When Eum-chun stepped into Hong's courtyard, a dozen people were rushing about. Hong's spirit daughter, Pure Peony, primed the hourglass drum. Hong's male assistant shaman, Lump Head, did what he did the best—eyeing pretty women, especially Hong's daughter-in-law, whom everyone called "Gae-dol's mom." She saw Eum-chun first and called out.

"Hurry, give us a hand!"

What a story that woman of the prettiest dimples had on how her son got to be called by that name. Before she had him, she'd had three miscarriages, and so when she became pregnant again, Hong held a healing rite for her and named the unborn child Gae-dol, a shortened form of *gae-do-ra*, or "Gods, leave him there."

Eum-chun went into the kitchen, where her mother and Gae-dol's mom sat frying mung bean pancakes.

"Didn't bring Mi-na?" her mother asked.

"She's happy at home with her books." Eum-chun pressed the pancakes with the back of the spatula she took from her mother. They sizzled in the spattering oil. Her mother took a cigarette from her trouser pocket and lit it.

Eum-chun looked into the courtyard. A hired hand was sweeping the dirt with a millet-branch broom. Another man polished the wood-footed bowls and plates on the side ledge. They were lucky they didn't have to set up a bamboo pole with rice paper-strip pom-poms glued on it. Since Aunt Hong was a "possession" shaman, not one who inherited the business from her family, her gods found her shrine even without a pole.

Even with the smell of sesame seed oil in the air, Eum-chun detected the scent of the incense coiling from the shrine to one side of the hallway sitting room. The smell hypnotized her. Buddha-taught Nothingness—the great big calm—touched her as though she had walked into an ocean. She felt in the roots of her hair that this was an important night, not just for Soo-yang, but for her and Gui-yong, too.

Aunt Hong's younger son sprinkled ocher dirt on the ground, chasing away evil spirits. After that, he spread out extra straw mats in the courtyard for the dozens of neighbors who would flock to watch the ceremony.

He laid the clay tub in the middle of the yard. Two knives held down by ropes stood, blades up, on the rim of the tub.

Hong would later dance barefoot on the blades.

When Eum-chun was finished with the pancakes, Aunt Hong came to the kitchen door.

"How about doing some ironing?" she asked Eum-chun.

"Yes, Aunt."

Eum-chun entered the wardrobe room of the shrine. She took out Hong's outfits and accessories from the three-tiered dresser. The indigo blue robe spangled with metallic sequins, a matching helmet, a spear for the Old General God, a gold robe for the Ancestor God, and crowns for the Sun and Moon Gods. After ironing, she must gather more head gears and tools—hats, veils, swords, fans, flags, and hand bells.

Steam from the iron warmed her face.

In a short while, Aunt Hong came to the doorway and asked, "Are you about finished with those?"

"Yes. I ironed your new padded socks, too. Will one pair be enough?"

"Yes. Will you check on the men sharpening the swords?"

"Yes, I will, Aunt." She looked up at Hong. Narrow, not pretty, with a large black mole on the chin, Hong's face looked burdened, her eyes hard. Eum-chun flinched. She wondered, if only for a short time, if Hong had discerned her secret wish for Soo-yang to not receive healing.

She stepped down into the courtyard. By the faucet, the backs of two men sharpening swords rippled as they rubbed the blades on the stone. The sharpening required silence. If they talked, the blades would cut Hong's sockless feet during the dance. She tiptoed along the rooms and glanced sideways at the men's faces. A woman approaching them straight on would break their sacred spell. The rectangular pieces of rice paper glued over the men's lips stayed in place.

She slipped back into the kitchen and joined her mother. Soo-yang and Gui-yong arrived at dusk. Eum-chun fed them dinner in a side room so they could be ready. Dozens of guests and neighbors crowded into Aunt Hong's courtyard to watch the ceremony, the biggest show in the eastern section of town. They faced the open-air sitting room where the feast table reigned in rainbow colors of the fruits, cookies, rice cakes, vegetable salads, meats, and the portraits of the gods on the wall behind the table.

Aunt Hong seated herself in the middle of the hallway, slapped her palms on the cowhide hourglass drum, and tested its tautness before she burst into invocation.

From ten thousand ri away, here I've come
From six regions and eight directions, here I've come

She followed it with the purification song.

Let the fire brighten the dark at night and
water purify at noon.

Cleanse with fire and water,
Like the phoenix wandering about,
Like the sun and moon shining forth
Through the divining process their wishes are fulfilled

Eum-chun's temples throbbed. Surrounded by a dozen spectators, Soo-yang sat by Gui-yong in the hallway sitting room by the altar. Eum-chun slid into the one empty spot left, a few seats away from them.

Kllllaaang, kllllaaang, the Lump Head assistant shaman hit the brass gong from the left of the altar and feast table. Another helper next to him broke into a tune on his bamboo flute. Pure Peony stood by Hong at the center of the sitting room and rubbed her palms together, bowing to the east, west, north, and south.

Lump Head prayed to shoo away impurity.

Let the clean one in and the unclean out
The impurity of great horse catches the horse
The impurity of the great cow catches the cow
The impurity of fire is in heaven
The impurity of water is in earth
The impurity of the dead and the living is in the
flying birds and crawling insects
The impurity of the white butterfly is on a strand of hair
Let the impurity pass slowly through

the rear and the front doors.

Eum-chun rubbed her palms, her eyes on the twelve gods painted on the wall scrolls. Aunt Hong's personal guardian Sun and Moon Gods sat in the center. The gods' robes, even on the warrior gods, fearsome with their spears, flowed like water, contrasting with their fiery eyes, whose corners slanted like scorpion tails.

The clock in the hallway by Aunt Hong's room struck midnight. The large and small gongs clanged through the air, over the roof, and toward Mt. Bugaksan, Seoul's guardian mountain to the north. That peak looked directly down into Changgyeonggung Palace. On that slope, one of the dethroned Joseon Dynasty queens had draped her white skirt from a pine tree. "One Heart," read the writing on her skirt—the words her husband-king had written to vow his unchanging love for her.

Powered by that history and the mountain's spirit, drum beats thundered. Still in the middle of the hallway in front of the feast table, Aunt Hong spun, her face spraying sweat. A hush came over the spectators.

"Look at her face. The wrinkles. The fire in her eyes!" a woman close enough to Eum-chun said. Hong twirled her body at a dizzying speed, her hands wielding the three-pronged spear in one hand and the bunched-bells in the other.

Boom. Baaarrrr aaaa. The Old General God possessed Aunt Hong. She pulled off her socks, flung them in the air, jumped off the hallway floor, and tore through the spectators in the yard to the tub, across which lay the skyward blades. Her robes, tunics, and sashes of violet, gold, black, and crimson fanned out like rainbow satellites orbiting her. She flew up and planted her naked feet on the blades.

"Aaahhhhhh," the crowd went.

"Possess us, possess us!" The assistant shamans screamed.

Eum-chun clamped her eyes shut. Did she dare to see Hong's feet bleed? If they did, Soo-yang's chance of being healed would be lost. Aunt Hong's assistants would then have to search for the source of the impurity that had caused the bleeding. Who saw an animal being butchered today? A cow, dog, chicken? Who touched its blood? Who killed someone's spirit with wickedness in their heart?

Music thundered. Weeping erupted. Eum-chun opened her eyes; Soo-yang was moaning into her hands.

Under the rainbow of her skirt and tunic hems, Hong's feet, rice-cake white, pistoned up and down. Shouts of "Possess us, possess us!" shredded the air.

No blood dripped.

Hong's eyeballs disappeared into her head. When it looked as if she might pass out and crash off the swords, she flew down, threw her silver bells and spear away at her feet, and rushed back to the hallway. She grabbed the red, blue, black, yellow, and white flags her helper thrust at her.

"Mother and Father Gods, my Sun and Moon Gods!" Hong shouted, pulling a red flag and tapping it on Soo-yang's shoulder. Still holding the flags in one hand, she snatched a rice paper triangle wad from the table and slid it into her own hair. The name of someone on Soo-yang's side of the family was written in it. That person's spirit now entered Hong, and when she spoke, a man's voice rolled out.

Soo-yang, my child!

"Possess us, spirit, possess us," chanted the assistants.

My lost-soul granddaughter!
Possess us, spirit, possess us.
Sadness is upon you!
Possess us.

Soo-yang rose and wobbled toward Hong, still covering her mouth with both hands. Tears and sweat made her face sparkle under the altar candlelight. Hong waved the red flag over her head three times clockwise and then counterclockwise. The man's voice poured out.

Look to the left and look to the right, possess us, possess us.

Look to the north and look to the south,
possess us, possess us.
All blocked, you are blocked, possess us, possess us.
A person of the year of the snake, possess us, possess us.
Come forward, oh, man, woman, or child, possess us,
possess us.
Of the snake sign, possess us, possess us.
Raise my Soo-yang out of the hole, possess us, possess us.

Someone in the crowd let out a gasp. Heads turned. Murmurs rippled. "Ssshhhhh," a spectator went.

Eum-chun's sign was a snake. She looked at Gui-yong. He held her eyes with a dead serious stare and shook his head.

Not you, he seemed to say.

It's me, yeobo. I'm supposed to save Soo-yang, she gestured to him with her eyes.

Soo-yang took another handkerchief out of the sleeve of her blouse and wiped her eyes. She put it back and bobbed her head in prayer. Hong spun around faster than a scarecrow in a gale, the flags in her hand swirling in sheets. Gui-yong moved his head out of the way of the flapping flags. Aunt Hong stopped and thrust the handles of the flags to Soo-yang so that she could feel them but not see the colors of the flags. Sweat beads formed above Soo-yang's eyebrows. She fingered the bamboo ends as though listening for a message from each. She chose one. Aunt Hong pulled it from the bunch. A fresh round of gasping and muttering swept across the crowd. It was yellow. It wasn't as bad as the white, but not good either; she might not die, but dark clouds would hang.

They slept at Aunt Hong's that night. Other than neighbors, no one could go home because of the midnight curfew.

The next night, Gui-yong slept in Eum-chun's room. When the light went off in Soo-yang's room and Mrs. Rhee's snoring began, Gui-yong and Eum-chun talked under their breath.

"No, no, no!" he said when she offered not to follow him into the new larger house.

"How can Mi-na get to school every day? Don't you want Soo-yang's stomach to get better, too? Not living with me will help."

"But you're not the person with the snake sign Aunt Hong meant!"

"How do you know?"

He threw his arm around her and blew a sigh into her neck. "I just want us to stay together, *yeobo*."

They hissed back and forth. He finally said, "If we must live apart and you must live in a one-room rental, it'll be for only a short time, understand? Until I scrape enough to find you a house. It may be small, only one bedroom, but it'll be near Mi-na's school. You won't have to live in a rental." They slept a long while before they woke and made love.

The moment her body arched and welded onto his, an image crowded into her head; it opiumed her. A scene played in her head: Soo-yang as the lady of the house, washing diapers, boarders' long-johns, and Mrs. Rhee's brown-streaked underwear. Gui-yong and Eum-chun honeymoon in her new rental. In the dark, with Mi-na asleep, they whisper like lovers; she runs her finger over the clean lines of his lips and chin, sandy like the salt sprinkled on seaweed. She's his pinky.

Wearing Holes in Books

August 1958

Soo-yang

"Thank you, Grain Bin God," Soo-yang's mother muttered, heaping her granddaughter's diapers on the scrubbing stone in Soo-yang's yard. On her washboard Soo-yang scrubbed her mother-in-law's brown-stained underwear. She batted sweat from her forehead with the back of her hand.

"I can't wait for September," Soo-yang said. "It'll cool, and mosquitoes' mouths will twist and not bite. Why are you thanking Grain Bin God?"

"The blessings he piled on you," Mrs. Chung said. "My feet break out in sweat thinking that what happened to Eum-chun's sister could've decimated you, too. Kyung-jin and Kyung-ae could've been turned over to Eum-chun!

You could've been sent back to me, weeping your eyes out. But look at you. The lady of the house. No first wife to lord it over you. Expecting another baby." The liver spots under Mrs. Chung's eyes grew dark and matched the color of her lips. "And your pomegranate tree," she said, "so fat with juicy fruit."

"Then on New Year's Eve this year, you won't have to hang a basket of your grandchildren's shoes from my doorway for good luck. You can skip that, right, Mother?"

"Oh, no, I won't. I've never seen anyone die of having too much luck, have you?"

They both laughed, but before Soo-yang had the time to close her mouth, Kyung-jin stumbled through the gate, blood flowing down his face. The red lines made the shape of the Chinese character meaning "enter." Soo-yang ran to him, stopped mid-gait, and bowled over. She shouldn't have moved so rapidly when a baby weighed her down. Mrs. Chung came over, threw one arm around Soo-yang, and pulled in Kyung-jin with the other.

"Jin-soo beat me!"

"Gods, help me." Soo-yang had hardened herself to her neighbors calling her a fox-faced woman behind her back, but did she have to tolerate their boys beating hers, too? Her little ones who'd committed no crime other than being born to a man's mistress? No matter how hard she racked her brain, she found nothing she could do without attracting criticism from everyone, especially Gui-yong and her parents. She dropped on her knees, parted his hair, and checked where the blood was gushing from. A gash showed above his left ear.

"Mother, put him on my back. I'll rush him to the doctor's."

"No, you shouldn't. He's too heavy. Put him on my back."

"No!!" Kyung-jin tore away from both of them.

Just then, Gui-yong stepped through the gate.

"Oh, get on your father's back. Quick."

"What happened?"

"Hurry, please. Take him! Let's go to Doctor Han's." Soo-yang pushed Kyung-jin up her husband's back. Before they rushed out the gate, she flung words at her mother. "Stay here, Mother. Kyung-ae'll wake up. Got more to thank Grain Bin God for?"

October 1958

Mi-na

"Parasite Day? Oh, goodie. Little Noodle Day! Yum, yum." Li-ho teased. She'd done that last year, too, and since then, Mi-na quit eating noodles, fat or skinny, white or buckwheat, seasoned or plain.

"I hate you, Li-ho," Mi-na had said.

"Goodie. That makes two of us."

Teachers passed out the powdered parasite medicine every year. Within hours, kids ran to the bathroom.

"Two fat ones."

"I had five. One dropped into my panties." Kids bragged as they did on Mouse Tail Days when they turned in tails to their teachers. They were excused from mopping and waxing the classroom floor for a day for each ten they turned in. Mi-na would rather do the floors all by herself than bring in bloody mouse tails.

After dinner, Mi-na sat on the floor with her legs stretched under a table loaded with textbooks and notes to review for the three exams she had tomorrow. That guaranteed this Parasite Day be the worst in four years, since the seventh grade.

Mother was knitting fiercely, using the faster style—skipping using the right index finger to loop the yarn around a needle in the left hand to form every stitch. Li-ho was doing what she did best—lounging in her bedding.

Mi-na dug her nails into her upper arm. She wanted to feel a pinch strong enough to distract her mind from Parasite Day. The worse she hated something, the harder and longer she pushed the nails. She bruised easily, so she moved to different parts of her body. A purple moss rose on her thigh. A purple daisy on the inner side of her arm. Why not do it to her eyelids, cheeks, or neck, where people could see? She was a chicken.

She shot an evil glance at her notes instead of letting out the sigh bulging up her chest. Mother would ask, "What's wrong?" She'd worry; Mother needed another worry as much as she needed a centipede to crawl in her bed.

"Blow out the light. I can't sleep." Li-ho whined.

After they separated from Father, Grandma, and Little Mommy three years ago, Li-ho came to live with them, as she'd done during the war. Their grandparents' one-room shack where Li-ho had lived stank; too many people, including Uncle Chang-gil and his family, ate and slept there. So Mother took in Li-ho.

This rental, cheaper than the last one, didn't have electricity. Even during the war, they had it. Now they used a kerosene lamp and candles. But they weren't alone. Even five years after the Armistice Agreement, one million people lived in cardboard box shanties, which sprawled up the outlying hills and mountain ridges cradling Seoul. Because the slums were perched on the hills, people called them "moon villages," as they were closer to the moon. She read in her landlord's day-old paper that her people's average income was fifty US dollars a year. That would come to $4.15 a month. One dollar per week. The allowance they got from Father was less than that.

"Mi-na, can you go see Father tomorrow?" Mother needed

money too desperately to wait for his next visit. She stooped under the lamp light, her knitting needles catching the light over the sweater she must finish and sell to their neighbor the next day.

"Can I see Father another day? When I don't have Parasite Day and three tests?" Mi-na wanted to ask Mother but didn't. Her tuition was overdue, and Li-ho's was three months behind.

"I'll send you money in three days. I promise upon my ancestors' graves," Aunt Jin-i had written, but no money came.

Embarrassed, Li-ho joked, "My mom's a toy cannon. She makes a loud noise, but nothing happens."

For the first couple years, Father had made weekly visits, but now he came less often. Did that mean Father's heart had tipped completely toward Little Mommy and their children? She didn't think so. He was busy out of his mind. On his days off, he piggybacked Kyung-ae and got her to sleep while Little Mommy cooked and washed and went to the market. Father doubled his workload to save up money to build Mother and Mi-na a house. At least Father and Little Mommy didn't have to wash Grandma's poopy underwear any more. A week after Mi-na and Mother saw Grandma at an ancestor worship ceremony last year, she passed away.

Bedridden, Grandma had lain on her back, her stomach

hollowed out like a banana. She held Mi-na's and Mother's hands and whispered to them. Without her fake teeth, her lips flopped in and out. They couldn't make out what she said, but they got the message from the tears that rolled down from her eyes.

"My Medicine Hand. I'm sorry I pushed your husband to get a second wife. I've loved you," she was saying to Mommy.

"I've loved you, Mi-na, even without a penis."

Maybe Grandma didn't say those words, but Mi-na believed Grandma wanted to.

The last time Mi-na saw Father, his eyes had looked glazed. That and the smudge on his face from unloading coal on his route had made him look far from the old joking father. What if he had a heart attack? He was only forty-four. Mi-na was too afraid to talk about that fear with Mother. She'd scold her: "What ugly words. They'll become seeds and make them come true!"

"All right, Mother, I'll go see Father," Mi-na said.

Byung-soon, her high school classmate and a friend since grade school, had given her a stay-awake pill so she could study all night for the exams. She'd already worn out her notes, but she wanted to review her books one more time. Nothing but A's every semester and the top score in every test would do. If she couldn't beat out seventy girls, how could she take on the hundreds of boys at Seoul National

University Law School in two years? Without doing that, how could she become the famous person Mother's fortune-tellers had predicted? If she didn't accomplish that, what would happen to Mother? She'd die, her tongue cracked from disappointment in having nothing to show for to women with sons.

Mother's life had been too pitiful for Mi-na to just ignore it and say, "I should do whatever I want. So what if I don't want to become Mother's dream judge?" For that matter, all women's lives in her country were wretched. They had no real choice but to obey men's laws. Were they heaven's laws? No, no, no. The gods wouldn't be this unfair to women and so fair to men. Look at Aunt Jin-i. Look at Little Mommy. Look at all other women who had to obey dumb rules like having to bear sons! *I must leave this hell hole, so help me gods!*

This room, one in a row of the newly constructed apartments for bottom-income people—many of them wounded soldiers hobbling on crutches or wearing black eyepatches—still had that new plaster smell. When no one was looking, she sniffed it. The smell took her back to the days before Little Mommy came. Father hired workers to build Mother a sauce jar stand in the yard. Men with brown arms and legs mixed cement, scooped it with hoe-shaped tools, and slathered the mix on the foundation. Mother served them lunch. The air smelled of happiness.

"Auntie, want me to walk on your back?" Li-ho said. She figured whining would likely make Mother say, "A do-nothing grasshopper! Get up and study like Mi-na." Massaging Mother's back by walking on it would bring her far greater benefits, like a roasted sweet potato for a snack.

Since Mother had been cooking all day at Great Aunt Hong's for an exorcist ceremony, which was where Mother had brought rice and vegetable salads from, her back hurt.

Li-ho did favors for Mother that Mi-na had grown sick of doing. Now, when Mother frowned with an ache somewhere several times a week, Mi-na opened her book. Who knew where Mother's aches came from? Some came from overworking, getting old ("I've lived one-half of ninety years," she sang like a song), money worries, and not seeing enough of Father. But their true source was the famed sonless-woman's heart knot. If Mi-na had been a son, Mother would dance to "Taepyeongga" and be too happy for aches.

"That'll be nice, Li-ho," Mother said. "But work on my legs instead." Mother stretched them out without stopping her knitting. While kneading Mother's muscles, Li-ho suddenly asked Mother, "Momma, how did that mirror get broken?" She flicked her head toward the one on the wardrobe, the only piece of furniture in the room, patched with rice paper cutouts. Mi-na remembered helping Mother cut the paper ten years ago but didn't remember how it broke.

"I felt dizzy one day and fell against it," Mother said.

"Did you bleed, Momma?"

"No, but I did step on a broken piece and got a cut. But it healed."

The edges of the blossoms had turned yellow. After Mi-na became a judge that everyone admired, she'd buy Mother a new mirror, or better yet, a whole new wardrobe.

Li-ho moved on to singing "A Spring Day."

Azaleas cover hills and mountains
Where azaleas bloom, my heart also blooms
Pretty maidens, when you pluck azaleas
Pluck my heart, too.

Li-ho's ability to remain cheerful was a gift either from the gods or from the intelligence of a dog, her horoscope sign.

Mi-na opened her calculus notebook.

"Li-ho, my legs feel fine now. Go to sleep."

Li-ho wriggled into the bedding. Mi-na wished she could snuggle under the comforter, too. A far-away train whistle echoed as a dog barked. She'd wait until after Mother began snoring to gulp the pill Byung-soon had given her.

She closed the calculus notebook and opened *The Introduction to Law* instead. Before studying for tests, she forced herself to read her daily quota of the extracurricular reading she'd chosen in order to prepare herself for the competition against the law students at Seoul National in two years.

> *The laws of Korea take full effect in all areas within its geographical and territorial boundaries. However, exceptions exist as follows.*
>
> *1) In the case of ships, airplanes, and other forms of transportation, even if they are outside Korea's geographical and territorial boundaries proper and in international or other countries' lands, waters or air, the laws of Korea take full effect.*

Boring! She'd love to become the lawyer Mother required her to, but every page of *The Introduction to Law* was an introduction to abstraction that made her want to run full speed toward a brick wall. But that was not an acceptable reason to stop studying the book. She finished reading the five pages, knitting her brows as though her brain were a fisherman pulling in the world's slipperiest fish. With that out of the way, she sharpened her pencils with a razor blade. The shavings curled and dropped onto a page of an old *Kyunghyang Daily* she'd retrieved from the pile her landlord had left in the outhouse for butt wiping. A headline caught her eye.

"The University of Southern California," it read, "confers

an Honorary Doctorate on Yim Yong-sin." She was one of Mother's idols. In the picture, Yim looked strong, square-shouldered, and straight-backed. In 1945, she founded the Korean Women's National Party. Her appointment as the president of what was now Chung-ang University followed. Five years later, she became the first woman member of the National Assembly. Now her alma mater had honored her with a doctorate. Mi-na didn't clip it. She did something more permanent: she burned into her brain how glorious the woman's face, cap, and gown looked.

Another train rattled by. The whistle stirred in her a violent yearning: *Gods, take me away from here! Drop me in a different world!*

A different world? Like what? The world of adopted kids Seung-hee tried to tell her about yesterday? A giggle pushed its way up. She cupped her hand over her mouth and stole a glance at Mother and Li-ho, who were both asleep now.

During recess, Seung-hee had pulled her away from the other kids and whispered to Mi-na, spraying excited spit into Mi-na's ear. Mi-na loved Seung-hee. To her, life was a never-ending opera. People loved, died, and wept. Nothing ordinary, like going to the bathroom and brushing teeth, lay in between dramatic scenes. She was a singer and dreamed of someday playing Carmen or Madam Butterfly.

"Our maid said she ran into Mrs. No," Seung-hee had said, pulling away from Mi-na's ear a little and using her soprano voice. "Way back, Mrs. No was one of your parents' old neighbors, I guess. Mrs. No told our maid you were adopted! I told our maid Mrs. No must have been on opium and hallucinated and made up the story. But of all the stories she could have imagined, why that one?"

Mi-na had plopped down on the ground and laughed. If that story were real, Mi-na would fly like a kite of the brightest colors. Her being a girl would not have sent her mother to a near-deathbed. It would not have made her father sleep with another woman. It would not whip Mi-na as though she were a donkey.

When she caught her breath after laughing silly yesterday, Mi-na told Seung-hee the rumor was an old one from ten years ago.

"Yeah, that's what I thought. I swear, our maid's the dumbest! She even said you had a twin brother!" Seung-hee giggled, too. *How sweet it'd be if she'd been adopted! Little Mommy's coming and Mother's collapse wouldn't have been her fault. Mother wouldn't be moping with aches every day.*

Mi-na stared at Mother's and Li-ho's sleeping faces. Mother couldn't possibly not be her blood mother.

"You look just like your mother," everybody said. She kept quiet, but she violently disagreed with that comparison. Mother's face was round and full like a pumpkin, not beautiful like Aunt Jin-i's.

Through kindergarten and first grade, Mother had

carried her piggyback and galloped around the block every day to wake her sleepy-headed daughter. Throughout her grade school winters, Mother had warmed Mi-na's shoes on the hearth ledge and, kneeling, fit them on Mi-na's feet for her walk to school. Byung-soon had enviously nicknamed her the Hot-Shoe Princess. No mother would've loved an adopted daughter that way.

Then there was Mother's conception dream. "A large peony descended from the sky and dropped right into my lap. Then I had you, Mi-na."

Srrrr aaakkk. Mother snored.

So the terrible truth was Mi-na had no such luck as to have been adopted, and there was no different world a train could transport her to. No matter where she went, she'd have to live her role as her mother's savior. She'd have to go to law school and become a leader everyone, especially women with sons, would drool over with envy.

For three years she'd taken afterschool ballet and art classes taught by her teachers for free twice a week. She loved them.

One day, her dance teacher said, "Mi-na, wouldn't you like to major in dance in college?"

Another day, her drawing teacher said, "You should go to an art school. I'll help you to get a scholarship to my alma mater."

But this year, with only two years left to prepare for the

Seoul National University law school entrance exam, she dropped both ballet and art. She missed the wood and charcoal chalk smell of the attic room where she'd drawn the plaster of Paris busts of Venus, Agrippa, and Tiberius. She missed doing pirouettes and hearing her teacher tap on the wooden bar, calling out "One, two, three."

Had she been adopted and all that happened to her parents not been her fault, she would "Swan Lake" her way through life. Doing it all day, day after day, would not tire her. Or she could become a woman Michaelangelo, drawing and painting every day. It sounded like too much fun, like listening to stories all day. Or she could plop into bed early with Li-ho and be content to be at the bottom of her class. She'd marry a handsome man who'd work and worry for both of them. How sweet it'd be to be satisfied with becoming a nobody—like the faint little stars in the Milky Way that Mr. Sung, the English teacher, had rhapsodized.

Mi-na lined the pencils on the table and read the pretest questions her teachers had passed out. First calculus while her head was clear. Then geography.

She swallowed the pill.

Mi-na took the bus to Jongno Road. She scooted toward the back and slid into the one empty seat. She read *The Introduction to Law.*

Interpretation, Clarification and Expansion of Laws: In some cases, laws require interpretation, clarification, and expansion. The purpose of this exercise lies in making the intents and purposes of laws clearer and to provide appropriate bases of their application to potential situations.

A pencil chewed from one end to the other would taste better than this. Reading novels translated into Korean, like Hemingway's *The Old Man and the Sea*, was fun. Even if she were smart enough to enter law school, could she study law books like this for four years and keep studying them even after she became a lawyer without dying of boredom? "A prominent lawyer dies of . . . monotony," she imagined a headline.

In all fairness, compared to the fate of Mother and Little Mommy and thousands of women of their generation, she should consider herself lucky. At least she had some genuine options other than jumping into a well or hanging herself from a tree. If she died of boredom from working as a lawyer, at least it would've been the life she had chosen. Chosen? Would she have chosen that life if it weren't for having to redeem Mother's pathetic life? Of course not. So did she really have any more choice than Mother's generation had?

She looked out. Fragments of posters from the presidential

election of over a year and a half ago flapped on the doors of shops and telephone poles. One showed the forehead and one eye of the leading opposition presidential candidate, Shin Ik-hee. President Syngman Rhee had to be the luckiest man politician alive. During the campaign, his opponent Shin dropped dead from a heart attack. She should take more vital interest in politics and economics. How else would she become what fortune-tellers had predicted?

More people got on, and people's knees and briefcases knocked against hers.

At Jongno 5-ga Street, she elbowed her way off the bus. She walked past a hole-in-the-wall. Through the windowpanes spared from the signs for the specialty, hangover cure soup, she saw men bent over steaming bowls.

In her classroom, Mr. Hyun piled white packets on his desk. He took the kettle off the potbelly stove and poured boiled barley tea into a cup.

"Yoon Soo-mi," he called. The first victim. She had a hunched back and was the shortest girl in class. She went up to Mr. Hyun, who dispensed the sour-tasting powder into her mouth and handed her the tea. She swallowed. The rest of the girls followed. Yesterday, Kim Bang-ja, the tall girl every one called Steamed Bun because of her fat face and pinprick eyes, asked the science teacher, Mr. Ji, "Do they have Parasite Days in America?"

"No."

"In Japan?"

"Not there either. They stopped using night soil to fertilize crops."

Mi-na would give up eating red bean pudding if she could go to America. Not Japan, though, even if it meant no Parasite Day. During World War II, the Japanese forced Koreans to change their names to Japanese ones. They confiscated land from Korean farmers. They made Mother's and Aunt Jin-i's fingers bleed from working in a silkworm factory. They had the Ear Tomb in Japan, where the trophy ears of the Koreans the Japanese killed during the Imjin War of 1592 were on permanent exhibit.

Her stomach cramps started during Mr. Sung's English class. Instantly, from day one, the tall, thin new teacher had made the girls' hearts beat as wildly as a newborn puppy's. They followed him, sniffing the lilac scent that puffed from his black suit, white shirt, and black tie. Why couldn't her stomach behave until Mr. Greasy Smile's geography class? But, no, her stomach squeezed during Mr. Sung's story about stars. He'd gone on a school picnic, he said. He was a pear-skinned, timid first grader.

"Purple bell flowers were everywhere," he whispered, as though communicating only with an invisible presence hovering by the window. "We boys rolled down a hill for fun. The purple petals of bell flowers brushed against my eyelashes. I laughed as though they were clowns. We ate seaweed-wrapped rice. We sang a psalm that went, 'Nature wears clothes as splendid as Solomon's.' My cheeks turned hot. At night in my bed, the purple flowers appeared before my eyes. A breeze lifted the cloth wrap someone had lost. It flip-flopped a little ways and came to rest against one of my flowers. The flower asked: 'Where did the songs of the children go?' I felt the disappearance of all laughing things. A tear rolled out of my eyes. Then another. I never went on another picnic." He breathed a sigh only those in the front row could hear.

"Before that school picnic came to an end," Mr. Sung went on, "I used to want to become like the North Star, Polaris, the brightest star in the night sky all year round. Someone famous. Someone everybody admired. Lost people can find their way by looking at Polaris. But after that picnic, I wanted to become like those bell flowers in the valley no one sees. I wanted to become one of the faintest stars that make up the Dragon Stream, the Milky Way. Doesn't 'the Dragon Stream' sound more poetic than 'the Milky Way'? The stars there look hidden, but there they are, more powerful than the North Star, because they want nothing for themselves and they're not puffed up and self-important. They have burned off all their self-glorifying thoughts. When you reach such a state, you can hear what the bell flowers, daffodils, and stars tell you."

Her belly prepared to explode, but the parasites must wait.

Mr. Sung read William Wordsworth's "The Daffodils" in English.

I wandered lonely as a cloud
That floats on high o'er vales and hills,
When all at once I saw a crowd,
A host, of golden daffodils;
Beside the lake, beneath the trees,
Fluttering and dancing . . . .

"Daffodils and bell flowers," he said, "each one exquisite, and a whole field of them magnificent, like the little stars in the Milky Way."

A star drove its sharp corner into her belly. She doubled over. How could she say the embarrassing word "bathroom" to Mr. Sung? She bit her lips, rushed to him, and mumbled.

While running to the outhouse building across the school yard, something like a wet rubber band flip-flopped between her legs. She slowed and waddled the rest of the way. Once inside a stall, she tore a piece of newspaper from the pile on the floor, and standing over the hole, she threw the paper around the thing and pulled it out. Even after flinging it into the tank, her hands shook so wildly that it took a long time to pull her panties up. She washed her hands at the faucet. It was the first time a parasite had dropped out like that. She felt like sitting by the sun-warmed junipers alongside the Quonset gym, but if a teacher saw her outside, she'd be called to the principal's office. She stood at her classroom door for a moment.

So then trying to become ten times better than a boy would be like struggling to become the North Star. Aiming to become the object of others' adoration was impure, shameful. Wouldn't becoming a nobody happen soon enough if one failed to become a big star? She banged her fist against her forehead. She wanted to crack open the meaning of Mr. Sung's logic and understand why it was superior to the fortune-tellers' and Mother's idea of success.

She felt as though she were hanging upside down from a steel bar and water and sand were being poured into her eyes, nose, and mouth, the way the Joseon Dynasty punished criminals. Breathing became a struggle. Was she stupid to stay up all night to get the highest score in every exam? Should she believe Mr. Sung? Wouldn't embracing his ideas make her a coward who had run away from a dream she feared she might not achieve? She'd cause Mother to collapse again. The parasite was gone, but all other things that clung to her lived on.

After school, she took the city bus to the City Hall. She quit squinting and opened her eyes wide. She mustn't look like she'd had a Parasite Day, for Father's sake. She brushed her bangs to the left with her free hand. Father liked seeing her forehead. Inside the Transportation Division, as she passed the hallway windows, she smiled at her reflection. She'd smile like that for Father. When she got to the office, the woman at the desk said Father had gone on a run to Chuncheon and would return two days later. If Mother didn't make a payment on Li-ho's tuition, Li-ho might get sent home tomorrow.

"Ooooeeeee!" Li-ho would howl, happy to skip school. She liked practicing ballet and Korean dance, which were held in the same room as Mi-na's dance classes, but hated sitting in a class more than she hated eating sow thistle salad. But Mother would slap her headache band around her head and stay in bed for days, sick with worry. She'd grit her teeth and her eyelids would pull so tight Mi-na would be afraid they'd split.

In her seat on the half-filled bus, she opened *The Introduction to Law.*

She didn't have the fortune of being an adopted kid and not having to be her mother's savior, so she'd better study the book, even if it killed her.

Mr. Sung was wrong; the stars in the Milky Way were nincompoops. They didn't become big stars because they couldn't.

The Nature of the Interpretation of Laws:
An interpretation must exhibit objectivity since the interpretation provides how laws are to be applied.

But because an interpretation does not serve as a tool to discern right from wrong, it cannot be said to hold scientific accuracy and objectivity as science does.

She looked out the window. At the Dongdaemun rotary, men lined up before the glass-cased news bulletin board. The Japanese planned to send a group of Korean immigrants living in Japan to North Korea. The Japanese claimed the Koreans wanted to repatriate to the North, although some of them were originally from South Korea. College students, who were always demonstrating, had held demonstrations against that, too, their leaders usually political science or law students.

Some high school students, including girls, joined their activism, and Mi-na should, too. How else could she achieve distinction in the most admired fields, law and politics? But she possessed neither the courage nor the interest. She wished she were spinning herself in pirouettes, sketching the bust of Venus, or reading *The Old Man and the Sea.*

October 1959

Eum-chun

Eum-chun and Jin-i sat in Aunt Hong's small worship room. Eum-chun ballooned with pleasure over this surprise visit from Jin-i; so would the girls. Jin-i brought a large dried codfish as a snack for the girls, a new dress for each girl, and money that would tide Eum-chun over until Gui-yong gave her his contribution. Today Hong would tell Jin-i's fortune, as well as where Jin-i's son Joon-ho, Superior Tiger, was. Hong might touch upon Mi-na, too, and why she seemed moody these days, hardly speaking to Eum-chun. At first she had blamed the teenage years, which made girls rebellious. Mi-na always had her nose in her books, but when not reading, Mi-na's stare into space looked chilling. What could she be thinking so hard about? Had someone leaked to Mi-na about her adoption? *Buddha, have mercy.* Some thought Mi-na was old enough and had been loved in double measures by her family to be able to handle the shock of discovering the adoption. Still, Mi-na should never know. If Eum-chun's logic was selfish, so be it. Mi-na was her girl, her one beloved who belonged only to her. She must show the world that girls could reward their parents tenfold over sons. Already, not only had she been the top in her class of seventy girls year after year; she was also the highest scorer three times in the recent schoolwide college pretest. Eum-chun ran into high-school-age boys who dropped out of school every day. What were they doing? Getting boxed in their ears by their fathers and sent out to pick up trash from the streets and bring cigarette butts to their fathers, who couldn't afford new cigarettes.

Perhaps Hong would say a word about Gui-yong, too. He had lost weight and his eyelids looked lazy, as though he was having trouble keeping them up. Was Soo-yang being excessively demanding . . . in bed? *That bitch. Was she begging me to wring her neck until her bones sang the notes of breaking? Eum-chun! The Voice of Heaven! What nastiness!* The ten years of having taken turns with Soo-yang in sleeping with the love of her life had sharpened rather than dulled the blades of Eum-chun's emotion.

"Here. Tie a red string around this." Eum-chun handed the bundle of prairie grass to Jin-i. The crisscross wrinkles on Hong's forehead deepened in concentration while she shook a small vase. The rustling of a persimmon tree brushing against the eaves outside accompanied the jostling of rice grains in the container.

"Aunt Hong, anything about my Joon-ho?" Jin-i asked. "In my dream, I saw a dragon. It crawled slowly on its belly out of the ocean and dragged itself up on the beach toward me. Doesn't that mean there's some new lead, Auntie?"

Jin-i looked beautiful as ever, her lips as shapely as her

widow's peak. Alcohol didn't seem to have damaged her looks, but she was pushing forty. She couldn't go on drinking and fooling with men without ruining herself, inside and out, especially her skin.

Eum-chun took the bundle of grass Jin-i had tied with a red string and planted it in the sand she'd poured into a high-footed brass bowl. She also set an incense stick into the sand and lit it. A thin blue line zigzagged up. Hong's gods would smell it, descend from the heavens, and settle on the treetop. With one swift flip of her wrist, Hong fanned out the rice grains across the cherry wood table. Each piece, moved by the gods Hong had prayed to, found its rightful spot. By examining the shapes created by the grains, Hong would discern a message for Jin-i.

"The boy has a new name," Aunt Hong said. "That's why you couldn't find him. His father gave him a name containing the character for *wang*. The rest of the name is too blurred to read, but there's a *wang* in it."

Wang meant "king." King what? King Tiger? King Dragon?

"Aunt, please try to read more of the name." Jin-i's lips trembled. Eum-chun patted her shoulder. Once Aunt Hong spoke, that was it. Her gods didn't give an oracle in dribbles. For further direction, Jin-i would have to wait for another time. Without knowing the boy's new name, snooping in elementary schools in Busan and Seoul and the towns in between and asking the principal's office clerks to check the student rosters would do no good. The bribery money she'd pressed into the clerks' and principals' sweaty palms had been for nothing. All that money could have gone to paying for Li-ho's tuition and food.

Eum-chun ran her palm down Jin-i's back as Jin-i wept into her handkerchief. Aunt Hong muttered her prayers. None of them said it, but they all thought Joon-ho was lucky to not know of his birth mother. He was a fish that had gotten away and become a golden dragon. Let him go. Let him be legitimate. Let him become the president of the country. If it became known he was the son of a mistress, he couldn't.

"Now, what's troubling you?" Hong asked Eum-chun. "Mi-na's on your mind," Hong said. "Let me see. Mi-na's birth hour is between one and two in the morning, right?" Hong gathered the grains into her right hand, rested it on her temple, and closed her eyes. She kept her hand on her head for a long while.

She opened her eyes and said, "Mi-na's as innocent as a newborn piglet! Doesn't know a thing about the adoption. People itch to tell her. But your Jade Leaf is all yours."

Hong swept up the rice grains, returned them into the vase, and put the vase on the altar; she was finished. Hearing word about Gui-yong would have to wait until next time.

Jin-i leaned toward Eum-chun and rested her forehead against her sister's shoulder. Jin-i's occasional genius for kindness struck at moments like this; Eum-chun could allow her tears of joy to run without feeling too guilty about Jin-i's bad news about Joon-ho. Under the thousand stars and blinding rays of the sun, Mi-na was completely Eum-chun's. *Thank you, Buddha and Aunt Hong's gods.* Even if Mi-na hardly spoke to her in anything other than one-word responses, having her under her roof was good enough. Listening to her breathe as they lay on their bedding was sweet enough. Eum-chun's life as Mi-na's Mommy was as warm as a bowl of newly-harvested five grains—rice, millet, beans, wheat, and rye— expertly cooked by Eum-chun herself to that prized chewy texture and sweetness.

Yellow Sky

August 1960

Mi-na

Father came and stayed overnight. Each time he had visited them in the last five years, their room and lean-to kitchen didn't look so shabby anymore. Life consisted of only pinched pennies, watery bean sprout soups, and the books and notes Mi-na crammed into her head. But with Father's tall body stooping to get into their room, life suddenly smelled good, like the gasoline scent on his skin and coveralls. Even if his face was smudged from doing repairs on his truck and other city government equipment, his tired smile and the snacks he brought flung her into a party mood.

In the summer, he brought watermelons set in straw

slings. Mother didn't slice and serve them plain, as she did on the days Father wasn't there.

"Li-ho," Mother said, "run to Mr. Lee's and get some ice. Quick." She yanked up her skirt, reached into her slip pocket, and fished out a few tattered notes. Mother cut a hole into the watermelon, splurged on sugar, and set it on ice. Watermelon made the best summer snack.

Mother worked her magic with dinner, too. She made ordinary whiting fish stew taste like a special-ordered dish from the Golden Lotus Chinese Restaurant. Mother was also a psychic about the timing of Father's visit. Three and a half days before his arrival, she made radish kimchi. Sure enough, he came when the kimchi fermenting juice percolated to his liking—between too fresh and too ripe.

Today, too, his voice calling out "Li-ho!" transformed Mina's evening. Studying after dinner for tomorrow's college entrance pretest would go that much faster, because she'd want to get it done quickly and go to sleep earlier.

How could she give up Seoul National Law School and take the exam for Sogang College instead? Less-than-a-year-old Sogang had no law school. American Catholic priests had founded it, and it had only one building that contained classrooms and a library. The only other structure was the residence for the Jesuits. Furious objections from Korean educational leaders had risen. Declaring their already established, first-ranked universities to be up to par with the leading universities of advanced countries, they questioned, "Who do Americans think they are? Why should they have to come and found a new college? The only result will be that the smartest students will go to the United States for graduate degrees and never return. A disastrous brain drain!" Despite all the wrangling, the college opened its doors in 1960. She'd have to choose English or philosophy or some other major that was unlikely to lead to realizing the success and fame required of her. But suffering through law school might drive her to take extreme measures, like jumping into the Han River.

"What do you think, Byung-soon?" Mi-na had asked a few days ago. "Will my going to an unknown college and studying English kill my mother sooner than my entering Seoul National University's law school and then killing myself?"

Byung-soon gave her typical reply: "I don't know."

What Sogang meant to Mi-na was personal: it offered her the speediest way to escape her native culture. How ironic that to achieve such a non-scholarly goal, she'd have to study mountains of books in English and win a scholarship to an American graduate school. The priests promised the award to those with a B average or better. America! A world where Mi-na could start from scratch, where her gender might not prove to be her worst enemy.

Father didn't announce his arrival by shouting "Mi-na!" anymore.

"Because you're a young woman now, not a child," he said. He didn't tease her anymore either. He still joked with Li-ho, particularly about her dog sign. Because she padded around, hummed, and made yipping noises, he called her a puppy.

A few visits before, Li-ho had protested, "I'm a young woman, too, Uncle." Father laughed so hard he lost his voice. When he got it back, he held up his pinky finger.

"You're the size of this," he said. Li-ho made snake eyes at him. Father smiled and winked at Mi-na.

They planned to save the roasted sweet potatoes Father brought today for an evening snack. Mother cleared the table while Mi-na scooped water from the boiling pot into the brass basin and mixed cool water for Father to wash his feet in. Mother squatted over a small pail of water in a corner of the kitchen and washed herself, first her face and then between her legs, more scrupulously than usual. Tiny smacking sounds came as she soaped herself.

Mi-na planned to quit studying at about midnight, two hours earlier than usual. Father would snore next to Mother. Because the room was too small for four, she and Li-ho would sleep under her desk. She'd keep her legs curled so as to not kick Mother's feet.

If she waited until her parents fell into a deep sleep before going to bed herself, she might stay asleep until morning. Her parents would wake up and have their private time.

She felt nervous she might wake up in the middle of those moments.

After tonight, Mother would not have her aches for a while. Li-ho wouldn't have to massage her arms and legs. Mi-na would be relieved of the guilt of letting Li-ho take care of Mother.

Sometime during the night, Mi-na awoke and heard her parents talking.

"Is Kyung-jin making better grades?" Mother asked.

"No. I wish he studied like Mi-na." He changed the subject. "There's a place . . . I'll take you there," he said.

"Where?" Mother asked, but she sounded as though she already knew what he meant. Was Father close to having enough money saved up? Mi-na's eyelids fluttered, wanting to open.

"I'll take two days off at the Chuseok harvest festival. We can go look at the piece of land." His voice came out low and relaxed, carrying a tiny drag Mi-na hadn't noticed before. She wondered if he was overly tired from doing double shifts. But she liked that sound. She'd heard such a drawl from foreign actors, like Gary Cooper, during romantic scenes. Her parent's cover rustled; Mi-na imagined him pulling Mother tight against him.

September 1960

Gui-yong

He started out on his run to Cheorwon. He drove around the roundabout by City Hall, but before he made it halfway around the circle, he felt as though he was being lifted up by a gale, and was then plunked into the middle of a vast ocean. He and his truck both floated, but water had taken over inside the truck, and he fought hard to breathe. The tide thrashed him down hard on the beach. His truck went ahead of him. Slowly, his heart squeezed. Eum-chun's face grew large before his eyes. "Sweetheart," he called out. "Let's go see the plot for your new house." "*Yeobo*," she said, "Don't go yet." "I'll wait for you over there," he said to her. (*There where? Did he mean in death? Was he dying?*) His truck idled, the tire rammed against the curve, the engine still running. People rushed around his truck. (*What were they gawking at?*) His head rolled and rested on the windowpane he'd left down. Then came Soo-yang's face, the tuft of hair in a corner by her part fanned out like he blew on it. "*Yeobo*, Sweetheart," he called out to her. That's the first time he called her that, and it didn't feel right. Even in his dreams (*Was he dreaming?*) he knew he'd never used that word for her. No, he didn't mean to do that. She was known as "Kyung-jin's mother," and he always called her "Kyung-jin."

When Kyung-jin was home, they came to him together, then he talked to whichever he'd meant. The other turned away and went back to whatever she or he had been doing. What a strange system, but done all the time. He breathed his one last breath. "*Yeobo*, Sweetheart. I'll wait . . . for . . . you. Over . . . there." He meant the woman with the moon face and flowing eyes. They didn't bring us wealth, but they did bring us . . . Love, you say? *No, yeobo. Not just love. A joy ride that'll never end. Don't cry, yeobo. I'll wait for you. If not you, who else would I wait for?*

Mi-na

When Mother heard the news of Father's death, she became weightless. Little Mommy had sent word through a neighbor boy. There were only six days till Chuseok, which was when Father was planning to take her mother to survey the plot he was going to put a deposit on for her new house. The boy and Mi-na helped Mother stumble from the yard into the room and laid her down on a mat on the floor. Before leaving, he said, "The lady and her children are waiting for you to come to the morgue at the hospital."

Mi-na sat by Mother and looked at her open mouth, the teeth and tongue, a gaping hole full of words and sounds battling to burst out but not making it. Mi-na had her mouth closed, but her head felt as though it were a halved gourd, seeds lined neatly to be scooped out and cracked open to the reality and meaning of Father's sudden death.

She looked out into the ribbon of space between their room and the fence. People spoke of the ways the sky looked at the moment a disaster struck.

Cheongcheon byeongnyeok, they said. Lightning bolted across the bluest sky.

Nal byeorak, they said. Raw lightning hit between their eyes.

Haneuri muneojyeotda, they said. The sky broke and fell into crumbs.

Haneuri norata, they said. The sky turned yellow.

Over the fence of their rental, toothy at the top with the rotting wood, the sky did look yellow—a lovely shade of jaundice.

"Shhhhhh." Mi-na warned Li-ho to be quiet. "Listen for Mother's footsteps." From her desk drawer, Mi-na pulled out a sheet of rice paper and a pen, needle, thread, and square piece of red silk.

"Help me make a talisman and pouch. I'll draw the picture. I'll sew the bag, too. Your job's to tell me if you hear Mother so I can hide these."

"What are you making and why are we hiding it?

"I'm making a long-life charm."

"For Momma? Why do we have to keep it a secret? Won't she be happy we're making her the charm?"

Mi-na couldn't tell Li-ho the truth. The magic pouch would be for Little Mommy. She'd give it to her at the Forty-Ninth Day ceremony being held for Father. On that day his soul would be released from limbo and be allowed to enter heaven.

At the funeral, Mother and Little Mommy had cried themselves out, holding onto each other as though they were sisters. Since then, Mi-na faced a dilemma about afterlife. Buddhists believed in reincarnation. Confucians were philosophers, but they honored their dead by offering worship rites and treating their departed as though they were alive and continuing to watch over them. Shamanism and superstitions depended on souls' existence through afterlives. So then, Father's life would continue. He was waiting for Mother. Would he wait for Little Mommy, too? Whether he would or not, when Little Mommy died, she'd find him and once again come between him and Mother.

No! I'd rather choose hell than join Mother and Father in heaven if it meant having to live with the three of them again.

She was neither a Buddhist nor a believer of shamanism or ancestral rites. But as long as she didn't have proof a person's life didn't continue after death in one form or another, she couldn't ignore the possibility of her parents' three-way marriage repeating itself.

Clearly, Mother would have to die *before* Little Mommy for Mother to get in her years with Father alone. The sooner Mother died and the longer Little Mommy remained on earth, the longer Mother and Father could enjoy their happiness as the mandarin duck couple again.

Then how fast do I want Mother to die? Even if her motivation for wishing Mother an early death was for Mother's own good, Mi-na's insides felt as though they'd broken out in a rash. For now, all she could think of doing to help prolong Little Mommy's life was making this talisman.

How Mi-na would hand it to her without anyone noticing would be tricky. If anyone, like Mother's brother, Uncle Chang-gil, caught her, he'd turn red in his face and grab her.

"You give it to her and not your own mother?" he'd demand. "You lost your mind? What kind of a daughter are you?" He'd slap her across her face. Worse, if Mother found out . . . Mi-na didn't want to know what might happen.

Someone coughed outside.

Mi-na threw a blanket over the project. Li-ho cracked the door open and peeked.

"Our landlady going to the outhouse."

"Oh." Mi-na peeled the blanket away.

"So why do we have to keep this a secret from Momma?"

"I want to surprise Mother. So promise to keep quiet. Even after I give it to her, never ask her if she got it or talk about it with her. Never. Charms work only if you keep silent. Understand?"

"All right. What do you want me to do, other than listening for Momma?"

"Here, start sewing the pouch. Stitch along here first."

"This is pretty fabric. Where did you get it? When?"

"You're asking too many questions. Just do as I tell you."

Mi-na copied on to the rice paper the charm symbol for "happiness at home" from Aunt Hong's note that Mi-na had sneaked out of her shrine. She didn't find the picture for long life so she had to settle for "happiness at home." That should help Little Mommy to live a long life. But the image was made up of several lines, connecting circles, and a character that resembled a Chinese word crammed with a dozen different strokes. It was difficult to copy, but she finished the drawing and folded the paper in eight ways, down to the size of a fingernail.

"Give it to me. I'll finish sewing."

"Good." Li-ho flopped on the floor as though the few stitches she had sewn had exhausted her.

After sending Father off to heaven during the Forty-Ninth Day ceremony, Mother, Mi-na, and Li-ho said goodbye to Little Mommy, Kyung-jin, Kyung-ae, Kyung-chan, Kyung-soo, and the baby. The perfect moment to give the amulet to Little Mommy never came. There were too many eyes. Mi-na must find the chance.

Down the path a little ways, Mi-na turned and saw Little Mommy standing alone with just the baby in her arms. Her children had gone into the house, Kyung-jin taking Kyung-soo inside. A perfect time! Mi-na ran back to Little Mommy and squeezed the gift into her hand

"Here, put it away quickly and keep it a secret."

"What is it?"

"Open and look."

When she saw what it was, Little Mommy squeezed her eyes shut and a tear beaded out. "Mi-na, you should give it to your Mother. Oh, you probably already gave her one. She must live a long, healthy life."

"Yes, I gave her one. But don't tell anyone I gave you this. Promise? I want you to live a long life, too."

"Mi-na! What're you doing?" Mother called out. Nosey to perfection, Li-ho was running back toward Mi-na to see what she was up to.

"I have to go. Sew it to the inside of your blouse. Remember, it's a secret." She turned as she went *shhhh* with her finger across her lips.

Mi-na wheeled Li-ho around and together they trotted down the path. Mother watched them from where a dozen stairs began.

"Did you forget something?" Mother asked.

"I forgot to give Little Mommy the new pencils I brought for Kyung-jin."

"Oh, I don't know if he'll like them, but she will," Mother said. Like Li-ho, Kyung-jin didn't like studying.

They went down the steps. The path was too narrow for the three to walk abreast, but they squeezed in together. When Li-ho moved her arm to throw it around Mother, Mother lost her footing, and the next thing Mi-na knew, Mother sprawled across three stairsteps.

"Mother!"

"Momma!"

Mi-na got down by Mother's head.

"You all right?"

"Not hurt, Momma?"

They pulled her up to sit on a step.

"I think I'm all right. Let me catch my breath."

Mi-na brushed hair out of Mother's face. Li-ho rubbed her back. After a while, Mother got on her feet and declared she was in one piece.

Mi-na felt relieved. Why? Didn't she wish for Mother to drop dead? The sooner, the better? Wouldn't it have been a happy moment if Mother had a heart attack or broke her neck and died right there and went to Father?

True, but Mi-na didn't mean for Mother to die today. Then when? In a year? Two?

Back home, Mi-na brought a small bowl of rice wine from the kitchen and handed it to Mother.

"Want a leg massage, Momma?"

"You're one clever girl to know what I need, Li-ho."

Mother sat with her back flat against the wall, stretched her legs out, and took the drink.

Saying goodbye to Father and believing he entered the Heaven in the West had been rough. Somehow, the limbo where Father had stayed had felt closer to earth. Now Father was really gone. Mi-na would take the rest of the day off from her books.

"How about a song, Li-ho?" Mother asked.

Did a monkey need an invitation to eat a banana? Li-ho lit into the lyrics of "Chunhyang." Mi-na should've known she'd sing that. Their school musical was next week, and Li-ho was playing the part of Lee Mong-ryong, the nobleman who falls in love with the daughter of a *gisaeng*.

Chunhyang, my love, what will you turn into when you die?

Don't be a wide ocean washing away; be a never-changing lake,

And instead of a white crane or blue heron, I'll be a mandarin duck.

You'll recognize me, and, quack, quack, we'll float 'n dance.

When you die, you be a wild rose,
I'll be a butterfly; I'll glue my lips to yours,
So linked and afloat on a spring breeze
Tweeeet this way, tweeet that way, we'll do our love dance.

Unable to resist the bouncy rhythm, Mother put the wine bowl down and, still sitting on the floor, kicked into a shoulder dance, mounding her shoulders and dropping them to Li-ho's tune.

Mi-na must leave the timing of Mother's death and her fall into Father's arms up to Buddha and Great Aunt's Sun and Moon Gods.

For now, she shouted out a refrain.

You'll recognize me,
Tweeeet this way, tweeet that way
We'll do our love dance.

Epilogue

A Hemp Robe and Juniper

2005

Mi-na

"Honorable Ms. Chon!" A reporter practically knocked down Mi-na on his way to snap pictures of an assemblywoman. Mi-na had read about her, the chair of the Task Force on South Korea–US relations.

"What do you think of the demonstrators' demand to tear down General MacArthur's statue in Incheon?" Cameras flashed. For weeks, anti-American activists blasted their demands into their megaphones to get the government to send the 35,000 US troops packing. It was clear the young generation didn't comprehend that without the US military presence, Korea might not have enjoyed fifty years of peace and laid the golden egg—the Miracle on the Han River.

Since her childhood years in Masan during the War, Mi-na felt President Truman, General MacArthur, and the UN troops had saved her life. Didn't the demonstrators realize they had rescued the lives of their grandparents and parents, too? If their families had perished, these rebels wouldn't be alive, let alone screaming, "Fuck Americans!"

Had Mi-na accomplished Mother's dream and become a judge or a National Assembly member, the media would have dubbed Mi-na's visit "a native's return in a golden robe," as a common saying went. Even from her grave, Mother would mouth to the mothers with sons, "See? Didn't I tell you my daughter would become ten times better than a boy?" Sadly, not having achieved any national distinction, Mi-na blended into the crowd feeling as though she were wearing a hemp robe.

She walked past Ms. Chon. The distraction over the crowd delayed Mi-na's reaction to her surroundings—the brilliance of money and technology crystallized into every detail of the Incheon International Airport. Mi-na swiveled 360 degrees and scanned the stunning interior. She could not believe this was the same country that had reeked with the odor of 200,000 unwashed war orphans covered with lice.

Despite the blinding modernization and stacking of economic power her motherland had made herself famous for, as far as she knew her people had not completely molted off patriarchal values. They still had people like Little Mommy frozen as the "virgin daughter" on their parents' registry. Even though Mi-na's mother had been dead for fifteen years, as recently as two years ago Mother remained on Father's registry as his wife and as mother of Mi-na *and* Little Mommy's five children.

She had passed up several opportunities to teach in her homeland—she dreaded placing herself back in that tiger's den that scantily afforded real choices for women, where women largely followed collective male values. But she recently gave in to the urge to embrace an opportunity to touch the umbilical cord stage of her life. Perhaps by digging into the rectum of old times, she could gather a few negatives of her life as projected onto others' lenses and, in the process, construct a deeper and more objective sense of her former life, those of others around her, and the culture that had begot them.

Her children's careers bloomed in international education, religion, art, and engineering. Her husband, Matt, would visit her during her semester break. Having met in graduate school in St. Louis, she married him—an Illinois native, a Cubs fan, and a scholar of US-Asia relations—as much for what he was not as who he was. He was as far away from the males of her native culture as she hoped.

She looked forward to catching up with Little Mommy on the lives of her four sons and one daughter. Kyung-jin, married now, lived a hellish life because of his chronic migraines, which plagued him since childhood. The illness caused him to resign from his job as a heavy machinery operator. Now, he and his wife, Jae-in, a level-headed woman with throaty laughter, ran a tent bar during the graveyard shift. Sleeping during the day gave him a clear-enough head to work nights.

Mi-na was happy her mother had fifteen years with Father in the afterlife, without interference from Little Mommy. The talisman for long life Mi-na had made for Little Mommy had obviously worked. Mi-na had sent her money to buy good medicine, too.

She planned to spend some time with Li-ho. Joon-ho, Superior Tiger, her half brother, was scheduled to visit Korea from Canada this fall. Aunt Jin-i finally located him before she passed away. She and Li-ho would sneak a look at him, now an executive of a large corporation, just as Li-ho and Aunt Jin-i had done before she died. Aunt Jin-i had never revealed herself to him as his birth mother. She settled for the satisfaction of knowing he enjoyed at least three of the five ingredients for happiness—health, wealth, and good teeth. As for the fourth, long life, it remained to be seen. The fifth, producing many boys, was where he fell short. He had only daughters.

Two days after her arrival, Mi-na headed to Emille Restaurant to meet with Little Mommy. The cab passed

Gwanghwamun, the Gate of Enlightenment, one of the only two landmarks Mi-na recognized. The other was Namdaemun Gate, with its flying wing-shaped roof line. Dwarfed by the skyscrapers that shot up to twenty, thirty, even sixty-three stories high and packed every block throughout the city, the gate looked like a baby turtle. In the city bursting at the seams with thirteen million people squeezed into a space the size of Denver, she didn't feel like a native but like an alien.

Mi-na stared out from the air-conditioned taxi. The sun was surely melting the sidewalk bustling with lunch crowds. At least monsoon season was over.

If you had to live your life over, would you marry my father again? She rehearsed what she would ask Little Mommy. No. Too sappy. *Were you happy with him? Was he a good husband to you? Did you resent my mother? When did you know you'd not be kicked out of the house?*

She hoped Little Mommy's stomach ulcer and Kyung-jin's migraine hadn't worsened. They had gone to good herbal as well as Western-educated doctors but received no relief. The way their illnesses kept their teeth sunk into them reminded Mi-na of what Mrs. Bang and other neighbors had delighted in gabbing about.

"A demon possession. What else can it be? Serves that fox-faced pinky right," Mrs. Bang said. But, even as a child, Mi-na didn't think Mrs. Bang was right. Little Mommy didn't write the rule about every family needing to produce a son even at the cost of running polygamous households and relationships. What made even less sense was why Kyung-jin needed to pay a price, not only with physical pain but also with the shame heaped upon him by his countrymen. And the hell he went through to marry the young woman he had fallen in love with! Mi-na remembered hearing about that ordeal through letters from home. The bride's family put up an insurmountable barricade, insisting, "No daughter of ours marries a man born to a live-in mistress of a married man!" What finally broke that down was Eum-chun's stepping in on his behalf, meeting with the prospective bride's parents and vouchsafing the virginity of Kyung-jin's mother at the time she became Gui-yong's mistress. Only in deference to such an unconventional and honorable plea from Gui-yong's first wife did the bride's family soften.

The thoroughfares rippled with cars. The made-over face of her birthplace both pleased and sickened her. She was glad her countrymen had finally triumphed over what she regarded as their genetic defect—factionalism, or the Rose of Sharon factor, as she liked to call it. Korea's national flower bloomed a few at a time—metaphorically mirroring Korea's headstrong separatist drives. Enviably, Japan's cherry blossoms burst open in unity—a perfect show of cohesiveness. Somehow transcending such millennia-old infighting, Koreans had surfaced with their economic stunt act. On the other hand, they didn't seem to have sufficiently dealt with some of the caustic effects of their Confucian worldview, leaving Korea among the handful of strongholds of that heritage. As a result, 30,000 female fetuses were aborted in 1994 alone.

As the cab crept past the steel, chrome, and concrete Press Center Building, clouds rumbled from the direction of the Han River. Charcoal clouds hung overhead and were about to unleash a deluge. Monsoon season must have not exhausted itself.

The cab headed toward the Mt. Bugaksan neighborhood where the Blue House was nestled. There, in 1968, North Korean assassins had wielded their assault rifles to eliminate President Park Chung-hee.

Instead of the question she asked a cab driver yesterday—"Do you think North Korea will really attack the South again?"—today she asked, "What do you think of the Iraq War?"

He joked, "You know what we call President George Bush?"

"No."

"We call him Geogee Bushee."

She laughed. The Korean words that sounded closest to his first and last name, *joji* and *busi*, meant "to destroy" and "to trash," which is what the cab driver meant to say

President Bush did in Iraq. She hoped the criticism was aimed at Bush policies and didn't reflect widespread anti-Americanism.

Mi-na got off where the southern hem of the Changgyeonggung Palace stone wall swept up to the north. Emille Restaurant was half a block up and across the palace grounds. An aerial photo of this neighborhood showed the palace complex as a patch of a meadow in a forest of skyscrapers.

If it hadn't been for Li-ho's recommendation, Mi-na wouldn't have chosen Emille Restaurant. It was named after the historic Emille Bell, which carried a horrendous legend. In 771, when the bell refused to ring, a three-year-old girl given to a monk by her mother as an offering was dropped into the soup of the red-hot metal. The bell rang and became a cultural icon with the stature of the bells of Notre Dame.

Mi-na came early to wander around this historic neighborhood before doubling back to the restaurant. The lunch crowd didn't mob this stretch as it did in Insa-dong a few blocks away, where souvenir hunters haggled with the vendors at old-homes-turned-antique-shops. Juniper bushes greening sidewalks everywhere puffed their sweet resiny scent. During her elementary school calligraphy classes, she and her friends used to mash juniper leaves and add the oily fluid to the ink they made by rubbing ink sticks on slate ink wells. She didn't remember whether they had done it for the scent or for the oil that made the ink spread on rice paper more smoothly or just for kicks, but the fragrance was as powerful as ever. She recently learned about juniper's properties and how it detoxified harmful materials in the body. "Physically and emotionally cleansing," one source on herbs noted.

Willows, gingkos, and pines drooped over the blocks-long wall spined by a narrow slate-tiled roof. During the five centuries of the final Joseon Dynasty, beyond these walls and the lotus-carved lattice doors of pavilions and halls on the other side, kings and their Confucian scholar cabinet members had passed out edicts, while an axe, an amulet believed to ensure the conception of a prince, had shone under every queen's and concubine's pillows.

The green awning of Emille Restaurant appeared a half block down. Last night, in a fit to refresh memories about her native heritage, she'd read about the bell.

> *Completed in 771. Now housed in Gyeongju National Museum. Because of its famous long echoes, whenever the bell is struck, it heals multitudes from the one hundred and eight sources of tribulations. The sacrificed girl's cries of "Emille, emille" (because of Mommy, because of Mommy) can be heard in the echoes.*

Why was a girl sacrificed? Since boys were deemed so much more precious, wouldn't one of them have made a more valuable offering deserving of the approval of the gods of bells? Too bad the spirits apparently weren't too discriminating and accepted an inferior gift.

To the right of the restaurant door stood a wooden structure. Behind its grillwork, a life-size replica of Emille Bell sat on a stand in the shape of the mythical animal *haetae*. The carved pupil-less eyes of the creature stared at her blankly, neither giving nor taking.

Inside the air conditioned foyer, she brushed her hair off her sweaty neck. She kept her hair long and loose, a small act of rebellion against the Korean customary short hair for older women. "Bedroom hair," Koreans called it, showing their disapproval. It was also how men and women during the Joseon Dynasty draped hair down the front of their white robes when begging for absolution from the king.

Little Mommy hadn't arrived yet. Mi-na followed the hostess dressed in an oatmeal-colored traditional hemp blouse and skirt and sat by a window. A Japanese-style garden dotted with miniature pines and a stone lamp edged up to it.

While the server poured chilled barley tea, she picked up the *Korea Times* from a magazine rack.

"No Trembling at the North Korean Nuclear Threat,"

read the editorial. It argued from the perspective of an old saying: "Elbows bend inward." In the seventy million North and South Koreans who had been enemies for fifty years flowed the same blood, and their elbows would bend only one way; inward, in an embrace of their blood relations. Give North Korean "brothers" economic aid, the Nobel-Prize-winning former President Kim Dae-jung insisted in his Sunshine Policy, and they'd swoon peacefully into the arms of the South.

"Ha! Rots of ruck," she mocked.

"You came early!"

"Little Mommy!" She should've called her Little Mother, but "Little Mommy" is what popped out. They took each other's hands for a few moments. Little Mommy, looking thin, sat across from Mi-na and smiled halfway, as usual. After Mi-na ordered the Queen's Supper for Two, the waitress handed them chilled towels on a wicker tray.

"How are Kyung-jin and his family? Kyung-chan, Kyung-soo, Kyung-hyun? Their wives? Kyung-ae and her husband?" They laughed at how the names tumbled out.

"By the way, who gave names beginning with 'Kyung' to everyone except me? Was it Father or some fortune-teller?" she asked Little Mommy. "Does that mean the Chinese character for brilliance, *kyung*, didn't apply to me? I feel like I was a changeling dropped at our doorstep!" Mi-na laughed but Little Mommy didn't.

"Nothing's new with me and Kyung-jin," Little Mommy said instead. "Medicines keep us alive. Other children are getting by." She wiped her fingers with the towel and dropped it in the tray. She'd always been modest about herself and her children. But as much as Little Mommy saw herself as having led a lowly, difficult life, Aunt Jin-i would've drunk anyone's piss if it'd have meant a chance at raising her own son as Little Mommy had raised hers.

"She couldn't die with her eyes closed because she never embraced Superior Tiger as her son," Li-ho had written about Aunt Jin-i's death. "I closed them for her."

"I'm not complaining," Little Mommy said, as if she read Mi-na's mind. "Life's been good. I'd be punished if I asked for more."

The food arrived. Mi-na piled thread-thin strips of carrot, green onion, fried egg yolk, and smoked beef onto the crepe in her palm, rolled the wrap, and handed it to Little Mommy, an old-fashioned gesture of affection.

"By the way, have you kept the talisman for long life that I made for you? It must have disintegrated. That was forty years ago!"

Little Mommy fumbled in her purse and produced a button-like object wrapped in a plastic bag.

"I had to put in it a bag to keep it from falling apart. You can still see the red fabric. Look."

Mi-na held the bag in her hand and, without taking

the charm out, fingered it. Gods listened to the prayers of innocent and simple-minded sixteen-year-olds. Over the years, her desire for Little Mommy to leave her parents alone in heaven hadn't diminished.

"And thank you, Mi-na, for the money you sent me to buy good medicine. No other stepmother would be as lucky as I to have a daughter like you." Little Mommy reached for Mi-na's hand and patted it.

Mi-na didn't respond, feeling guilty.

"Eat plenty," Mi-na said. "You need to put on some weight. Remember what Grandma said about eating beef? How one piece of meat keeps a thousand ghosts from devouring you?"

Little Mommy nodded. "'Eat plenty' were the first words your mother spoke to me my first night at your father's house."

"Really? I'm glad my mom and I hit on the same idea! How did you feel when you heard that?"

Little Mommy didn't answer, her face turning stiff.

Mi-na filled another crepe and bit off one end. She waited until Little Mommy ate the pumpkin soup, two crepes, and marinated beef before plunging ahead.

"I've been wanting to ask you about old times. I hope I don't make you uncomfortable. What were the circumstances of your coming to my father, for example?"

Little Mommy looked at her emptied soup bowl and

arranged her chopsticks next to it. Mi-na worried about whether the question sounded as though she were asking, "Why did you ruin our lives?" Little Mommy dabbed a corner of her mouth with her napkin. She lifted her eyes as though they were made of tofu. Fixing them at a hole somewhere behind Mi-na's shoulder, Little Mommy remained silent. She looked as if she hadn't heard Mi-na's question, but she had. Thoughts riffled across her face. Mi-na dropped her eyes to the table; perhaps having no eye contact would ease Little Mommy into speaking. More silence. Much longer than hesitation or reflection. It was clear that the question had startled her and that she didn't wish or know how to answer. Maybe she should have waited until after she saw Little Mommy a few more times.

"Mi-na. I have . . . something . . . more important . . . to tell you." Her words stumbled out in groups.

What could be more important?

"Whatever it is, go ahead. Anything will be fine." She winced a little.

"Your parents took the story to their graves. I should take it to mine, too."

Dear God. A spot in her spine felt like chilled soup.

"Does it have to do with Aunt Jin-i? Superior Tiger? We found him!"

Little Mommy sighed. "I worked up the courage to tell you today because before your father passed away he asked me to tell you if your mother died without doing it."Mi-na poured tea into Little Mommy's and her own cup. She drank hers. Even if it was midday, she should have ordered wine. A large bottle.

"Mi-na, you were adopted."

Without forming words with her tongue, but with her eyes instead, Mi-na bounced what was said back to Little Mommy. "Me? Adopted?" Her people believed shocking news caused a person's spirit to shred into pieces and fly out in a hundred directions. Even though Mi-na didn't believe what she heard, her insides felt singed.

The next moment, Mi-na smiled. *Not this again.*

When Little Mommy didn't join her in making light of what she said, Mi-na slowed her breezy response. She pushed away the fish cakes, locked her hands on the table, and studied Little Mommy's face for meaning. When their eyes met, tears pearled in Little Mommy's eyes.

Mi-na jumped in. "Little Mommy, you know that's not true. We heard rumors like that before. Remember?" Mi-na reminded her of the episode she had with Mrs. Bang's daughter's sore-loser tantrum when Mi-na was six.

"I remember. Do you remember how after that, your mother wrapped her head with a headache band?" Little Mommy poured out the story. "She was so scared you'd find out. The whole family was. When he heard, your father shook fists at Sun-ja's house and even yelled at your mother.

Well, under his breath. He didn't want to wake you up. He yelled like a water demon at Grandma, too. Never seen him like that. He said we'd have to move to another province if your mother and Grandma couldn't keep our neighbors' mouths sewn up."

Of course Mi-na remembered Mother's headache band, but she wrapped it around her head as often as she ate rice cake. How was she to remember that particular time and why she did so? She looked out at the garden. No, she couldn't have been adopted. Not after having yearned for that to have been true all those nights of staying up studying, gulping stay-awake pills, and boring herself to death reading the damn *The Introduction to Law*. Not after she'd heard a million times about how she could have saved Mother from collapsing the night Little Mommy came and from falling sick every so often throughout her seventy-six-year-long life by being born a boy. Not after kneading Mother's legs and walking on her back to relieve her of the aches Mi-na believed had shot straight from her not being a boy. No, she would not accept it.

The lumpy clouds she'd seen from her taxi unloaded a downpour, and tiny mouth-shaped cups bubbled up from the ground where the rain hit the sand. They jabbered words Mi-na couldn't comprehend.

Mi-na wet her throat with tea. She wasn't a little girl. She was a woman of a certain age, a wife, mother, and teacher.

According to Confucius, she was the age to realize her heaven-given mission in life and "understand others' words easily." She'd remain calm and muster wisdom. She should remember how, unlike Westerners, her people never told children about their adoption unless it took place within the family, like an uncle adopting his nephew. As a person of a wise age, she shouldn't lose her senses. But her calf muscles tightened underneath the table. Pain crept up along her spine, too, but strangely, her head felt nothing. It felt as though it had frozen, just as her laptop had done a month ago. She'd pressed the control, delete, and alt keys. When that didn't do the trick, she tried various other keys. When that didn't resurrect it, she jabbed at the power button. Even that didn't work.

"You have to press the power button for eight seconds," said the techie on the Geek Squad.

Eight seconds. She took her eyes off the torrent outside and looked at Little Mommy's face. Her eyes were dry now. In eight seconds, Mi-na's brain would start connecting and processing. The shreds of her ghost would settle back inside her. What Little Mommy had said would turn out to be some family news about her granddaughter's upcoming wedding. Mi-na had a habit of tuning people out while they talked. Eight seconds passed. Little Mommy's words still buzzed. She didn't hear the rain anymore. The mouth-shaped sand cups flattened into a smooth line.

Little Mommy reached for Mi-na's hand and covered it. Then came words in tidal rhythms again, rising and quieting to whispers. "Since you're now a mother and professor, too, I thought you'd want to and should know. Your father couldn't bear to tell you himself. Among the few things I heard about your birth family, they had sons, you being the middle child and a twin with a boy."

"A twin?!"

"Yes, your grandma said so."

Yes, of course. People didn't keep a twin boy and girl together. Didn't want the girl to drain luck from the boy. Didn't want them to become incestuous.

This meant her gender hadn't been the root of her problem, having to gallop when boys walked and fly when they ran. It was deception that led her to live a wrong life. Had she lived with the birth family, her sex wouldn't have mattered. They already had boys to feed them through old age. But then again, her sex had mattered. It was she, not her twin brother, who had been cast away.

"Was I just found at our doorstep? Where did those people live?" she asked. What difference did it make? She rubbed her dry lips together. She had called her birth parents "those people." What else should she call them?

"I don't know where they lived or what they do now. Your parents and grandma didn't either. A relative's neighbors of your grandmother's—some such connection—brought you.

No one dared tell you, not even Li-ho."

So Li-ho had known. It figured. She hid her secrets in the tunes she hummed and the words she jabbered. She pulled her hand from under Little Mommy's and waved the waitress over.

"More tea, please." The blue and white tea pot arrived, a dragon twisting across its belly. They drank the tea.

Outside, by Emille Bell, Mi-na hailed a cab for Little Mommy, handed the driver money, and bowed to her. Little Mommy honored her by telling her what nobody else did.

"Don't worry, Little Mommy. I'm all right. I'll call you. Let's have dinner with all your children."

Even though it was way past *sambok*, one of the three hottest dog days of the summer, the heat and humidity sucked the life out of her. But that felt right. The ridiculous blue of the western sky also matched the incredulity of the day. It was known as "a fox's wedding day," a day that suddenly changed from downpour to sunshine.

How would Matt take the news she'd just learned? She felt the urge to head to Ahyeon Hill near Sinchon, where Li-ho lived. How could Li-ho not have told her? Bitterness firmed inside her like a fist.

It felt right to climb a distance far beyond a middle-aged person's endurance. Being thrust into boiling bronze would feel right, too. Her flesh being cooked would negate all other sensations. Her lunch with Little Mommy would go *pooff* and be gone.

Perhaps she could find a dog stew shop, which she had heard were now officially illegal and therefore rare. The soup, which was thought to increase energy, might keep her upright.

Because of the enormity of what Little Mommy told her, she didn't ask her any more questions. Just as well. Little Mommy wouldn't have answered them or might not have known how. Deep down, Mi-na already knew the answers. Father maintained a good relationship with Little Mommy and their children. He gave himself up to feed them and send them to school. Little Mommy cared for Father as her husband and yearned to have her name written side by side with his on his family registry.

She started on the stretch that hugged the walls of Changgyeonggung Palace, the same sidewalk she'd covered earlier. The stones, tiles, gingkos, oaks, and pines looked the same as before. The junipers smelled the same, too. But there was something new. It moved. She shaded her eyes and scanned the ground. Scattered throughout, steam crept up like tufts of hair from the sweating asphalt and sidewalks. The dozens of rising foggy clumps looked so surreal they struck Mi-na as ascending from the dead in the underworld. *Shaken adrift from old bones.* They whispered, *Go, fly, let go.*

The Internet site on the Emille Bell reported:

For five hundred and fifty years, at the first moment of each New Year, the Emille Bell was rung. But to conserve the old bell, it was silenced after its final ringing in 1992.

She made a U-turn and headed back to the restaurant. She couldn't remember if the imitation Emille she'd seen at the restaurant had the protrusions referred to as nipples. She hadn't looked carefully enough. She had no reason to, nor did she now, but the compulsion to find out fogged up like the steam in the street.

The online site posted this about the nipples:

The original Emille has four sets of nine protrusions around its shoulders. Some scholars argue the "nipples" are purely decorative, while others attribute the bell's exceptionally haunting echoes to them.

She wondered why the nipples had been placed at the bell's shoulders.

She'd been betrayed, lied to, and deceived. When confronting a liar, her people asked, "Did you wet your lips before lying?" The question sounded strange at first. Did wetting the lips make the act of deceiving less of an offense? Later, it dawned on her: they were differentiating between a habitual liar and one driven to tell untruths despite or because of one's best intentions. For the former, lying didn't require a moment's hesitation, not even the time to wet one's lips. Did Mother wet her lips before describing her conception dream about the peony descending from heaven and landing in her lap in order to make Mi-na believe she was Mother's flesh-and-blood daughter?

She'd been betrayed by Father. He'd loved her with a lie caught between his teeth when he grinned. She'd been betrayed by Aunt Jin-i. Her sweet lips had sung Mi-na's praises as her one and only favorite niece. She'd been betrayed by Li-ho those nights they slept huddled under one comforter and through all those songs they sang while squatting over a one-hole outhouse together.

More was said about the bell:

> *The original Emille Bell also featured bands of carved vine stems and leaves, symbols of long life and the blessings of boy children. Four lotus blossoms decorated the bottom band. The bichon angels flew at the mid-level. The lines and curves were so delicate, they produced an optical illusion—that the bell was made of silk, not bronze.*

In order to be moved by such a benevolent deception, several million people visited the National Museum each year and stood in awe of the bell. Illusions hoisted ordinary people to a height where they could inhale the scent of the deities. When they left the museum, they felt in their veins the power to transform their lives, sometimes in ways they might not recognize.

As for Mi-na, she wasn't heading back to the Emille Bell for a dose of delusion. After all, didn't her entire life consist of one unbroken tightrope line of it? She wondered if the Emille Bell's nipples would reveal truths to her she didn't know she wanted to know.

Mother had cared for her as one would prize one's molars. That might not sound like much to outsiders, but her people thought having good teeth was one of life's five essential blessings. Mother spiced raw beef with extra green onion, garlic, and black pepper, in exactly the amounts Mi-na craved, and put a morsel into her mouth. She was four. When Mi-na had a nightmare of worms inching toward her and climbed up on Mother's belly, she kept her there until the sun popped out. She was five. Mother, thinking Mi-na was asleep, planted a kiss on her cheek. She was fifteen. Even if she had pulled out all her hair and woven it into a pair of shoes for Mother, as heroines did in ancient stories, would they equal the love Mother had poured down on her? No.

She passed the picture windows of a photography studio and saw herself, her image too obscured by the display of portraits for her to tell if her face showed desperation, denial, anger, or gratitude. The Emille appeared at the end of the block.

Father had loved her, too. His lap felt toasty like a bed of roasted chestnuts. She was three. Rice was sweeter eaten off his spoon; the fried sea minnows he put in her bowl crunched with extra crispiness. She was four. Even after he had sons and a daughter, for whom he'd chosen names beginning with "Kyung" to show their blood unity, he still looked at Mi-na lovingly, his eyes cooking up a funny thought. "How are you going to catch a husband," he said, "with that forehead of yours, sticking out?" She had been five, ten, thirteen.

Steam kept rising from the asphalt. It whispered again, *Go, fly, let go.* What should she let go?

Li-ho, the queen of chatting and humming, had loved her. Mother said Li-ho slept with a chicken's neck on her pillow, meaning she was an early riser. She awoke before the cocks crowed and poured bits of stories, songs, and jokes into Mi-na's sleeping ears, but never one word about the adoption. She certainly must've been told by adults, "If you tell Mi-na, she will kill herself. You want to see her die? Then tell her." Poor child. Her heart must have turned to ash from trying to keep that secret from flying out. Even if they didn't share one drop of ancestral blood, Li-ho was her sister. She was her other half. She was like her slave, always at her beck and call. They were children together through the war and teenagers together through the years in one-room rentals, some with electricity, some without. They were college students together. The year Mi-na received scholarships from two different sources, one went to pay Li-ho's tuition. The truth would never unmake Li-ho as her sister.

Mother's old wardrobe had disintegrated and Li-ho had gotten rid of it, but not before she pried the mirror out, packaged it in a padded box, and mailed it to Mi-na in the United States.

"I thought you'd want to keep this memento of your mother," her note had read. When she returned home, she planned to redo the yellowed plum blossom cutouts, frame the mirror, and set it on the table in Mother's corner.

Why did the Emille Bell need nipples? Why thirty-six of them?

She turned into the entrance pathway leading to the restaurant.

What was her birth family like? Was not raising the twin boy and girl together the only reason for giving her away? Mi-na remembered stories of such pairs who had been raised together but didn't become incestuous. So that fear didn't tell the whole story. The one way the family would have kept her was if they were lepers. They would have lived in a colony, and a child of lepers couldn't be given away. She wondered if her parents were still alive. Should she try to find them? They obviously didn't attempt to find her, or didn't succeed. Did her birth mother hide behind her school walls and crane her neck to catch a glimpse of her? Aunt Jin-i had done that for years at the schools she thought might be Superior Tiger's, without being sure she'd recognize him. But then again, he was a boy. Did Mi-na's birth mother wipe away tears when she said goodbye? Did she let Mi-na's mouth close around her nipples one more time before sending her away?

She stood in front of the bell shrine.

The final passage on the bell read:

> *Eventually, the experts decided the ringing of the Emille once a year wouldn't cause significant deterioration. So beginning in 2002, the bell has been rung at the last moment of each year. The official bell ringer strikes a wooden mallet at the precise spot that makes the bell produce the longest lingering echoes of "Emille, emille." "Because of Mommy, because of Mommy."*

She wrapped her fingers around the bars and squinted at the bell inside.

When she thought of some benefits of having lived someone else's life and in the culture that had driven it, the impulse to see the dark side of her adoption slowly softened.

After all, "because of Mommy," yes, because of Mother's obsession, Mi-na pursued education with matching ferocity. None of Little Mommy's children had gone beyond high school. Mi-na had lived in the shining pool of her parents' love. But despite these magnificent blessings, the untruth she had lived made her feel as though she had been an alien who'd flitted through life without ever having touched the soil where humans lived.

The thirty-six protrusions shimmered in the sunlight slanting through the grillwork. Besides thrusting from the wrong places, like shoulders, the number was absurd, unless they were designed to serve a purely decorative or unknown function.

She gazed at the bell, but no optical illusion occurred; through the heat and humidity, the nipples remained bronze, neither silk nor a woman's flesh. The afternoon sun burnishing the metal produced an intensity that felt like it might melt the bell back into boiling liquid.

When she took a breath that felt as though it had traveled from the bowels of the earth, she smelled juniper—nothing but juniper.

For a late starter like me, my novel could only burst into being with spirited and creative coaching. Among my coaches were Vicki Lindner, Kent Nelson, Don Snow, Alyson Hagy, Michael Pritchett, Catherine Browder, and Judith Kitchen. Also, heartfelt thanks go to the Silver Sage writers in Laramie, Wyoming and the members of a writing group in Kansas City, Missouri.

My deep gratitude goes to the editors of literary journals where the earlier versions of sections of this novel appeared or won honors. These editors include Richard Burgin of *Boulevard*, Laurence Goldstein of *Michigan Quarterly Review*, Robert Stewart of *New Letters*, and David H. Lynn of *The Kenyon Review*. I am indebted to other editors who provided succinct critiques of my work in personal notes. Among these mentors are Michael Lennon of James Jones First Novel Fellowship, T.R. Hummer and Stephen Corey of *The Georgia Review*, and C. Michael Curtis of *The Atlantic*, whose letters I have kept for over a decade. Without their encouragement and critiques, *The Voices of Heaven* would not have developed to its current shape.

Tim Seldes of Russell & Volkening Literary Agency of New York kept his faith in this manuscript for years, and his wise counsel for revisions fueled the last lap my manuscript made to the finishing line.

I thank my editor, Daisy Larios, for her meticulous work and Hyung-geun "Hank" Kim, the president of Seoul Selection, for his extraordinary vision and single-minded dedication to making the truth of the culture and history of Korea known to the world.

Most importantly, I thank my husband, Michael J. Devine, for having provided year-round, multipurpose support for a much longer period of time than should be expected of any spouse. Perhaps he felt motivated to see this project through—even to the bitterest end—because it was he who planted the seed for this book in the first place and prodded me relentlessly until I reluctantly accepted the call to write. Once I got started, he kept his faith in me. Without such dedication on his part, I would not have persisted.

Photo by John English

A Korean War survivor, **Maija Rhee Devine** earned a B.A. from Sogang University (Seoul) and an M.A. from St. Louis University. Her works have appeared in *The Kenyon Review, Michigan Quarterly Review, Boulevard* (Best Short Story of 2002), and *North American Review*. Honors include an NEA grant, a finalist for the William Faulkner Creative Writing Competition and Emily Dickinson Poetry Award, and nominations to the Pushcart Prize and O. Henry Awards. *The Voices of Heaven* has won four book awards/honors including the long list for the 2014 Chautauqua Institution Book Award; Silver (Multicultural) and Bronze (War & Military) for the 2013 ForeWord Reviews Book of the Year; Honorable Mention in the 2013 Eric Hoffer Book Award; Bronze in the 2014 Independent Publisher Book Award (Best Adult Fiction E-book); and the AAUW of Kansas City, MO, 36th Thorpe Menn Literary Excellence Award.

In her TEDx Talk (http://youtu.be/GFD-6JFLF5A), she discusses her novel's relevance to today's Korea. Also authored by her is a poetry book, *Long Walks on Short Days*. Her next projects are a novel and a book of poetry about the Korean comfort women of WWII. She is married to Michael J. Devine, who retired in 2014 as Director of Harry S. Truman Presidential Library, Independence, MO.

Credits

Publisher	Kim Hyung-geun
Editor	Daisy Larios
Designer	Jung Hyun-young
Cover illustrator	Kim Ji-hye